MW00561733

The Body Farm

ALSO BY ABBY GENI

The Wildlands

The Lightkeepers

The Last Animal

The Body Farm

Stories

Abby Geni

COUNTERPOINT
CALIFORNIA

THE BODY FARM

This is a work of fiction. All of the characters, organizations, and events portrayed in this novel are either products of the author's imagination or are used fictitiously.

First Counterpoint edition: 2024

Library of Congress Cataloging-in-Publication Data
Names: Geni, Abby, author.
Title: The body farm : stories / Abby Geni.
Description: First Counterpoint edition. | Berkeley : Counterpoint, 2024.
Identifiers: LCCN 2023052625 | ISBN 9781640096264 (hardcover) | ISBN 9781640096271 (ebook)
Subjects: LCGFT: Short stories.
Classification: LCC PS3607.E545 B63 2024 | DDC 813/.6--dc23/eng/20231109
LC record available at https://lccn.loc.gov/2023052625

Jacket design by Jaya Miceli
Jacket illustration of silhouette © Shutterstock / Nowik Sylwia
Book design by tracy danes

COUNTERPOINT
Los Angeles and San Francisco, CA
www.counterpointpress.com

Printed in the United States of America

1 3 5 7 9 10 8 6 4 2

For Patsy

Contents

The Body Farm

The Rapture of the Deep

Eloise hated and adored her scuba gear in equal measure. On the deck of the *Aphrodite*, she stripped it away like the plating of an exoskeleton—her monocular face mask, her breathing apparatus, and the sticky second skin of her wetsuit. Sunset stained the sky, reflected in choppy shards across the surface of the ocean. There would be no more diving today. The ship was chugging toward shore.

With a frown, Eloise stowed her gear below deck. The metamorphosis was complete: she had devolved once more from a splendid aquatic life-form into a boring land mammal. On the one hand, her scuba equipment was a remarkable gift, a marvel of science, allowing her to spend hours in the belly of the sea, moving in three dimensions and carrying a mini-atmosphere on her back. On the other hand, she suffered withdrawal at the end of every single dive. Her coworkers knew not to talk to her for the duration of the voyage back to shore. She needed that time to mourn, to accept the burden of gravity once more.

Back in her hotel room, she showered the salt off her skin. The evening air was filled with the roar of waves, the ocean breaking against the beach on the other side of the trees. Eloise wove her hair into a frowsy braid. Daily immersion in seawater had changed its consistency from limp ash-blond to spongy copper. Voices and laughter carried on the breeze from the hotel bar. Stefan and the others gathered there most nights to blow off steam and trade shark stories. Eloise rarely joined them, though her fish tale could have topped them all. She slipped a hand under her T-shirt and ran her fingers along the elaborate scar on the right side of her rib cage: the precise imprint of a tiger shark bite. Four hundred and sixty-seven stitches. A mottled red ribbon of teeth marks. Her torso no longer smooth but topographical. Her belly button torn away.

On the nightstand, her cell phone lit up and buzzed. Eloise picked it up, observing that she had missed thirty-four calls during today's underwater sojourn. All from her brother. There were a few texts too: *Call me back.* And later: *The ten-year anniversary is next week. Can you please get in touch so we can figure out what we're going to do?* And later still: *I won't pick a fight, I promise.* Finally: *You are such a goddamn brat.*

Eloise considered several replies before turning her phone off and sticking it in a drawer.

°

In the morning, she led the way down the winding trail through the trees to the beach. The sun was just rising, and the sand glowed bronze between the trunks. Eloise brushed aside the low-hanging branches. Behind her, José tripped on a tree root and swore. Alana and Beth were murmuring together in low voices. At the back of the caravan, Stefan moved with a lithe, easy grace. As always, he carried the bag of gear slung across his shoulders, clanking faintly with each stride.

When Eloise reached the beach, she noted the dark patches by the horizon: moody, dangerous places where the waves prevented sunlight from reflecting. She observed the bite of the wind and the heavy clumps of seaweed tossed up on the beach. The air was filled with energy. A shiver tracked up her spine.

The marina lay half a mile down the shore. Alana and Beth set the pace, walking side by side on the firm, packed sand at the water's edge. They had been best friends since joining the team a few months earlier, two marine biology grad students from different universities united by a summer of fieldwork on the sea. Eloise treated them with politeness and reserve; she never got attached to the interns who came and went, as ephemeral as mayflies.

José and Stefan, on the other hand, had been her colleagues for nearly a decade. The three of them had traveled the world together. They'd tagged sleeper sharks in Alaska, stealth predators with an eerie, silent glide. They'd braved the storms and wild surf off the Farallon Islands to track the diminishing number of great white sharks. And now they were in North Carolina to chart the astonishing migration of the *Prionace glauca*.

The shore was deserted. It was not yet hot enough for the tourists—reeking of sunblock, toting towels and small children—to collect there. Eloise noted the melting body of a medusa rolled ashore in a rubbery paste. Alana and Beth were so far ahead now that the rising sun reduced them to shadow puppets. José strolled in their wake, smoking his daily cigarette—one per morning, Eloise knew.

Stefan caught up to her, the gear clattering on his back. He was pale and dark, a slim reed of a man, exactly her height. Years in the United States had done little to erode the sharp edges of his Polish accent.

"Listen," he said, nudging her with his elbow. She turned to him, expecting some detail about their plan for the day—coordinates, oxygen sats, timing.

"Your brother called me," he said.

Eloise stepped into the sweep of a wave, as warm as bathwater.

"Did you hear me?" Stefan said. "Your brother called me last night."

"I'm going to kill him."

Stefan raised his eyebrows.

"How on earth did Noah even get your number?" Eloise asked.

"He didn't say."

A seagull soared overhead, making its lonely cry. Stefan was watching her steadily. They rarely ever talked about personal things. Their relationship had been forged in the silence of the deep ocean; they always dove together. Eloise knew that Stefan was left-handed, a quick thinker, and clearheaded in a crisis. But she did not know if he had any siblings. She'd never mentioned Noah to him before.

"What did you tell my brother?" she asked carefully.

Stefan averted his gaze. "He asked me to make you call him. He wanted to know where in Africa we were working right now."

"Oh, hell."

"He seemed to think we were tagging requiem sharks somewhere in the Indian Ocean."

"That's what I told him," Eloise said, the words tumbling out. "Yes, I lied, but you have to understand that Noah is persistent. He lives in D.C., and I figured he would drive right down if he knew I was just a few hours away. He's smart, so I had to make something up that he would actually believe, and he wouldn't fall for just any—" She broke off, shaking her head. "I'm sorry you ended up getting involved."

Stefan shifted the bag of gear from one shoulder to another. His expression was inscrutable.

"Did you tell Noah the truth?" Eloise asked, adding quickly, "It's okay if you did. You don't have to lie for me. I know he put you on the spot."

"I didn't tell him anything. I said I'd pass on the message, and I have."

"Thank you." She reached for his hand and gave it a squeeze.

"It isn't my business," he said, offering an answering squeeze. Then he dropped her hand, and they walked in silence to the *Aphrodite*.

◦

Eloise had learned to scuba dive from her mother. Ada had been an adventurer, always outside, eager for new experiences, dazzled and elated by the natural world. She'd backpacked through the Amazon rainforest. She'd skied with expert daring along The Tunnel in Alpe d'Huez. She'd skydived at least once a month. The walls of Eloise's childhood home were decorated with framed snapshots of Ada perched on rocky cliffs, scuba diving in caves, or free-climbing trees.

Eloise had spent her youth hiking up mountains and white water rafting. She and her mother were kindred spirits, excited to tackle a black-diamond trail, gasping in tandem at an eagle in flight, saying yes to every new experience. Eloise begged to sky-dive with her mother, but you had to be eighteen years old. Scuba diving, however, was legal at ten years of age, so that was when she learned. She spent the best days of her young life underwater at her mother's side, kicking through clouds of sand in the chilly California surf off the coast where she grew up.

And then there was Noah. Eloise often wondered if her brother resembled their late father, who died before she was old enough to form memories of him. She'd only ever seen her father in pictures: a bearded, narrow face, eyes hidden behind Coke-bottle glasses. He left a sizable estate, which their mother used to care for her children and fund her adventures. Eloise had never missed having a father; her mother was enough, and they were so delightfully in sync, two peas in a pod.

But she did wonder where careful Noah had come from. An old man at the age of eight. He flatly refused to scuba dive or even snorkel, remaining on the shore. He would wait for the walk signal before crossing the street, even when there was not a car in sight. He saved every penny of his allowance, never wasting it, as Eloise did, on adventure comics or toy sharks. As soon as he was old enough to stay home alone, he let his mother and sister spelunk and backpack without him.

Eventually they both went to college—Noah for accounting, Eloise for marine biology. In their absence, their mother had decided to free-climb Hyperion, the tallest tree in the world. At the summit, 380 feet in the air, Ada took a selfie, beaming, her cheeks bronzed by wind and sun. Eloise sent back a heart emoji. Noah texted, *Please come down from there.*

A month later, Ada died while skydiving. Her parachute failed to open, a freak accident. There was nothing she could have done to save herself, despite her years of experience. Eloise got the call in her dorm room. Upon hearing the news, her first response was to laugh. The voice on the other end of the phone had to be mistaken. Her mother could not be dead. Her mother was more alive than anyone else in the world.

°

The canned air tasted sweet, like cinnamon. Weightless, Eloise pumped her powerful flippers, circling the interior of her cage. Stefan filmed it all from thirty feet away, the lens poking between the bars of his own cage. Eloise waved at the camera. Stefan waved back. She had the feeling that José, on the deck of the *Aphrodite*, watching the live feed on the snowy monitor, was waving also.

She shook her bag of chum, emptying bright scales and fish juice into the sea. She was calling the blue sharks to her—graceful creatures, sky-colored, with long, flowy tails. They filled the North Carolina waters in the summer. Eloise was here, fifty feet below the surface, to document the profundity of the blue sharks' migratory path. The females, once pregnant, crossed the entirety of the Atlantic Ocean to give birth in the warm seas off Italy and Spain. Then they coasted on the Gulf Stream all the way back to the Yucatán. And then, as if that were not enough, they swam north along the eastern shore of Mexico and the United States to return to the icy depths near Massachusetts, where they mated and began the whole journey over again.

At this depth, the sunlight began to fail. There was no land in sight, the shore miles away, no seabed visible below, only water deepening into black. The blue sharks came in a group, six or seven, maybe—Eloise could not be sure in the erratic dappling of wave-broken glow. They emerged like clumps of cobalt coalescing from liquid to solid. By shark standards, they were skinny creatures, pencil-shaped, with sharpened conical snouts. Their oversized eyes, perfectly round, seemed surprised in sunlight and hollow in shadow. They swam toward Eloise with the classic *Selachimorpha* waggle, noses swinging back and forth, tracking the faint trails of blood from the chum.

Twenty feet from the cage, they stopped their forward progress and began to circle. They ignored Stefan's cage completely; there was no intriguing smell coming from there. Sharks were mechanical creatures. They circled when they were interested and bit when they were curious. Most recorded shark attacks were not attacks at all, merely an inquisitive animal checking out a strange object in the best way it knew how, as innocent and guileless as a dog sticking its nose into a compelling pile of garbage. If startled, sharks voided their bellies in a cloudy explosion and swam off. When there was blood in the water and a throng of them gathered close, with a helpless figure at their center, they boiled gradually into a frenzy. And—Eloise's favorite—when sharks were turned upside down, they went momentarily into a coma.

Clearly the blues did not like her cage, an unfamiliar object in their domain. Eloise knew that her body bewildered them too, roughly seal-sized but shaped wrong—gangly, almost amphibian. Still, the chum drew them inexorably toward her. By degrees, they narrowed their orbit around the cage. Stefan signaled to Eloise, and she opened up the second sack of chum, tossing a handful into the open water. The bloody pulp sank slowly, twirling in the light. A brave but undersized shark cut loose from the pack and swallowed the mess whole.

They were all around her now. Eloise readied her tagging pole and tossed more chum through the bars. She loved their dance, how they were always coming back to her, maws agape, never losing focus. They could actually feel her on their skin; the bow wave she made with the smallest motion registered to them like a caress. She threw a glob of chum into the open sea, and when a shark came rocketing to gobble it up, Eloise lifted the pole and struck. The telemetry tag flashed orange, clipped like an earring to the animal's dorsal fin. The shark did not appear to register the impact. The flesh of the dorsal fin was impervious to sensation, lacking blood flow or nerve endings. And anyway, there was chum in the water, so nothing else mattered.

Another shark approached the bars. The blues had snub dorsals, scarcely bigger than a human palm, but Eloise's aim was precise; she had not missed her mark in years. As the speed of the animals increased, the telemetry tags bobbed gaily from their backs. Each stroke of their scythe-shaped tails brought them a little closer. Not a muscle wasted. Eloise tagged another, and another, and soon the chum was gone, and the sharks glided away, dissolving into the blue.

∘

As the boat chugged back to shore, Eloise stood alone at the prow. Alana and Beth were below deck, reviewing the footage from the day under Stefan's tutelage. The team did not always film their efforts; it was a biweekly thing at most. Their sponsors at the Marine Environmental Laboratory, who controlled their funding, liked to see documentation every so often. Verification of their dollars at work.

Eloise was thinking about her mother. This was Noah's fault, Noah and his calls, his texts, his insistence on marking the ten-year anniversary of her death, as though a memorial could ease the profundity of this grief.

Eloise and her mother had made so many plans. Skydive together for the first time, Eloise strapped to Ada's belly like a kangaroo joey. Visit the Arctic during the season of the midnight sun.

Scuba dive in the Great Blue Hole in Belize, an eerie, yawning abyss as round as a coin and more than three hundred meters deep, surrounded by a plateau of shallow, turquoise sea.

Ada had been there once as a young woman, and she described it to Eloise with glee—the way the sunlight disappeared and the pressure of the water did strange things to the mind. That far down, it was necessary to have a buddy or, better yet, a group, in case the dreaminess overtook you and you forgot to check your air. Divers had died in that crevasse, hundreds of them, lulled into soporific unconcern, eventually suffocating, their bodies entombed forever in the black water.

The rapture of the deep, it was called. Ada had experienced it too, she told Eloise. She dove the Great Blue Hole with four companions, all of them descending slowly to equalize the air pressure in their ears and sinuses. She had not felt the change coming until it was too late. Voices warbled around her, high and sweet. Mermaids? Sirens? Tiny lights flickered and shone in her peripheral vision. At first she'd thought they were bioluminescent organisms, but then she understood they were stars. This had not troubled her. She felt sure the water would only grow more euphoric the deeper she dove—more splintered with light and richer with melodies.

One of her fellow divers had tapped her shoulder then, and the group returned to the surface. Ever since, Ada had been itching to get back there and try again.

°

The next day, the sea was empty of sharks. Stefan and Eloise floated in the same cage, bumping elbows, each armed with a tagging pole. When he was not serving as cameraman, they usually worked side by side, while José remained on deck as their overseer and guardian angel. Stefan dumped a bag of chum into the sea. Eloise clapped her hands and yelled inside her mouthpiece. Sharks were attracted to the agitated movements of wounded fish. If the smell of blood was not enough to summon them, it often helped to add simulated death throes.

Minutes passed. Long columns of light shifted through the water. A few Atlantic spadefish, two feet long and striped like zebras, came to nibble the sinking chum. Stefan checked his watch and shrugged. At last he signaled to José, who winched their cage out of the ocean several hours earlier than planned. The *Aphrodite* was crowned by two long-necked derricks, a double-headed dragon. Each crane could easily lift and maneuver a midsize shark cage made of utilitarian aluminum (lighter than steel, noncorrosive in salt water, and foul-tasting to sharks).

As the ship motored back to shore, Alana and Beth unearthed a boom box from a cupboard and set it up on deck. A set of dusty CDs offered the greatest hits of eighties pop—no other choices. José swiveled his hips and snapped his fingers to the synthetic beat while Alana and Beth waltzed grandly with each other, giggling. Stefan joined the party, not exactly dancing, more swaying in place.

Eloise leaned over the bulwark, staring into the empty ocean. Quiet days left her unsettled. It had been the same on the fateful afternoon when she had been maimed by the tiger shark.

The team had been in the Gulf of Mexico then, tagging every shark they could get their hands on, regardless of species, as part of a worldwide study to determine how climate change was affecting fish populations. For a week, Eloise and Stefan tagged threshers, hammerheads, and makos. The creatures were greedy for chum, and the work was nonstop. Every night before bed, Eloise had to ice her biceps, sore from overuse.

Then came a quiet day. She remembered it perfectly, every detail etched into her brain. The sea was clouded with sand after a morning of wind and storms. A few mackerel passed by at a distance. A gelatinous mesh of moon jellies bobbed along the surface above, translucent in the sunlight. The sharks appeared to have left the area entirely. Not even the omnipresent blacktips, four feet long and incurably curious, came to check out the armloads of chum Eloise and Stefan hurled into the water.

So Eloise had decided to go for a swim. It had been a long time since she'd scuba dived just for pleasure. She'd been cooped up in the cage for so long that she felt like a goldfish in a tank. She communicated her intentions to Stefan—they had created their own sign language over the years—and he replied that he would stay in the cage and maintain watch.

At the time, Eloise had only ever seen tiger sharks at a distance. They were solitary creatures, passing by occasionally in the deep ocean, charcoal gray and bulky, the juveniles banded with those trademark stripes. She knew that tiger sharks were the most unpredictable members of their species. Their migrations were irregular, their diets variable. Unlike other sharks, they could be intentionally aggressive toward humans. Eloise had once read about a tiger shark that had solved a murder mystery. After a week in captivity, the beast suddenly went wild, thrashing and vomiting. Finally it coughed up a human arm that had been severed medically at the shoulder and bore a distinct tattoo that matched it with a missing man. Without the tiger shark's assistance, no one would ever have found the corpse, sliced into pieces and scattered in the sea.

On that lazy afternoon, Eloise kicked toward shore, watching the ocean floor rise slowly to meet her, ridged like the roof of a mouth. Curtains of beige sand drifted idly on the current. She saw a school of grouper moving along the seabed, mouths molded in permanent grimaces. She saw a silver tarpon dart by. She did not see the tiger shark, not until it was too late, a blur on her periphery, a glint of teeth, the inky cave of its mouth opening, the shock of impact. She saw her own blood coiling dark against the water before she felt the pain.

Stefan saved her. He'd watched the whole thing unfold from inside the shark cage. Eloise later heard about how he swam fearlessly into the open water, pulling his dive knife from its holster. The tiger shark did not react to his approach, intent on the kill. Stefan had stabbed it in the eye. Nothing else would have stopped it, and even that might not have deterred it forever; Eloise had seen sharks shake off worse injuries to continue hunting. There was a perpetual debate in the marine biology community about whether sharks felt pain at all.

Stefan never got his dive knife back. The tiger shark had thrashed away from him, the blade jutting out of its flesh like a horn. It let go of Eloise's body. Stefan folded her in his arms and swam toward the surface, trailing clouds of blood.

°

Around midnight, Eloise called her brother. Rain silvered the air outside. The mumble of someone's television set penetrated the thin walls. Eloise sat curled in a ball on the bed, holding her phone in both hands like a child.

"Finally," Noah said by way of greeting.

She closed her eyes. She had not seen her brother in three

years, not since the aftermath of the tiger shark. Once her wounds had healed enough for her to leave the hospital, she had recovered at Noah's house in the suburbs of D.C. It all came flooding back now—her brother's anxious face, the fog of medication, and the pain, a loop of burning wire in her flesh, electrified every time she inhaled.

"Hello? Are you there?" Noah cried.

Eloise found her voice. "That was a cheap goddamn trick, calling Stefan."

"It worked, didn't it?"

"Well, stop it," she said. "Stop leaving me messages. Stop texting me. Don't bother the people I work with. It's enough."

Noah sniffed—a sound from childhood, the percussion of his breathing. He suffered from hay fever and sinus infections, constantly congested.

"Where are you?" he said. "You're not calling from Africa."

"It doesn't matter where I am," she said. "I don't want to do a memorial. You can mark the ten-year anniversary however you want. Just leave me out of it."

She heard the creak of Noah's mattress and pictured him sitting up in bed, fumbling for his glasses. There was a painting of a forest on the wall above his head. Eloise knew it well; she'd spent long hours in a drugged stupor staring at the crudely rendered branches, the leaves that appeared to have been daubed on with a sponge. After the tiger shark had crushed her chest and filled one lung with water, Noah insisted that she take his bed to recover in comfort. He slept on the couch for months as she relearned how to move her arms, how to walk, how to breathe.

"You're being selfish," Noah said peevishly. "Everything isn't about you. A lot of relatives have been asking if I'll be doing some sort of memorial for Mom. Even some of her old hiking buddies contacted me. You aren't the only one who loved her."

"So invite them," Eloise said. "Invite everybody. Have the biggest, saddest party in the world. But stop badgering me about it. I'll be busy that day."

Noah sighed, and she imagined him rubbing the bridge of his nose, where his glasses left tiny indentations at the end of a long workday.

"We both have to cope in our own way," she said, trying to put some gentleness into her voice.

"I believe this is what Mom would want," Noah said. "Something in her honor. I know you think you had this special bond with her, but—"

"I *did*."

"But you aren't the only one who misses her," he continued, his voice rising. "I wish you would listen to me for once."

"I'm listening. I hear you. You do what you need, and I'll do what I need."

"Selfish *and* hardheaded," Noah said. "You never change, do you?"

Eloise hung up and hurled her phone against the pillow.

°

Noah hadn't cried when their mother died. He only grew paler and more cautious. He was alarmed when Eloise dropped out of college. He was apoplectic when she took her first job as a shark tagger, traveling to Alaska with Stefan and José to count the sleeper sharks. Her team visited the Great Barrier Reef and the Indian Ocean. Their work was instrumental in getting angel sharks and great hammerheads declared endangered species. Eloise had never felt so vital, so fulfilled.

At first, Noah insisted that she text him proof of life after each and every dive. But gradually, grudgingly, he seemed to come to terms with the fact that he could not monitor her so closely as to keep her safe. At least he knew exactly *how* she was risking her life, a small mercy, he told her once. Their mother had done everything—climbing, skiing, mountain biking—while Eloise settled on one thing.

When she dove, she felt the way she used to in her mother's company—dazzled by the glory and strangeness of nature. When she dove, she felt as though her mother might still be there with her, temporarily out of sight, like the time they'd been separated by a coral reef. Eloise, twelve years old, stayed where she was, kicking in place as she had been taught, waiting patiently until her mother came to find her. She remembered the moment when Ada swam around a bulbous arch of rock and blew her a kiss.

During her convalescence in her brother's house, Eloise had been troubled by fish, haunted by them. Lying in Noah's bed, each of her 467 stitches gripping her flesh like a cat's claw, she felt fish flooding around her. She felt them in her throat when she drank. When she meant to be taking notes or writing letters, jellyfish and whales spread out beneath her pencil. And always, when the bedroom was dark and she was trying to sleep, she heard the swish of giant tails, as though sharks were passing in and out through the open window.

After her recovery, Noah had begged her not to go back to shark tagging. He got down on his knees, eyes filled with tears—the first time she'd seen him cry since childhood. Their mother's death could not move him to weeping, but this did. He pleaded with her to find another line of work. Something sane.

Eloise explained, as she had done so many times, that her job was the great passion of her life. She assured him that this sort of injury would not happen again. She was wiser now, more savvy. Besides, tiger sharks were vanishingly rare.

The argument escalated. Noah informed her that her risk-taking was a hazard to his health, the source of his high blood pressure. Eloise retorted that she had no choice; her yearning for the ocean while landlocked in her brother's bed had been more unendurable than the agony of her wounds. Noah screamed that she was just like their mother. Eloise roared back that she couldn't think of a higher compliment. He accused her of having a death wish. She told him that he had never really learned how to live. Then she banged out of his house and had not seen him since.

°

She spent the next hour pacing her hotel room and having imaginary arguments with Noah, gesticulating furiously at no one. When her phone rang again, she snatched it up and yelled, "What? What now?"

"I didn't mean to lose my temper," he said. "I didn't intend to pick a fight."

She settled cross-legged on the bed. She knew this was the closest thing she would get to an apology.

"I don't know why I got so . . ." Noah trailed off. "You bring that out in me. It's like I'm fourteen years old again. Just trying to win the damn argument. I'm sorry," he added stiffly.

Eloise was startled into a laugh. "Are pigs flying? Did hell just freeze over?"

"The memorial wasn't the only reason I was calling," he went on, ignoring her. "I honestly don't care if you come. You don't even have to plan it with me. I just wanted . . . I thought . . ."

She waited, but he did not finish the sentence. The rain had dwindled into mist outside, a damp, chalky gray that erased the world beyond the window.

"I've started dreaming about her again," Noah said. "I see her at the top of that redwood. Or on a mountain. She's laughing and talking and not paying attention. She starts to fall—it's the same every time."

"I have that dream too," Eloise whispered.

"I watch it happen in slow motion, kind of. You know how dreams are like that sometimes? How everything gets really slow and out of focus?"

"Yeah."

"I try to grab her arm," Noah said. "I try to stop her from falling. I never get there in time."

"Neither do I."

In the distance, a church bell tolled a single doleful note. One o'clock in the morning.

"What are you doing up so late?" Eloise asked softly. "You never even make it to midnight on New Year's Eve."

He blew his nose like a goose's honk, another nostalgic echo from the past. Poor Noah—antihistamines, nasal sprays, and sinus rinses every night.

"How's work?" he asked. "I assume you're still chasing sharks around?"

"I thought you weren't going to pick a fight."

"I'm not. I'm having a normal conversation. Work is a normal thing to talk about."

"Huh." She adjusted her pose against the bed frame.

"*My* work is going well," Noah said. "The business has expanded, and I've hired more staff."

"Nice."

"It is."

There was a small, awkward silence. To fill it, Eloise asked, "Do you like the people you work with?"

"They're great. Solid citizens. This last tax season was like a tsunami. But we banded together and got through it."

Eloise thought about Stefan and José, who had saved her life from the tiger shark. Stefan carried her out of the ocean. José put pressure on the wound and radioed for a helicopter extraction. She would have bled to death without their swift, skillful intervention. She trusted them, respected them, all the way down to the bone. She intended to work with them until they all retired or died in the field.

But they were not family. They were something else—comrades-in-arms, maybe.

She had not realized how profoundly she missed Noah. It was like putting on corrective glasses after years of a slow drift into astigmatism. You didn't understand how much you had lost until the world slipped back into focus, every edge crisp and defined.

"Can we just . . ." Noah began, then paused. "Can we chat sometimes? No arguing. Just catching up. I wish you'd answer the phone once in a goddamn while."

When she did not immediately reply, he went on quickly, "Or we could text. If phone calls are too much, I'd be happy with just—I don't know—a meme or something. A selfie. You don't even have to use words."

Eloise laughed. "Words have never been my strong point, have they? Yes, we can text. I'll text you tomorrow, okay?"

He exhaled sharply, a crackle down the line. "You promise?"

"I'd pinkie swear if you were here."

Another silence bloomed, but this time it did not feel strained. Tendrils of mist pooled in through the window like ghostly fingers.

"I wish you understood why I do this," Eloise said, all in a rush. "I wish you would come diving with me sometime. It would open up your mind in ways you can't even imagine."

Noah laughed. "I wish you would get a job where nothing could possibly eat you. But we can't always get what we want."

°

In the morning, Stefan saw it first. Eloise was tired from her late-night conversation, thinking about Noah and their mother, not paying attention to her surroundings as her cage drifted downward. Descending into the sea was less perilous than ascending. The former could, at worst, cause sinus pressure and earaches, while the latter could trigger the bends: joint pain, paralysis, brain damage, even death. To be safe, José always winched the cages up and down at a steady thirty feet per minute.

Stefan was filming today from his separate aluminum cube. Eventually Eloise noticed him waving and gleaned from his posture that he had been trying to get her attention for some time. He pointed down.

The ocean beneath them teemed with shadows. It was a school of what appeared to be dozens of fish. The haziness of their forms told Eloise that they were at some distance, so they must be large creatures, bigger than humans. Too thin to be whales, too broad to be tuna, too sluggish to be dolphins. Stefan aimed his camera into the deep. Eloise flattened herself prone on the floor of the cage, peering eagerly down into the gloom.

They were blue sharks. As the cage sank, she could distinguish their whiplike tails and thin backs. At least forty animals swam together in a planar formation, strewn like pockets of afternoon sky across the twilight beneath. Eloise had never seen blues—or any sharks—behave this way. She climbed to her knees on the bottom of the cage and glanced questioningly at Stefan, but he was busy filming.

The cage descended farther. Eloise could see now that there were more sharks beneath the upper layer. Silhouettes beneath silhouettes, shifting like the gemstones in a kaleidoscope, overlapping and eclipsing one another, never still.

There were hundreds of them.

Both cages dipped into the school simultaneously. Sinking through the bodies, Eloise felt a tug of vertigo. The sharks were traveling northward, all cruising at the same languid pace, while she and Stefan fell slowly through their ranks. Everything around her was moving; there was no fixed point to use as reference.

At last the cage stopped, having reached the predetermined depth. Eloise kicked off from the bottom. As far as the eye could see, slender figures swam in synchrony, eerily similar in size and shape, differentiated only by the occasional scar—a torn dorsal fin or the gouged track left by a fishhook. There seemed to be no end to their ranks. Eloise had read about this phenomenon, blue sharks that crossed the sea in massive schools, but nothing could have prepared her for the reality of it. A scrap of manmade orange flashed among the bodies. Some of them sported her tags, but only a few, amazingly few, a tiny fraction, a visual representation of the tenuous connection between the human world and the much wilder world beneath the surface. The ocean brimmed with more life than even Ada could have imagined.

Eloise peeled off her dive glove and held up a pink hand. She had always wished for a lateral line, the sensory organ that allowed fish to detect pressure and vibrations through the water. In this moment, she did not need it. She could feel the sharks on her bare skin. The sea trembled with the weight of their bodies. Except for them, the ocean was absolutely deserted—not a fish or turtle in sight. Every living thing for miles had taken shelter when they felt the bow wave of this monstrous horde.

And the blue! Never had there been such a comprehensive study of a single color. The sharks were turquoise up close, navy in the distance, with every shade from teal to sapphire in between. Only blue was permitted here, erasing any rogue color that dared to interfere. Eloise's tags shone as brief and bright as signal flares before the density of bodies snuffed them out. White and black were not tolerated either: the sharks blotted out the light above and blanketed the inky depths below. In this moment, blue transcended mere pigmentation to become something more—a statement of intent, a revelation of secret knowledge, a new theory of the universe.

Strangest of all, the sharks swam without urgency or desire. Mouths slightly open. Eyes glassy. Minds unfocused. They were not hunting, not fleeing, not mating, not pupping, not engaged in any behavior Eloise recognized. Sharks were always expressionless, but this was something else: a robotic repetition of manner, an absence of will. Like a swarm of bees or a flock of birds, the blues had sacrificed their individuality to form a blended whole, greater than the sum of its parts, a single organism. But what was its function? That was the question that cracked Eloise's mind open. Bees pollinated, birds migrated, but here was a school of sharks that consumed an ocean with their numbers, a thousand discrete entities merging into one, a collective entity, an aquatic supremacy, wonderful and terrible, godlike in its power and unknowable in its purpose, beyond human understanding.

Eloise looked at Stefan, who lifted his hand to his brow and mimed an explosion. There was no protocol for this. She could not possibly tag this many animals. She would not have known where to begin.

And so she twirled in the middle of her cage, trying to take it all in. Sometimes there was no possible response but celebration. She laughed as her mother had laughed at the top of the tallest tree in the world. She could not stop turning, sharks above her, sharks beneath her, laughing and laughing inside her mouthpiece.

Stefan lifted the camera, and later that day Noah got a text from his sister, no message, no words, just a link to a video on the Marine Environmental Laboratory website. And there, once he discovered his reading glasses pushed up to his hairline, Noah saw Eloise underwater, recognizable by her leggy contours even beneath the wetsuit and face mask—and behind her a galaxy of sharks, more sharks than Noah had known existed in all seven seas. The sunlight failed before their numbers. A sound rose from his chest, halfway between a chortle and a sob, as his sister spun in a circle, her arms flung wide, then turned to the camera and blew him a kiss.

A Spell for Disappearing

Do not attempt this magic lightly. You must be willing to risk everything to succeed, even your health, even your safety. Witches have died performing this rite.

You are stacking shelves when it happens. Rain patters against the windows as you wheel a cart loaded with books between the aisles. You head for the nonfiction section, your long skirt swirling around your ankles, your bracelets jangling faintly. You have worked at the library for more than a decade, and it is your favorite place, especially in the rain. There is a mystical quality to the silence today, a kind of otherworldly hush.

As you round the corner, something slams into you from behind. Your midriff collides with the cart, knocking the wind out of you. Books thud against the carpet.

"Herregud, jag är ledsen. Är du okej?" a deep voice asks. A large hand closes around your elbow, steadying you.

"I'm fine," you say, correctly interpreting his question.

The man bends down and picks up the fallen books, handing each one to you with a brush of fingers. He is beautiful—there's no other word for it—strong jaw, eyes like gemstones.

To your surprise, he's staring at you the same way you're staring at him, with dawning admiration. No one has ever looked at you this way before.

"My name is Ulf," he says, his words tinged with a slight accent. "You must let me buy you a coffee as an apology. Yes? I will not take no for an answer."

Gather your strength before attempting the Spell for Disappearing. This magic requires focus and stamina. The rite will unfold over a period of days, sometimes weeks, and you will not be able to rest until it is finished.

You wake to Ulf's mouth on your nape. It is not yet dawn. His hands fumble hungrily down your waist, gripping your hips. You feel the sharp rim of his teeth and moan as he pulls you against his body. Your sleepiness makes one sensation of the warmth of his skin and the honeyed glow of the predawn air.

He pins you facedown to the bed, his palms crushing your wrists into the mattress. You spread your legs invitingly, obediently, though you are still sore and damp from last night's lovemaking. Ulf does not hesitate. He is a talker during sex. During your whirlwind courtship, you have grown to enjoy it. His accent makes his words delicious. In a mix of English and Swedish, he whispers to you, telling you he craves you, telling you how amazing your *fitta* is, telling you he would die without you. "I need you, I need you," he murmurs. "*Du är så skön*, just like that, so tight, *gillar du det här?*" He reaches his orgasm, biting your shoulder hard enough to bruise.

"And a good morning to you," you mumble into the pillow. "Let's sleep a little more, okay?"

But Ulf takes hold of your hips and turns you on your back. He strokes your breasts, teasing your nipples, then kisses determinedly down your stomach, toward your tangle of pubic hair.

"And now it's your turn," he says. "*Mitt hjärta, min skatt, mitt liv.*"

The sun is rising, throwing shards of light against the wall. You close your eyes, torn between fatigue and anticipation.

Ulf has been in your life for five weeks. You have not had a solid night's sleep for five weeks. He grins wickedly up at you from beneath his mop of flaxen curls.

"I will be a student of your body," he says.

Your alarm clock sounds. You fling out a hand and whack it blindly off the table. This is how all your mornings begin nowadays.

The Spell for Disappearing has been handed down through generations of witches. Through trial and error, it has been refined to its purest and most potent form.

Your mother was a junkie, your father a blank space on your birth certificate. And so you were raised by your grandmother, who taught you to pick mushrooms and bind the wings of injured birds. Together you nursed an abandoned litter of raccoons until they were old enough to be released into the alley, their natural habitat. Together you made poultices and teas from garden plants: feverfew for headaches, chamomile for wounds, goldenseal for stomach ailments, and valerian for sleep.

Together you weathered your mother's occasional appearances. It was always the same—she would show up in the middle of the night, sweaty and disheveled, banging on the door and screaming that her only daughter was being kept from her. Your grandmother would usher you back to bed, where you would lie awake, listening to your mother's unfamiliar voice rising and falling, dipping into sobs, and eventually petering out into whimpers. She was usually gone by morning, along with a substantial portion of the cash your grandmother kept in the cookie jar beside the kitchen sink.

You did not have many friends as a child, since the neighborhood kids believed your grandmother was a witch. They weren't wrong. Raised in Reading, Massachusetts, a few miles from Salem, your grandmother came from a long line of herbalists and healers. She gave you your love of books. She taught you that your ancestors were persecuted as witches only because people did not value or understand botany and biology. She taught you what she knew about plants, about the body, about life on this planet, great and small. She taught you that men were afraid of women with knowledge and that women should seek knowledge in all its forms.

"It's all butterflies," your grandmother used to say, meaning that even the most remarkable things had logical explanations. You spent your summers collecting caterpillars, watching as they consumed the carrot leaves you picked for them until, driven by some internal wellspring of instinct, they climbed and held still, melting into jelly, thickening into a papery chrysalis, paralyzed for a somnolent week, and finally emerging as an entirely new creature, an explosion of color and wings.

Not a miracle, but evolution. Not witches, but wise women.

"It's all butterflies," your grandmother said, meaning that only fools believed in magic.

This spell requires a cursed object, ideally metal or stone. For best results, use a ring that has been marked by deceit or murder.

June brings rain to your small midwestern town. You and Ulf are strolling arm in arm, soaked in a gleaming drizzle, stopping every few feet to kiss. You could devour this man; you could live only on this wild love, forgoing food, water, and shelter. Your Viking, over six feet tall, with a craggy brow and golden curls. He has dual citizenship, he told you: his mother American, his father Nordic. He grew up in Uppsala, Sweden, and his English is accented but clear. The occasional malapropism serves only to endear him to you further. "It's a piece of pie," he will sometimes announce cheerfully, combining *easy as pie* and *piece of cake*. You never correct him.

You are thirty-eight years old, and you have never been in love before. You understand that now. Ulf is a revelation. Previous boyfriends might as well have been holograms, lacking flesh, breath, and pheromones. Even Zach, your partner for nearly five years, could not make you shimmy inside the way Ulf does with a single glance. You and Zach were polite lovers, doing crossword puzzles together and jogging side by side on the weekends. Your friends sometimes asked when you and Zach would marry, or even move in together, but neither of you had the inclination. The relationship stagnated, and eventually you parted, mostly due to boredom.

Before Ulf, you had come to believe that you would remain a solitary creature. You always wanted children, but it didn't seem to be in the cards, so you boxed that desire up and hid it away.

You expected to settle into middle age like your grandmother, resigned to her widowhood, surrounded by wildflowers and stray cats.

Now, beneath a lamppost, Ulf kneels, looking up at you, his skin milky in the light, his eyes white-blue, the irises frosted with ice crystals.

"I cannot wait even one more second," he says, pulling a small velvet box from his pocket. "Join your life to mine. We must be together always."

The ring is too small for your finger, and you do not like diamonds, certainly not boxy ones like this. You would have preferred something simple, but that does not matter now; nothing matters except this tidal wave of joy. You slide the ring onto your pinkie, and Ulf promises to have it resized "but immediately."

"My darling," he murmurs, kissing your eyelids, your throat, your palms. "My only love."

Names have power. In all things, give out your own name judiciously and infrequently, even among other witches.

You are striding out through the front doors of the library, late to meet Ulf, when a woman emerges from behind a tree, startling you. It is a hazy summer evening, the breeze slow and laden with humidity. You attempt to sidestep the stranger and keep walking, but the woman forestalls you, holding up a hand.

"I have to talk to you," she says.

"I'm off duty," you say kindly. "If you go in through the double doors, the librarian at the front desk can point you in the right direction."

"I'm Ruth Morgan." The woman offers her name like a question, as though hoping to see an answering flash of recognition.

She appears to be in her thirties, dressed in a denim vest and a skirt that swirls in the wind. Her skin is an earthy red-brown, her hair cut short and touched at the temples with gray.

"Do I know you?" you say. "I'm sorry, I don't remember. I'm usually pretty good with faces."

"No," Ruth says. "We've never met."

"Oh. Okay." You are beginning to feel unsettled. There is something in the woman's manner that you don't understand. "Listen, I'm late to meet my fiancé," you say.

You start walking again, wondering what Ulf has decided to cook tonight. He promised you a marvelous feast of Nordic recipes. It still feels odd to call him your fiancé. The resized ring is heavy on your finger, and it seems to have its own will, sometimes snagging on the stray strands of your scarf, sometimes glinting as though attempting to catch your attention.

A hand grabs your arm. You grunt in shock as the strange woman pulls you backward, her fingers cold, her grip painfully tight.

"Let go of me," you cry out. "What the hell do you want?"

"Your fiancé," Ruth says. "I need to talk to you."

"Who *are* you?"

She gives you an appraising look that scrolls from your toes to your ponytail. You bristle at the intimacy and arrogance of her gaze.

"Believe it or not, I'm here to help you," she says.

"Oh, really? How's that?"

"He isn't who he says he is."

There is a moment of silence. The breeze dances down the hill, tugging Ruth's skirt into billowing folds. You have one just like it at home, in a slightly darker shade. Her bracelets, too, remind you of your own, a row of silver bangles. There on the sidewalk, you experience the uncanny sensation of doubling. Like you, this woman has discreet tattoos peeking out beneath the edges of her clothing. She might be your distorted reflection in a funhouse mirror.

"You know Ulf?" you ask.

"Not by that name, but I know him." Her voice is weary. "God, I know him."

You have the sudden urge to put your fingers in your ears. You don't want this to be happening.

"I can tell you love him," she says. "I recognize the look."

For the first time, there is compassion in her face, or maybe pity. You find this more alarming than anything else she has done so far.

"Everything he says is a lie. You're in serious danger," Ruth says.

"No," you say. "Why are you doing this?"

"I know you don't believe me. You're not the first woman I've tracked down. They never believe me at first."

"What are you talking about?"

She reaches in her pocket and pulls out a card. "Take this. It has all my information. He's a pathological liar. He's violent. You'll start to see the signs now, if you just open your eyes. Call me when you're ready to talk, okay?"

You don't take the card, keeping your arms folded tight across your chest.

She snorts impatiently and rummages in her bag. After a moment, she extracts a photograph, shoving it under your nose.

"Look," she says. "I'm not making this up. I've known him since we were kids."

The picture is soft and creased around the edges, old and well-worn. A pair of teenagers lean against each other, a candid shot, neither of them smiling. There, unmistakable, is a younger Ruth, a smattering of pimples on her chin, hair in pigtails, midriff bared beneath a crop top. Beside her is a young man who vaguely resembles Ulf, but an American version, greasy-haired, dressed in a basketball jersey, his arms looped around Ruth's waist, pulling her close to him. His pupils are crimson pinpoints in the flash.

"That could be anybody," you say.

Ruth shudders, an odd convulsion. "It's always the same," she murmurs, as though to herself. She tucks the photograph back into her bag and closes her eyes. Then she begins to unbutton her vest. You watch in alarm as her fingers dance determinedly downward, revealing the freckled brown skin of her sternum.

"Don't worry, I'm not about to flash you," she says. Tugging her collar to the side, she shows you a mark above her heart, a wide scar, filmy and pink.

"He did this to me," she says, without looking at you. "He did this when I left him. I had my suitcase packed. He grabbed me on my way out the door."

The shape is unmistakable: an iron pressed against her flesh. For a moment you can hear the sizzle of scalding metal. The wide bottom seared the middle of her breastbone, while the point nestled in the hollow beneath her clavicle. The burn appears to be several years old, healed but still shiny, forever swollen at the edges.

Ruth buttons up her vest. You open your mouth and close it. There is no script for this.

"Ulf," she says. "He went by another name when I knew him. Ulf means *wolf,* you know, in those Scandinavian languages. Mr. Subtlety at his finest."

Without warning, her fingers dart forward, striking like a snake. She pinches your palm.

"What the hell?" you shout.

Ruth yanks off your engagement ring, holding it up to the light.

"God, he's nothing if not consistent," she says. "You'd think he'd buy a new ring, but he seems attached to this one. The thing must be cursed by now. He had it resized again, right? I'm guessing it was too small for you. The last woman had little squirrel paws."

You snatch the ring back with shaking hands. "You're crazy. You must be crazy."

"I cannot wait even one more second," Ruth says softly. "Join your life to mine. We must be together always."

Then she leans forward and tucks her card into your purse.

Before performing the rite, you will need these elements: eggshell for awakening, seeds for rebirth, earth for permanence, bone for strength, water for change, and blood for life.

Your mother died when you were eight. An overdose, as expected. You attended the funeral at the side of your stone-faced grandmother, feeling as though you ought to cry, since she seemed unable to.

A week later, you rode your bike to the little occult shop on Main Street—the one your grandmother so often sneered at—and purchased a crystal ball with your own pocket money. You propped it up on the desk in your bedroom, which had belonged to your mother in her youth and was still decorated to her taste rather than yours. You stared into the depths of the orb for hours, hoping for a glimpse of the future or an image of the past, but there was only murky gray. You turned the glass ball this way and that, moving it from sunlight to shadow, discovering lighter and darker gradations of gray, now ash, now charcoal, until your eyes burned with tears.

In retrospect, you are not sure what was driving you. Perhaps it was an unwillingness to face the truth of what you had suffered. Perhaps it was a rebellion against your grandmother's levelheaded practicality. Perhaps it was a desire to connect with the long line of witches who came before you. Perhaps it was a childish way of honoring your mother.

Even now, you know very little about her, beyond the addiction she could not overcome. But what is heroin if not synthetic magic, an escape from reality, a manufactured dream-state? You have seen pictures of your mother before she began using: long dark curls, a shy smile. You inherited her hair, her eyes, and something else, something stranger, something that kept you up late at night reading books about witchcraft that you checked out from the library without your grandmother's knowledge.

The crystal ball was only the beginning. You sketched sigils and incantations in your journal, which you privately thought of as your own book of shadows. You read about circle-casting, smudging, and pentagrams, which were not satanic symbols as you had been taught but five-pointed stars representing the four elements and the human spirit. You learned that real witches did not use the terms *black* and *white* magic, which had racist overtones, speaking instead of "baneful" magic, intended to cause harm. You spent so many days alone, reading in your mother's old bedroom with its frilly pink lampshades and flower-printed wallpaper. You would listen to your grandmother humming downstairs and the children at the neighborhood park screaming with laughter. You would turn the page, learning about sacred altars and the astral plane.

There had to be more to life than life. While other kids rode their bikes to the park or experimented with shoplifting, you kept track of the solstice and the equinox, Lammas and Beltane. When you were bullied or ignored at school, you imagined your astral body flying up through the ceiling and far away, leaving your mortal flesh behind. You wrote a list of intentions and burned it at the new moon. You pricked your finger and watched the blood collect in a bowl, drop by drop.

To this day, you have told no one about that time—it is too intimate, too precious. More than anything, you wished for a coven: a collective of witches, bonded by faith and sorcery, closer than family. More than anything, you wished for love—real love, the kind in songs and storybooks. After all, what could be more magical than two souls adrift in a heedless universe, happening to collide, and not just collide but open to each other, turning toward each other in a mutual dance?

The Spell for Disappearing may alter your perceptions. You may find that you can see through time. You may find that the true names of objects and people enter your mind unbidden. While working the ritual, you will be more powerful and astute, entering a heightened state.

You almost tear Ruth's card to pieces. You almost stuff it down the garbage disposal. You almost hand it to Ulf, telling him everything, letting him take the reins and relieving yourself of this bizarre, dreadful burden.

It is Ruth's scar that stops you—the precise outline of an iron, glowing neon in your memory.

Over dinner that night, you are quiet. Ulf whips up a sensuous repast, complete with a carafe of wine and acoustic guitar on the stereo. He raises a glass and toasts your good health. Over and over he calls you *min fästmö*, the Swedish word for *fiancée*. In response, you smile vaguely, pushing the food around on your plate. You have never treated him this way before, as though he is not the most interesting thing in the universe. Your obvious distraction sends him into a tizzy of praise—"my darling, so beautiful, so unique, *min skatt, mitt liv*." For the first time, you sense a false note somewhere. Ulf tells you that the engagement ring is perfect on your finger, that you are alight with love, as though he is willing these things to be true.

"Listen, *min fästmö*," he says. "How would it be if we went to Canada for our honeymoon? It is not so romantic as other places, perhaps, but I have a cabin there. It has been in my family forever, and it is my favorite place, yes, my very favorite place in all the world. Shall we go there together, as man and wife?"

"Perfect," you say absently.

There is no sex that night.

"I'm too tired," you tell him.

"Then let me fill you with energy, *min fästmö*," he says, nuzzling your neck and breathing in your ear.

"My head hurts," you say, harsher this time.

He pulls away like you slapped him. For a moment he stares, his eyes cold and narrow. Then he recovers himself, flashing a seductive smile.

"Poor thing," he coos. "Let me tuck you in. I'll massage your temples. Back home in Uppsala, *min farmor* taught me just how to heal a headache. That is Swedish for *my grandmother*. She would have loved you!"

You pretend to fall sleep. When Ulf slips out of the room, switching off the light, you take Ruth's card from your pocket and turn it over in the darkness, warming it between your palms.

A coven is needed for this magic to reach maximum efficacy. Alone, you will not be able to manage the rite. Ideally there will be a full cohort of twelve. But if you do not have the time or opportunity to gather so many witches, even two, working together closely, can achieve strong results.

"I don't know why I'm here," you say for the third time.

You are seated as far away from Ruth as possible while sharing the same park bench. A man pushes a stroller along the path. A lawn mower starts up in the distance. Ruth tips her head back, drinking in the sunshine with her eyes closed.

"Ask me anything," she says.

"I should go," you say, but you do not get to your feet.

"Want to know his real name?" Her eyes are still closed, her chin lifted.

You don't answer.

"Jeff Watkins," she says. "We grew up together."

"You grew up in Sweden?" you ask helplessly.

Ruth turns to you, her forehead crumpled. "No," she says. "No. I grew up in Dayton. And so did Jeff."

"I don't understand."

"He changes his identity," Ruth says. "He likes to be different people. I think it's almost . . . I don't know, I can't diagnose him, I'm not a medical professional, and he's . . . well, he's beyond the pale. Changing his whole persona seems like something he *has* to do, like a compulsion. He's pretended to be a California surfer. He's pretended to be a good old boy from the Deep South. Once he was an upper-class Brit. He remakes himself each time."

"But he speaks Swedish," you say.

"Nah. He's never even been to Europe. He probably just memorized some catchphrases, got a translation app on his phone.

You don't speak Swedish, do you? How would you know the difference?"

"Look," you say. "I'm not saying I believe you. But if I did—I mean—why? Why would he do this? Why would anyone?"

Ruth sighs. Her hair is a rumpled pixie cut, and she keeps smoothing it, a nervous habit.

"I should be better at this," she says at last. "God knows I've done it enough times. Here's the deal. You have money, right?"

The question hits like a gut punch.

Yes, you have money, but no one knows this. You have never told another living soul.

You lost your grandmother when you were twenty-two, in graduate school, getting your degree in library science. It was sudden, a car accident. A major trucking company was at fault, and there was a substantial settlement. All your grandmother's property went to you. Her house was worth over a million, to your surprise. Despite its dilapidated roof and rambling garden, the surrounding neighborhood was up-and-coming and the acreage was precious.

You added the totality of your grandmother's estate to the settlement from the trucking company. You have not touched that money, which has been sitting in the bank, accumulating interest at an astonishing rate, for over a decade.

You do not speak of it. Your friends, your coworkers—whenever someone asks about your family, you wave your hand noncommittally and change the subject. You have worked your entire adult life, put away money of your own, and saved carefully. You cannot bring yourself to spend one penny of the sum you were given as recompense for your immeasurable loss. Even magic cannot restore the dead. You cannot wish your grandmother back, but you will not grant the premise that cash could ever replace her raucous laugh, her perfect posture, her soft hands.

"How did you know?" you gasp.

"They've all got money," Ruth says. "Jeff is good with computers; he finds these things out. It's blood in the water. He can sniff it out a mile away. You're loaded, aren't you?"

She glances at you, finding confirmation in your face.

"You ran into him someplace random, I bet," she continues. "He bumped into you, spilled your drink or something, and your eyes met. Love at first sight."

"Kismet," you say. It was Ulf's word, and you had to look it up.

"Whirlwind courtship," Ruth says. "Quick marriage. He's already picked a date, right?"

"Next month," you whisper. "He said he always wanted a July wedding. 'Why wait?' he said."

"Right. And no prenup. You see?"

"But he pays for everything. He told me that his salary is amazing—he always picks up the check—he insists . . ." You cannot breathe. A wheezy whistling escapes you, and Ruth scoots closer, rubbing your back like a mother soothing a colicky child.

"It's difficult to hear, I know," she murmurs, but her tone is mechanical. How often has she said these exact words before?

"Go on," you say, steadying yourself. "Tell me what I need to know."

Ruth stares at you as though assessing your mettle. Then she nods.

"Jeff and I both grew up dirt-poor," she says. "But you're right, he does have money now. This is his job." She points to the diamond ring on your finger. "He can afford to pay for everything at the start of each relationship. It's his investment. It reaps *huge* benefits."

"And after? Once he's—married?"

"Well." She shakes her head. "He's got a temper. He can only be sugar and spice for so long. He keeps up the performance until the papers are signed. Then the true colors come out."

"True colors?" you echo on a high note.

She pauses, biting her lip. "Slaps and punches. Black eyes, broken nose."

"Jesus."

"He threw one woman through a glass door. Put her in the hospital."

You wrap your arms tightly around your middle.

"So you get divorced," Ruth says. "And he gets half. Sometimes more. One of them—one of his brides—her family had this beautiful cabin in Canada, on a lake. They'd owned it for generations. It was her favorite place in the world, she told me. I found her too late. After they were already married. His lawyer nabbed the cabin in the divorce."

A young couple strolls down the path in front of you, holding hands in companionable silence. You resist the urge to separate them by force.

"It's a lot to take in," Ruth says sympathetically. "Sleep on it. Think about it. And when you're ready to leave him, call me."

When—not *if*.

The sun breaks through the clouds, dappling your skin. There is a question hovering in the air. Finally you find the courage to ask it.

"Did he do this to you? Take your money? Lie to you?"

Ruth bows her head.

"I was the one he loved," she says after a moment, her voice expressionless. Her hand lifts to her chest, rubbing the scar beneath her T-shirt. "He pursued me since elementary school; he told everybody he was going to marry me. He would show up at my house with flowers, throw pebbles at my window. My friends thought it was the most romantic thing in the world. But I always said no. He scared me somehow. That anger. And—" She breaks off. "I felt like there was nothing behind his eyes, you know?"

You watch her, waiting. Her gaze has slipped inward.

"I finally gave in," she says. "He wore me down. Or maybe he got better at hiding who he really was. We dated for a few years in high school, then got engaged after graduation. I didn't have money. Not a red cent. There was nothing for him to gain. So I think he loved me, as much as he's capable of that emotion."

You realize you are holding your breath.

"He gave me that." She points to your ring again. "Then he gave me this." She points to the brand left by the iron.

Be conscious of what you eat and drink before performing the rite. Vegetables are best, as they will strengthen your flesh and nourish your spirit. It is wise to avoid heavy foods and sweets.

Haggard, you stumble through work like a zombie, making mistakes, earning concerned looks and a few reprimands. The world around you is unreal, flattened, like the set dressing on a stage, a facsimile of an actual place. The backdrop of the library might as well be made out of cardboard. Your coworkers are actors reading lines: "Hey, did you forget to check the inventory?" "You're looking a little green, are you okay?"

You are not okay. You are engaged to a villain. You have no doubts anymore. Your conversation on the park bench with Ruth was only yesterday, but that is long enough for the truth to sink in, all the way down to your bones.

You will break up with him. *When*, not *if*. You will choose a public place to do it. You will get your locks changed first. You will be brave, like Ruth. Maybe you will install a new security system. Maybe you will get a guard dog.

It felt too good to be true because it was too good to be true. You will survive this, you tell yourself. It will not be difficult to untangle your life from Ulf's. The man has been in your orbit for only two months now.

At lunchtime, he texts you: *I will pick you up at 4. We must go to the bakery and try wedding cakes. I prefer chocolate, but I will defer to you.*

A wave of nausea crests beneath your breastbone. You barely make it to the toilet in time, expelling everything you have eaten that day, vomiting until the sides of your stomach clang together and there is nothing left to come up.

Be prepared for strange and unpredictable bodily changes. The Spell for Disappearing has a way of altering and warping the flesh. Before, during, and after vanishing, your anatomy will undergo extreme stress and may swell, ache, or scar. You will emerge transformed.

Sitting on the toilet, you clutch the pregnancy test in both hands. It will take five minutes to give you results—enough time to make a cup of tea to soothe your stomach, peppermint, as your grandmother taught you—but you can't seem to move. You are trapped like a fly in amber, pants around your ankles, legs going numb, gaze fixed on the window of the pregnancy test, an oval the size of a grain of rice.

This is the most reliable brand on the market. One blue line means business as usual. Two blue lines means that the world, already sideways, has turned all the way upside down.

You run through your list of symptoms again. Fatigue, which

you assumed was due to your all-night marathons in bed with Ulf. Hot flashes, possibly attributable to Ulf's good looks. A vague feeling of nausea when smelling grilled meat over the past couple of weeks. A few moments of eerie light-headedness that you assumed were lovesickness, back when you were still in love. And one intense bout of vomiting earlier today. Nothing conclusive. Your period is a few weeks late, but that's not unusual. Your cycle has always been irregular, easily thrown out of its rhythm by stress.

The past few days have been extremely stressful. Since Ruth stepped out from behind that tree, you have inhabited a waking nightmare.

You left work early, telling your coworkers you were sick. You texted Ulf the same, hoping that he would give you space—a moment to breathe, to think, to find your footing. Instead, he bombarded you with messages, asking how you were feeling and offering to come over with medicine. You made excuses: *I don't want you to catch whatever this is, I don't want you to see me like this, it's gross.* He was undeterred, volunteering to lay a cool cloth on your brow, calling you his *fitta*, his *skatt*, his *liv*, words he learned from a translation app and was probably misusing.

I'm going to nap, I'll text you when I'm up, you wrote finally, then turned off your phone, relishing the silence.

Now your gaze is locked on the tiny window like a laser. You spin your engagement ring, a nervous tic, digging a shiny groove into the flesh of your third finger.

A sound from downstairs startles you—a key turning in the lock. Ulf calls out, "*Mitt allt?* Are you awake now? I have a surprise for you."

You glance back at the pregnancy test and muffle a cry in your palm. Two blue lines. Sperm and egg. Blood and bone.

Ulf's footsteps climb the stairs, quick and eager. You splash water on your face, ashen in the mirror. Then you realize you are still holding the pregnancy test. You lunge toward the trash can, intending to stuff it down beneath the soiled tissues and used cotton balls. But what if Ulf searches the garbage? You have no idea what he's capable of. The damn thing is too bulky to flush.

"*Mitt allt*?" Ulf repeats playfully, just outside the door. "I know you are in there. I can hear you breathing."

The window. You always leave it slightly ajar, even in cold weather, to reduce steam and odors. You lean across the sink and hurl the pregnancy test into the alley behind your house.

The knob rattles. Ulf pounds on the door with his fist, making you jump. "Are you all right? I am growing worried. Open, please."

You obey. He fills the bathroom with his bulk, holding out a bouquet of flowers, and you bare your teeth in what you hope is a smile.

The moon is a potent force in the lives of witches. You must learn how your own magic responds to each phase. Most practitioners find their abilities to be strongest during the full moon and weaker during waxing and waning. The new moon offers its own dark power, erratic and mysterious.

In the dead of night, you call Ruth, who answers after one ring, as though she was waiting. She sounds fully alert, not a hint of sleepy slurring.

"Are you alone?" she asks.

"Yes."

"Good. Where is he?"

"Asleep upstairs. I told him I wasn't feeling well and I wanted to be on my own tonight. He wouldn't go. He said he couldn't stand the idea of abandoning me when I'm under the weather." You pause, a chill tracking down your nape. "It's like he knows I'm on to him. He won't leave me alone for a second."

A low chuckle. "How can you tell when he's lying?" Ruth asks. "His lips are moving."

You settle on the couch. The moon hangs in the window, a delicate crescent. You are not yet ready to tell Ruth about your pregnancy. Speaking the words aloud will make the situation real.

"How many women has he done this to?" you ask instead.

"Twenty-three, including you." Her answer is immediate, no need to tally it up in her head. She knows the count; she carries it with her.

"Holy shit."

"Yeah, he's prolific. And I haven't always been able to stop him. He gets around; he's clever. He's gotten married eight times."

"Eight? Seriously? Isn't that illegal?"

"Oh, no. He gets divorced each time. No bigamy. Right side of the law."

The house is absolutely silent. For once, you are grateful for the loose floorboard outside your bedroom door that squeals like a banshee whenever you step on it. You've been meaning to have it fixed for years, but now it will be your lo-fi alarm. You are sure Ulf is sleeping; you waited to leave the bed until he was snoring, his mouth pooling open, fingers twitching. The board will tell you if he wakes.

"I broke up thirteen of his conquests," Ruth says. Her voice is a rich alto, filled with pride. "Saved thirteen women."

"Wow."

"Yeah," she says.

You count quickly on your fingers. “So eight of them married him. You stopped thirteen. That’s only twenty-one. What happened to the other two?”

Ruth sighs. “One lady figured his deal out on her own. By the time I found her, she’d already broken up with him. The other one . . .” She trails off.

You dig your fingernails into your palm. “What happened to her?”

“That’s the one he threw through a glass door. She was in the hospital for days. And she still didn’t want to leave him. Kept forgiving him. Even after I found her and told her everything, she kept trying to make it work. She told me to get lost. Told me she could change him. *He* left *her*, in the end. Once he had all her money.” There is a silence. Then, softly, Ruth says, “She committed suicide. A few months after he took off.”

The moon is tangled in the branches of a tree like a Christmas ornament. The crescent is so fine it seems that the twigs might scrape it, break it.

“Why do you do this?” you ask.

“Do what?”

“Help people. Save women. Don’t you have a job? How do you manage it?”

Ruth laughs. “I do have a job. I’m a coder, so I can work from anywhere. Thanks for asking.” You can’t tell if she’s being sarcastic or genuine. “And I didn’t always do this. After I left him, I didn’t think about him for years. I had my own shit to be dealing with. Then I heard he was married. And married again. And I heard that he broke a woman’s jaw. And got married again. Four women, five women. I realized what was happening. I went sleuthing and I saw that all the women . . .” Her voice dips into a murmur. “You’re all a little like me. Did you notice that?”

"Yes," you say.

"It's like he was looking for me over and over, then hurting me over and over. Dark hair, boho, intellectual, lonely—he'd find another one, swoop in, and take everything. I saw the pictures of these women on my laptop. All different but the same. Dozens of us laid out in a row like sisters or something. I couldn't sleep at night. The scar on my chest—" She breaks off, breathing hard. "I couldn't sleep."

You nod, then remember that she can't see you.

"I do this because I have to," Ruth says. "And now I sleep fine."

"Does he know?" you ask. "Does he know what you're doing?"

"Oh, no," she says in a rush. "No, I keep off his radar. I hope he just thinks he's losing his touch, that his plans keep coming apart, all these crazy women changing their minds on him. If he knew I was involved, he'd kill me."

She says this matter-of-factly. It's not hyperbole; it's the reality of her situation.

A creak from upstairs. You tremble involuntarily, staring at the ceiling.

"He's waking up," you whisper.

"Be careful," Ruth says, and the line goes dead.

The floorboard gives an inhuman shriek. You hear Ulf padding down the hall, calling your name.

You must speak the words of the Spell for Disappearing exactly. Any mispronunciation can be catastrophic, even fatal. While performing the rite, witches have been known to lose a hand, an eye, an entire limb, or their lives, because of a simple slip of the tongue.

For a week—the most difficult week of your life—you pretend to have the flu. You use the oldest trick in the book, holding the thermometer near a light bulb to fake a fever for Ulf's benefit. Your nausea, at least, is real enough. Morning sickness, however, seems to be a misnomer. The afternoons are the hardest, and you take to skipping lunch, since you won't be able to retain it anyway.

"Poor child," Ulf says. "Never have I seen someone so ill."

He won't leave your side for a moment. He hovers around you like a wolf circling an injured caribou. You can't call Ruth; he's always listening. You can't even text her, since Ulf has a habit of playfully grabbing your phone to "see what interests you so." In every interaction with him, you exercise rigid control over your body, imitating the same behaviors you used to do naturally: stroking his cheek, smoothing his hair. It is an eerie, mutual performance, a pas de deux, both of you miming love, both of you lying. He kisses your brow, thinking all the while about your bank account, or so you assume. You blink up at him, feigning fondness, wishing he would be run over by a bus or killed by a falling tree branch, something swift and accidental and not your fault. You are not friends or lovers but enemies locked in a bizarre pantomime. His goal is to hurt you; your goal is to escape him. Your hope is to survive him.

More and more, you catch glimpses behind his facade. His flirtatious winks, once so alluring, now contain a gleam of desperation. His exaggerated gestures, which used to seem intriguingly foreign, now strike you as hammy and implausible. How did you not notice these things before? Were you so flattered by his attentions that you could not perceive the instability of his accent, drifting occasionally into Russian or cockney? What has changed, the quality of his deception or your level of perceptiveness? You prefer to believe that Ulf is slipping—that he fooled you before not because you are a gullible stooge but because he was at the top of his game, a shrewd, practiced con man deploying his entire arsenal of charm. Now, however, he must sense that something is amiss in your reactions, and as a result he has begun to overdo his performance like a comedian onstage who stops getting laughs.

When he enters your bedroom, you close your eyes, pretending to sleep. You shudder away from his touch and blame the fever. You call in sick at work. Your boss is furious, but you don't care. They can fire you if they want to. What does it matter?

You are thirty-eight years old. You have always wanted children. This is your last chance to be a mother.

The fact of the baby burns like a bonfire in your mind, throwing everything else into shadow. All your life you have been searching for magic, and here, in your belly, a spark, a seedling, a cell dividing and dividing, a new creature spun into being, reworking your hormonal system, taking what it needs from your flesh, a miracle, nothing short of a miracle. You were not trying to get pregnant. You were falling in love, still using condoms, too sex-drunk to consider your ovulation cycle. Without your attention, without your conscious will, life has taken root inside you.

"It's all butterflies," your grandmother would say, but you know better.

And so you lie in bed, pretending to be sick, touching your belly, laughing and weeping in silence, making up your mind.

It is unwise to dabble in baneful magic. Jinxes and hexes offer power, but there is a cost. Remember the Rule of Three, which governs all practitioners of magic: any energy or intention that you send out into the world will one day return to you, threefold stronger.

After a week of fake flu, Ulf comes into your bedroom with a long face and sits on the edge of the bed.

"My love, I have terrible news," he says mournfully.

You feign disorientation, as though you've just woken up. "What? What is it?"

"I must leave town. I shall be gone all weekend. An eternity, when I am apart from you!"

"Oh no," you say. It doesn't come out right—too flat.

He flicks his gaze at you, a gleam of blue.

"I'll miss you," you add quickly.

"My work—it is overwhelming sometimes," he says. "But the salary—ah! How could I turn it down? And they rely on me so much."

You know better than to push for details. God knows what he'll really be doing out there.

As a child, you read about the negative side of magic, turning the pages of your library books with caution, as though even looking at the names of these dangerous spells could infect you with their essence. It frightened you to think that there were witches out there making hex bags, launching psychic attacks, or dabbling in necromancy.

But in your wildest imaginings, you never pictured someone like Ulf. A shapeshifter, a trickster, a sorcerer in his own right. He divined the secret presence of your wealth, something you have successfully hidden for almost two decades. He wove a love spell over you, captivating you, sweetening the air you breathed and electrifying all the colors. He remade you into a kind of living voodoo doll, a replica of the woman he once adored, the woman he really wanted to hurt. You imagine the long string of bodies in Ulf's wake, rag dolls cast aside, limbs broken, bank accounts empty, black eyes, hospital stays, medical bills, PTSD, panic attacks, scars.

"When do you leave?" you ask.

"The day after tomorrow," Ulf says, shaking his head in

sorrow. "But do not worry! I shall be by your side every moment until then."

"Gone all weekend," you repeat. A door is opening inside your mind.

Timing is critical in the Spell for Disappearing. You must be swift and decisive. Perform the rite without hesitation or pause. Any delay at the crucial moment can be lethal.

"Holy shit," Ruth says.

You are sitting in the back booth of a diner, screened from the door by a massive plastic fern. The restaurant is bustling, your voices hidden in the clatter of dishes from the kitchen and the warble of music from the jukebox.

"I told him I was going back to work today," you say. "I went to my ob-gyn instead. I'm eight weeks pregnant. It must have happened right away. Like the first or second time we had sex."

"Damn." Ruth lifts her coffee mug in both hands, brings it to her nose, inhales without drinking, and sets it down again. "I'm assuming he doesn't know."

"Of course not. You're the first person I've told."

The absurdity of this almost makes you laugh. Almost. Under normal circumstances, there is a pattern to this kind of disclosure: first the father of the baby, then family and friends. But your grandmother died over a decade ago, you don't dare to involve any of your work friends or book club members, and the father of your baby is a psychopath and a sorcerer.

And what is Ruth? As new as an acquaintance, as close as a blood relative, impossible to define.

"What are you going to do?" she asks. Without waiting for an answer, she says quickly, "I'd abort. Seriously. If you keep it, you'll be chained to him forever. He'll have rights over the kid. Do you want him involved in the life of your baby? What if he decides that the kid could be a new, fun way to hurt you? He'll get violent with you, and probably the kid too, it's just a matter of time. He'll take all your money and just keep taking. You'll never be free of him. What kind of life would that be?"

The waitress appears, setting down a plate of bacon and hash browns for Ruth and dry white toast for you. The smell of the meat turns your stomach.

"I've thought about all of that," you say, once the waitress is out of earshot. "I'm keeping the baby."

Ruth opens her mouth to argue, but you cut her off.

"He's leaving for a few days," you say. "He told me this morning."

She nods. "I was expecting that. There were legal complications with the last divorce, back in Michigan. He has to show up in person to make his case."

"I won't be here when he gets back," you say. "Will you help me?"

Ruth's bracelets flash in the light as she leans forward, gathering up your hands in hers.

You must divest yourself of all your worldly possessions. A spell of this potency requires a spiritual lightness. If you are weighed down by material objects, your magic will be diminished, and as a result, your disappearance may be painful, partial, or incomplete.

Barefoot, you stand on the front porch. A moving truck fills the street, casting its massive shadow across the lawn. Burly men stream in and out of your house, toting your furniture. They are as busy and indistinguishable as ants: black T-shirts, crew cuts, bulging biceps, unsmiling faces, a pervasive cloud of body odor. Feeling useless, you try to stay out of their way. Occasionally one of them barks a question: "Does this need to be bubble-wrapped?" or "Are you seriously giving this away?"

Yes, you're giving it away, all of it. Once the truck is loaded, the moving men will drive your belongings to Goodwill, and anything that remains unclaimed will end the day at the dump.

You wipe the sweat from your brow. The morning is coming to a boil, the heat climbing with each tick of the clock. Grunting, the men carry off your wrought iron bed frame, your oak bookshelves, even your books. You scheduled the moving company to come as early in the day as possible, hoping for an unobtrusive getaway, the work finished before dawn, your neighbors none the wiser. You underestimated the time it takes to empty an entire house. Dozens of joggers and dog-walkers have already passed by—wide-eyed witnesses. An elderly couple has even stopped to watch, murmuring to each other and pointing as though they're at a show.

Your phone buzzes in your pocket, and a jolt of panic runs down your spine. Of course, the text is from Ulf. It's always from Ulf. He has been away for only twelve hours, but he has sent nearly fifty messages and shows no sign of slowing.

I miss you, my darling. Tomorrow I will be in your arms again.

You send back a string of emojis: hearts, flowers, smiley faces. Hopefully this will appease him.

The sun climbs the sky. The air shimmers with plumes of heat. As though in a dream, you watch your possessions leaving you. A trio of men work together to balance your wide oval dining table. Another emerges from the house with your fridge-sized bureau strapped to his back. The truck is a hungry mouth, consuming your bicycle, your flower-printed couch, and the loom your grandmother left you.

Your phone buzzes again, and again you feel a thrill of fear.

Send me a selfie, Ulf writes. *Send it now, right now. I must see your face. I drown without you.*

You do not want to give him this, peeling off a layer of yourself and projecting it through the ether. You want him to have nothing of yours, not even your image. But you have no choice.

Careful framing is required, making sure that nothing suspicious is visible behind you, no glimpse of the truck or the men, just the big tree out front. In the photo, your smile is false, but you cannot summon a true one. You apply a filter that bleaches out the dark circles under your eyes and the taut lines of anxiety around your mouth.

That is beauty, Ulf texts back. You breathe again.

The process of disappearing will be arduous both physically and mentally. Remember that resilience is as much a matter of mind as it is bodily strength. You must be brave, even when the ritual becomes painful, even if the discomfort seems unbearable.

At the bus stop, you hover in the shadows. It is evening, the clouds underlined in fading gold. You do not want to be seen here; you wear a baseball cap and sunglasses and stay away from the bright lights of the depot. You don't think there's a security camera, but you aren't taking chances. Earlier today, you cut your hair in the mirror, chopping off your long dark curls without hesitation. You look even more like Ruth now, identical pixie cuts revealing shell-like ears.

At your feet lies a duffel containing the remainder of your

worldly possessions: a change of clothes, the turquoise bracelet your grandmother used to wear, and the crystal ball you purchased in your childhood, which turned up at the back of a cabinet as you prepared for the moving men. You have winnowed yourself down to the bare essentials. It is remarkable how little one actually needs.

Your phone rings in your pocket—a clunky flip phone with an old-fashioned electronic chime. No GPS function. Paid for in cash. Only one person has this number. You threw away your smartphone this morning.

"Are you okay?" Ruth asks.

"The bus should be here any minute." You check your ticket again. "We depart at seven thirty-five."

"Good."

"I'm so scared," you murmur.

"I know. But he won't find you. He'll never know what happened."

"His plane lands at eight. What if the bus is late? What if—"

"You'll be okay. We thought of everything."

"You promise?" you ask, hearing the childish note in your own voice.

To your surprise, Ruth laughs, the first genuine, full-throated laugh you have ever heard from her.

"This is exciting," she says. "I've helped so many women, you know? Getting an alarm system installed for them, driving them across town to move in with friends—I thought I'd seen it all. I even went with one to buy a gun." Her breath crackles eagerly down the line. "It's always the same pattern. I stick around until they're safe. And then Jeff disappears. Once he has the money, or when he realizes he's never going to get that money—poof. Gone in a puff of smoke."

"Right," you say slowly, considering this.

"I've spent so much time tracking that dude down," she says. "The women stay, and he goes. He runs, and I chase him. But this time—" Ruth gives another belly laugh, a deep burble of untamed mirth. "The tables are gonna turn. God, I'd give anything to see his face when he gets back. You're about to vanish into thin air."

You hang up, promising to call her from the road.

Fidgeting, you run through the checklist in your mind. Tomorrow the library will receive your letter of resignation. The change-of-name forms are loaded in your backpack. Your house is on the market. Ruth went with you to meet with the realtor, explaining the uniqueness of your circumstances. She accompanied you to the bank and helped you move your money into an untraceable account, safe even from Ulf's baneful powers of divination. You withdrew a healthy roll of cash, which will sustain you for the present, keeping you off the grid.

This is what the money is for. This is what it was for all along.

Eight weeks pregnant. You stroke your stomach, grateful that your baby is not yet developed enough to share any part of your anxiety. Near the end of a pregnancy, a fetus in the womb can absorb and echo some of its mother's emotions; her blood is its blood too, after all. But a two-month-old embryo is less than an inch long, with only the most nascent glimmer of a brain. It does not have bones or sensory organs, much less the neural architecture necessary to experience pain or fear.

Your child will grow up safe. Your child will never know a thing about her father. A blank space on the birth certificate.

You check your watch again: 7:32. Still no sign of the bus. Somewhere behind you, a teenager is playing a video game at top volume, filling the air with erratic, staccato chiming. The wind picks up, carrying the smell from the garbage bins beside the depot. Your stomach twists with nausea.

After a moment, you kneel, unzipping the duffel and groping for the crystal ball. You want its comforting weight in your hands just now. Beneath the streetlight, you see your own face reflected in the curve of glass. The combination of ambient darkness and overhead illumination brings your image into stark relief. You lean forward, and your reflection elongates. There are your grandmother's hooded eyes, her thin nose. You have never seen the likeness so clearly before, though people used to comment on it when you were a girl. Your features will age into your grandmother's, you can see now. The underlying bone structure has always been the same.

The streetlamp flickers, and your reflection changes. Now there are many faces inside the orb, some shadowy and ethereal, some crisp and solid. A few have pixie cuts like yours, but others blur into black, giving the impression of long dark curls. There are dozens of them, dancing in and out of view, shifting like light on the surface of water. Perhaps they represent the other women Ulf has harmed—Ruth and all your sisters, the coven you never knew you had. You lift a hand to wave to them, and the image alters again, your reflection warping and contracting before your eyes.

There, looking back at you, is a child's face. Plush cheeks, a rosebud mouth, a serene expression. You gasp aloud. Is this, at long last, a true glimpse of the future? You lean close, trying to see clearly in the murky depths, but the child remains stubbornly out of focus, a gauzy waif with blurred features. It is impossible to determine age or gender, though the face seems plump and healthy, maybe even smiling.

And then the bus thunders around the corner, huge and

shuddering, cutting a proud swath through the gloaming. Its headlights strike the crystal ball in your hands, erasing your image and setting the orb aglow. For a moment there is only light, a miniature sun cupped in your palms, shining with infinite possibilities.

Few witches have ever succeeded in performing the Spell for Disappearing. No one has ever managed to work the spell a second time, as it requires too much of the body and mind. This rite is one of the most potent and risky forms of magic known. If you are strong, if you are resolute, you will be able to vanish once in your lifetime—and only once. Choose wisely.

Across, Beyond, Through

For the first hundred miles, Eden is sound asleep in the back seat. Carl navigates the winding roads with the radio on low, a hiss of guitar chords and static. The sky is dark, the highway a shimmering ribbon of gray, but he is wide awake.

It is four in the morning. The highway fills gradually with fellow travelers, early commuters on their way to work. Carl welcomes the friendly blaze of their headlights. He keeps an eye on his daughter in the rearview mirror. Eden talks in her sleep, though not in any language he can understand. At fourteen, her coltish frame is too long to stretch comfortably across the back of the car. She tosses and turns.

Occasionally Carl catches a look at her face, splashed in the glow of oncoming headlights. It makes him wince each time. He knew that as the hours passed, his daughter's bruises would darken, all part of the healing process. Still, it is a shock to observe the pulpy mess that used to be Eden's right eye, her lip scabbed and swollen.

The sun crests the horizon dead ahead, lighting up every bird dropping and crust of ice on the windshield. And then, without warning, Eden hurtles into the passenger seat, her hand on Carl's shoulder, her bare foot fishing for purchase. She settles cross-legged beside him and yawns, smacking her lips. Her T-shirt is on inside out.

"We're really on the road," she says. "I thought maybe I dreamed that."

She flips down the visor and investigates her wounds in the mirror there. The black eye has taken on a sticky sheen, like mother-of-pearl. Her lip is spongy, split down the middle. She grimaces at her reflection.

"We'll get you an ice pack at the next oasis," Carl says.

"I thought I dreamed all of it," Eden says. "It seems like a nightmare, right?"

Carl nods. "Sure does."

"Mom punched me twice. Eye, then mouth. And then bam, open hand, right here." Eden lays a palm over her ear.

"I've never known your mother to hit anyone."

She cocks her head to the side, considering this. Her auburn hair, shoulder-length, swings with each gesture.

"Can you—" Carl pauses, unsure how to proceed. "Would you like to tell me more about what happened yesterday?"

"No," Eden says, without hesitation. Clearly she was waiting for this question, her answer loaded and ready to fire.

Carl knows better than to push. The highway winds among rolling hills, a wide prairie beaded with farmhouses. The sign for Pennsylvania appears around a curve. As they cross the border from New York, both Carl and Eden lunge forward across the dashboard, one arm outstretched, trying to be the first to enter the new state, if only by the length of a fingernail.

"I won," she crows.

"I'll beat you to Ohio," he says.

The sunlight flares across the windshield, offering light but no warmth. It is December, and the air is tinged with frost. Carl reaches for his thermos of coffee. He has not slept much in the past twenty-four hours.

The call came around 2:00 a.m. yesterday, waking him in his Las Vegas apartment. Eden's voice, incoherent with sobs. Carl staggered out of bed and switched on the light. It took him a while to understand what was happening. Eden cried in a way he hadn't heard since her babyhood, the sort of reckless, breathless wheezing that used to accompany a tantrum. He remembers fumbling for the clock and doing math—2:00 a.m. for him in Nevada, 5:00 a.m. for Eden in Utica on the other side of the country.

"Where's your mother?" he asked. "Can I talk to her?"

"She's been arrested," Eden screamed through her tears.

Carl threw on whatever clothes he could grab—a strange arrangement he is still wearing, crisp khaki slacks and an ancient hoodie with paint on the sleeve—and drove to the airport.

°

Dark pines stand out among the bare, skeletal trees. An arctic breeze buffets the car as Carl and Eden play Twenty Questions. He tries not to stare at her injuries, though it's difficult. Her lip is a chunk of pulped plum. Her eye is in the process of swelling shut. She has a concussion that will require care, and one eardrum is ruptured. They cannot fly across the country; the changes in cabin pressure could cause permanent damage to Eden's hearing, not to mention excruciating pain. So Carl rented a car and they are road-tripping through ten states over two days.

He has a high-stakes poker game on Tuesday, scheduled months ago. He's paid the entrance fee. The prize pool is over a million. It cannot be missed.

Lake Erie glimmers between the trees on Eden's side of the car. The Pennsylvania coast is layered with plateaus and valleys of ice, an otherworldly, uneven terrain caused by the movement of waves and sudden cold snaps and snowfall and the occasional thaw followed by refreezing. The deep water, however, seems unaffected by winter. Along the horizon, waves shift and dance, blue under blue sky.

Eden was not supposed to join Carl in Las Vegas until June. His apartment is not ready for her; it's still a bachelor pad strewn with empty liquor bottles and dirty dishes. Did he remember to hide his marijuana paraphernalia? He'll have to check as soon as they walk in the door.

Until now, his relationship with Eden has been one of summers and texting. They are buddies. They chat with their thumbs about TV shows they both watch, comic strips they both enjoy. Sometimes Eden sends him strings of emojis he can't parse. Sometimes he dreams about her—Technicolor, slow-motion moments of closeness, Eden as an infant clutching his finger, Eden as a toddler in his lap, Eden as a preteen riding on his back. He wakes up haunted, unsure whether these visitations are good dreams or nightmares.

She lives with her mother in Utica during the school year and spends her summers with Carl in Las Vegas. That has been the custody agreement up until now, anyway. For three precious months each year, Eden has hung her art on his fridge, critiqued his decor, woken him with a pillow to the face, challenged him to dance parties, and infused his life with sweetness and purpose. Their erratic closeness—periodic but intense—has allowed him to see her growing up in a different way. She does not age continually for him, but in surges, her shoulders suddenly wider, her face elongated, her vocabulary larger, her movements more assured.

He does not know what happened between her and her mother. He can only assume that his ex-wife suffered a psychotic break of some kind. He and June have a cordial, icy dynamic—cordial on his side, icy on hers. But she has always been a loving mother. She has never raised a hand to Eden before, not even a swat on the behind. Her discipline consists of time-outs and exhausting lectures on ethics. She is the sort of mother who cuts the crusts off the bread and peels the oranges she puts in Eden's lunch, even though Eden is in eighth grade and most of her friends just buy a hot lunch and a soda. June is doting and overprotective, lauding Eden's every achievement on social media. Even participation trophies and so-so report cards are touted like Olympic gold medals.

Carl cannot imagine what caused his ex-wife to beat their daughter so badly that Eden ended up in the emergency room and June in jail.

Pennsylvania is the shortest leg of their trip. They cut across the chimney of land that sticks up from the northwest corner of the state. When the sign for Ohio appears, Eden cracks her knuckles and rolls her head side to side like a gymnast preparing for a difficult routine. As they cross the border, both of them lunge forward against their seat belts, one arm extended.

"I won," Carl says.

"Your arms are longer. Unfair advantage."

A barbed wire fence separates a field of snow from another field of snow. Probably corn and soybeans grow here in the summer, proud thickets of green, but just now the landscape seems almost apocalyptically bare. Eden tips down the visor again to examine her reflection in the mirror. Beneath the black eye, her cheek has begun to swell, slowly turning mauve.

"It's gonna get worse before it gets better," she says.

Carl is in the process of passing a semi when his cell phone jangles to life.

Eden glances at the screen. "It's Mom."

"I'll handle it."

"I thought she was in jail."

"Your aunt probably posted bail."

"Oh no. Oh no." Eden tugs desperately on a lock of hair, a gesture Carl recognizes from her toddler years.

He pulls onto the shoulder, tires kicking up a wash of gravel that pings against the undercarriage. He waits a moment to steady his nerves before climbing out with the phone in his hand. The chill turns his breath to vapor. He takes a few steps down the road, glancing back at Eden's white face.

"You're a monster," June cries, in lieu of greeting. "Where on earth are you?"

"I'm bringing Eden to Vegas with me."

"I got home and the house was empty. The CPS people told me you'd taken her. How could you do this to me?"

Carl shivers. He did not think to bring a coat before boarding the plane; he has been a native of Nevada for long enough that he forgot what real winter is like.

"Are you there?" June shouts.

"I'm here. Eden is going to stay with me. It's all arranged."

"You're an asshole."

Carl gnaws on his thumbnail, baffled. June does not swear. She has forbidden Eden from saying *shut up* or *crap* or even the word *hate*.

"Is Eden . . ." June begins, then trails off. "How does she look? Is she—"

"She says you punched her twice and boxed her ear. Is that what happened?"

"Oh my goodness." June blows her nose. "Oh heavens. Look, you've got to bring her back here. This is all a big mistake."

"Did you hit her?" Carl repeats. His hands close instinctively into fists. Papa bear.

"It's complicated. I can't get into it right now."

"It doesn't seem complicated to me."

June's voice rises an octave. "I can't even *think* while you're holding my little girl hostage. You're going to turn around and bring Eden right back home. She belongs with me. I'm her mother. I know what's best."

Carl hangs up and glares at the phone for a minute, then turns it off in case June calls back. The little screen goes black between his fingers.

°

Ohio lasts for hours. Snow begins to fall, a powdery dusting, bleaching the air. Clouds cover the sky, the ground moon-pale, the whole world rendered in grayscale. Eden signals at trucks to sound their horns. Drivers in passing cars do double takes at the sight of her face. Her bruises are blossoming spectacularly. Whenever her mouth starts bleeding she dabs it with Kleenex, which is then deposited randomly around the car, along with ponytail holders, tubes of lip balm, socks, and hairpins. An adolescent nest.

And all the while, Carl's mind orbits the puzzle he cannot solve: What made June turn on her beloved child? He still remembers his ex as she was when he first encountered her—crackling with life, constantly in motion. He remembers her fiery red mane, now darkened to coffee brown and laced with gray. He remembers the way she hummed when she was thinking and chewed her pencils so intensely that she nibbled away every scrap of yellow coating, turning them into whittled, damp twigs.

Even then, he and June made for something of an uneasy alliance. She came from Southern Baptists who raised her on purity rings and father-daughter dances. Carl's parents, on the other hand, were hippies who urged him not to marry until he was at least thirty so he'd have plenty of time to sow his wild oats and find out what kind of life he wanted for himself. He and June met in an introductory science class at Utica University. They both needed it to fulfill their requirements for graduation and were both lost after the first session. Carl was prelaw, June majoring in philosophy with the goal of becoming a doctor of divinity. They coached each other through Physics 101 and ended up falling in love, each fascinated by the other's strangeness.

After graduation, they moved in together. In defiance of her upbringing, June was sexually active—a demon in the sack, actually—but she could not shake the guilt. Often she wept in shame after orgasm. Carl privately hypothesized that her fascination with the study of religious scholars arose from a desire to quantify the precise cost to her soul of each sin. He knew to tiptoe around the apartment without speaking whenever June was on the phone with her parents. They believed she lived alone. Fortunately they were proud Mississippians and refused to travel to the scary, unfamiliar North.

Then Eden came along. An accident, a statistical anomaly—June was one of the tiny fraction of women to get pregnant while on birth control. Abortion was out of the question, of course. Carl hadn't meant to marry so young, but he knew June needed this from him. And he loved her then, he did. They eloped as quickly as possible so her parents wouldn't be able to count backward from nine months and draw nefarious conclusions.

The real battles began during the pregnancy. Carl had finally come to terms with the fact that he did not enjoy the law. He was finding success as a poker player online. He'd begun driving down to Atlantic City on the weekends and returning with fat pockets. He wanted to try his luck as a professional gambler. He believed, rightly as it turned out, that he could make a good living.

June was horrified by this development. She insisted that he take a nine-to-five job instead, something with a schedule and benefits she could depend on. And so he did. Against his better judgment, he became a paralegal at a soul-crushing corporate firm. He did it for Eden, born a week after her due date, a nine-pound behemoth with a full head of red-blond hair.

The marriage limped along for a couple more years. June was at her best with Eden, changing her diapers with lightning speed, translating her mewls and grunts into plain English, and nursing her in the rocking chair for hours while she teethed. Carl can still see them there, Eden dozing at her mother's breast, June nudging the chair back and forth with her toes even as she dozed too.

Their split was more his fault than June's. Some might say it was entirely his fault. He continued gambling on the side, weathering the inevitable storms whenever June found out. Each time, she begged him to quit. Each time, he solemnly agreed, lying through his teeth and privately vowing to cover his tracks better.

Then came the affair. Her name was Marianna, another paralegal at the firm where he never wanted to work in the first place. Carl takes full blame for their tawdry, but satisfying, fling. He has always had difficulty denying himself pleasure. June walked in on them in bed together, and that was the end of the marriage.

His infidelity catalyzed something in June. She'd always been a Sunday churchgoer, but Carl's betrayal seemed to activate some latent zealotry. She switched from her broadminded Unitarian church to a fire-and-brimstone Baptist one on the other side of town. She started going three times a week. Overnight, it seemed, she became someone Carl did not recognize: born again, smugly saved, quoting scripture in every conversation, even with their divorce attorneys, and frantically organizing Eden's baptism, something she hadn't thought necessary until now.

The divorce was acrimonious but rapid. Carl escaped to Vegas and found his way to a kind of hedonistic serenity—sleeping with whomever he liked, avoiding serious entanglements, surfing the shifting waves of poker wins and losses, now broke, now flush, and following his bliss, as his parents used to say.

It was the right thing for him. But he does regret missing so many milestones in his daughter's life. He wasn't there when she was born. June had recently caught him gambling again and banned him from the delivery room as punishment. He was in bed with Marianna the evening Eden said her first word. He was settling into his new apartment in Vegas when Eden had her first ballet recital, a chubby three-year-old in a frilly tutu. He was at the casino when she lost her two bottom teeth on the same day; he had to content himself with seeing the gap in her smile over FaceTime. There are more things, surely, that he has missed—inches of growth, childish revelations, tiny heartbreaks, new ideas, moments too inconsequential to be mentioned over the phone but vital nonetheless. Impossible to reclaim.

In recent months, Eden has seemed further away than ever. She's a teenager, it makes sense, but still, it has turned his heart to water. She has refused to get on the phone, only texting. She has limited her responses to the bare minimum, sometimes just a cold, inscrutable *K*.

What has Carl missed during this period of near silence? How badly did he fail Eden by moving across the country all those years ago? He thought she was in good hands. He thought he was leaving her with the better parent.

°

At an oasis, Carl watches his daughter dash across an open field, chasing the chipmunks that gather around the picnic area in hope of scraps.

"I'm gonna catch one," she shouts. "I'm gonna name it Chippie."

Carl smiles indulgently. It will be good for Eden to work off some extra energy. Fourteen-year-olds are not calibrated to spend hours cooped up in a car. Giggling, Eden darts this way and that, finally disappearing into a grove of snow-covered pines. Carl zips up the coat he bought at the oasis shop, brand-new and stiff.

Right now Eden is refusing to speak about what happened, feigning normalcy. She's her father's daughter, with a fine poker face of her own. He will take his cues from her. He will let her come to him.

After a moment's thought, he pulls his phone from his pocket.

"Hello?" June cries, almost before the first ring has ended. "Yes? Is that Eden? Eden?"

"It's me," Carl says, settling at a picnic table. "We're in Indiana."

"What do you want?" June says coldly. "You don't need to rub salt in the wound, Carl. I understand that you're not bringing

Eden back here. You've made it perfectly clear, despite my expressed wishes."

"I was just calling to check up on you, actually." He keeps his voice gentle, picturing himself as a horse whisperer holding out a handful of oats to a skittish mare. Calm and nonthreatening.

When Carl arrived at the hospital yesterday, Eden's wounds had already been assessed and treated. He hurried into the recovery room and found his daughter curled in a fetal ball on the white bed, flanked by a representative of CPS on one side and a neighbor on the other. June wasn't there, of course. She'd been taken away in a squad car, while Eden left home in an ambulance.

The social worker gave Carl the broad outlines of what had happened: assault and arrest, prognosis and procedure. Mrs. Westerman, June's next-door neighbor, filled in the rest. She was a soft-spoken woman who kept laying her palm on Carl's forearm as she spoke. She'd insisted on accompanying Eden to the hospital, she told him. The poor child shouldn't be surrounded by strangers after such a trauma.

"Yesterday was a bad day for everyone," Carl says now. "I just wanted to make sure you were all right."

"Really?" June says suspiciously.

"I would love to understand what happened between you and Eden." He infuses his tone with warmth. The effort scalds his throat, but he needs to know what went down, and Eden isn't talking. Not yet, anyway.

"Well, that's a nice change, I have to say," June says. "I thought you were blaming me for everything."

"Why don't you tell me about it? I never got to talk to you at all. One of your neighbors mentioned that you were yelling about a murder as you . . . as the car drove you away. Is that what happened?"

He pictures Mrs. Westerman's wrinkled brown face, her eyebrows raised and pulled together with anxiety. She'd lived next door for years, she said, and always thought June was a nice, God-fearing woman. No, she didn't know what June could have meant about a murder. Yes, that was definitely the word—June shouted it over and over, pointing at Eden as the squad car pulled away.

"I suppose I did say something like that," June says. "It's a little hard to remember all the details. I was in quite a state."

"Did you . . ." He falters, wondering how to phrase this. "Were you trying to murder Eden? Is that what you meant?"

"Oh my goodness, *no*," June wails. "No, of course not. How could you think such a thing? I was trying to protect Eden. I still am."

Unable to speak, Carl closes his eyes.

"That's why you need to bring her back to me," June says. "This is an emergency. A family crisis. We should be on the same side, you and me."

There is a crunching of feet, and Eden emerges from the shelter of the trees, packing a snowball. She crouches low and begins to form the bottom layer of a snowman.

"What does Eden need to be protected from?" Carl asks, finding his voice. "What did you think you were protecting her from when you ruptured her eardrum and gave her a goddamn concussion?"

"Don't take the Lord's name in vain," June snaps.

"Sorry," he says, though his patience is starting to fray. "I'm just trying to understand. I've never known you to be violent, June. Are you saying that someone *else* was trying to murder Eden? That you were protecting Eden from someone other than you?"

"Yes," she says. "That's exactly what I'm saying."

"But Eden said you punched her. Mrs. Westerman said it was just you and Eden in the house. The police arrested *you*. Are you saying . . . I don't . . ." He stammers to a halt.

"When you see your child subjected to violence, you respond with violence," June says. Then she sighs. "But I went too far. I see that now. 'For the anger of man does not produce the righteousness of God,'" she adds, and Carl can tell from her tone that it's a Bible quote.

"You aren't making sense." He wants to scream at her, but he keeps his voice low so that Eden, now working on the middle part of the snowman, won't hear him.

"I'm in my right mind," June says. "Do you want to know what happened? I'll tell you what happened. Then you can judge me as you please."

"Fine," Carl says. "Yes. Tell me."

"I woke early for morning prayers. I always do. I was surprised to see the light on in Eden's room as I went downstairs. I usually have to bang pots and pans to get her up these days."

"Okay."

"I opened the door just to check on her. I thought she might have fallen asleep studying and left the light on. She has an algebra test coming up. Her grades have been slipping a little. I was going to get her a tutor."

"Right. Sure."

"Well!" June takes a shuddering breath. "I was caught off guard. There was Eden, *my* Eden, standing in front of her mirror in a pair of men's boxer shorts. I don't even know where she got a thing like that. And she was winding something around her chest. At first I thought it was a bandage, I thought Eden was injured. But no. She was binding her breasts."

Carl shoots a glance at his daughter kneeling in the icy field. The snowman is small and crooked but almost complete.

"Eden had the strangest look on her face," June says. "Kind of—I don't know, drugged, maybe. I didn't recognize her. Carl, in that moment, I swear I didn't recognize her."

"You're saying that . . ." He trails off, unsure if he has understood.

"Her breasts *just* bloomed. I brought home a B-cup bra for her only last month. I thought she'd be so excited. I was, when my time came! And here she was *binding* them. Forcing them flat against her chest. Crushing her femininity. It's violence! Where did she even get the idea to do such a thing?" June does not pause for an answer, continuing, "It's all this nonsense on the internet. It's like a contagion. Genderqueer this and orientation that. Saying your pronouns whenever you tell someone your name. And what is this business about *they*? How can one person be *they*?" Her voice climbs to a higher register. "I should never have let her go to public school. I knew in my *bones* that I should homeschool her. I blame you for that, Carl, I really do. You were so insistent! And now look what's happened."

"What did happen?" he asks unsteadily. "What happened next?"

June makes a tutting sound. "Eden was so preoccupied that she didn't even hear me come in. I asked her what she was doing. She grabbed her robe. She said it was nothing—just a game."

Carl shifts his weight on the picnic bench. Eden is gathering sticks, measuring them against one another to make sure the snowman's arms are even.

"I knew it wasn't a game," June says. "I knew that was a lie. It isn't the first time she's . . . This topic has come up before."

"It has?" he shouts, forgetting to keep his voice low. "And you didn't tell me?"

"Why would I? She's just a little confused. One time she mentioned something about it in the car. She said she didn't feel like a girl that day. I told her it was just hormones and adolescence. Their bodies go through so many changes!"

Carl clutches his brow. All those one-word replies from Eden. Strings of emojis, without substance. Never wanting to get on the phone, much less FaceTime. Of course she didn't feel she could share something so profound with him while they were hundreds of miles apart. The guilt is a body blow, knocking the wind out of him. Was Eden planning to tell him about this six months from now, when she came to stay with him in Nevada for the summer break? Would she ever have told him?

"She's been dressing more masculine," June says. "I didn't really notice it at the time, but now . . . There was a dance at school and I bought her the loveliest dress, new earrings, cute shoes. Then she went in jeans. I just figured it was a fashion thing." She pauses, humming a little, her thinking noise. "The other day she asked me how I know I'm really a woman. I didn't even understand the question. 'I am as God made me,' I told her. 'And so are you.'"

Carl wishes he could reach through the phone and throttle June. "So when you say you're protecting Eden . . ."

"From herself. We have to protect her from herself in this moment. She's in terrible danger, Carl. 'Train up a child in the way he should go,' the Lord says. Somehow the devil got into my home. I've always tried to raise her right. Binding her breasts! What's next? Pills to stop her periods? Disfiguring her body with surgery? I've read about what can happen."

"Oh god, poor kid," Carl says.

"*Lord's name in vain,*" June hisses.

He does not apologize. The blood is roaring in his ears.

"She's the fruit of my womb," June says. "I know my own daughter. I knew she was a girl before the doctor even found out, remember? I *felt* her there. I'm the one who birthed her and held her miraculous body in my arms. I'm the one who wiped poop out of her little vagina every time I changed her diaper." Her voice increases in volume, crackling with static. "Front to back, always front to back. I taught her that. I brushed out her tangles. Painted her toenails. We pressed flowers together. I took her to Disney World to meet the princesses from the movies. I know her better than anyone. Better than she knows herself."

Eden has finished the snowman, staring at it proudly with her hands on her hips. Carl pushes off from the picnic table, rising to his feet.

"She's a mixed-up little girl," June says. "This is the devil's work, you understand? We can't let her destroy her God-given body. That's what I meant by murder, Carl. The devil is telling my daughter—our daughter—that she's a boy. The devil is trying to murder my little girl."

Carl hangs up without saying good-bye. In the distance, Eden waves to him, then points to her snowman and takes a bow.

◦

They make it through Illinois without a single bathroom break. Eden wins the race across the border to Iowa, flinging out her arm before Carl even registers the sign. He wasn't paying attention, too busy watching her surreptitiously out of the corner of his eye. Eden's clothes give nothing away: jeans, a T-shirt, gender-neutral. He has decided that he will continue to think of her as "her" until Eden tells him otherwise. He can't take June's word about anything.

Night comes early, though the clouds are so thick that it's hard to tell when the sun actually sets. Eden curls in the passenger seat with her thighs against her chest, resting her cheek on her knees. Her eye is swollen completely shut now. The bruise has spread all the way down to her jaw. Iowa is a landscape of graceful, undulating hills. Carl knows it's time to stop driving when he begins to imagine that he's sailing a boat over ocean breakers. The fatigue has caught up to him, to both of them. Eden staggers up the steps to their motel room. In the bathroom, she brushes her teeth in drowsy slow motion.

"Get into bed, honey," Carl says. "Tomorrow will be a better day."

Eden laughs, then winces as her mouth begins to bleed. "You always say that."

Twin beds stand side by side. Eden picks the one by the window and climbs beneath the blanket. Carl sits on the edge of her mattress. All day he has been careful not to touch her unless she initiates contact. This is a child who has just experienced extreme brutality at a parent's hands. June was arrested for aggravated battery and aggravated child abuse. *Aggravated*—a nonsense word, given the circumstances. Carl can think of better terms. *Unforgivable. Indefensible. Deranged.*

"Want me to stroke your hair?" he asks. "Or would you rather I didn't?"

"Fine, if you want to," Eden says carelessly.

Her red-brown curls flow across the pillow. Carl traces each long ringlet with a gentle motion. It has always soothed her. As a toddler, this rhythmic petting was the only thing that could get her to sleep. At that age she habitually fought bedtime, growing increasingly teary while announcing more and more vehemently that she wasn't tired, right up until she conked out mid-sentence.

Carl feels a lump in his throat. He has always been the father of a daughter. All of his touchstone memories—teaching Eden to shuffle a deck of cards, applying temporary tattoos on her skinny arms, offering advice while she tried on dozens of pairs of soccer cleats to find the right fit—belong to the father of a daughter. He was the one who taught her the correct terms for her genitalia, something June shied away from. When Eden got her first period, June lectured her about Eve's sin and the burdens of womanhood, while Carl ordered flowers to the house in Utica with a congratulatory card.

Who is this child beneath the blanket? What has happened to the daughter he raised, the girl he thought he knew? *Murder*, June said, and Carl wouldn't go that far, but there is loss here, primal and disorienting. He dances his fingers along Eden's curls, just as he has always done, giving no sign of the ache in his chest, as powerful as an ebbing tide. It is grief, no more, no less. He swallows thickly. If there was ever a time for a poker face, it is this moment. Somehow he must pretend this child is still his own same Eden, not some stranger, an unknown quantity, a lanky teenage body made of mysteries.

"I wish I'd been there when you were born," he hears himself saying.

"Yeah?" Eden asks dreamily.

"It's one of my great regrets in life that I wasn't there."

"Why? Goopy baby. Umbilical stuff. Gross." The last word ends in a yawn.

With each brush of his hand, Carl can see the tension melt

from her shoulders. "I wanted to see you come into the world," he says. "It's the moment when you became real. When you separated from your mother."

"I guess."

"I took the birthing classes and everything. I was ready. But your mom didn't want me there."

"Well, she was mad at you, right?" Eden says. "That's basically all I remember from when you lived with us. Mom being mad at you."

He nods. "Sounds about right."

"I bet she just didn't want you staring at her coochie while she pushed a watermelon out of it. I've seen the pictures. I had a big head."

Carl laughs, still stroking her curls. A silence falls between them, filled with the soft, staccato knocking of the radiator.

"You know you can tell me anything," he says.

And just like that, the tension is back. Eden's shoulders hunch together beneath the sheet and she rolls over, facing away from him.

"Mom used to tell me that too," she says.

°

The motel alarm clock jangles at 3:00 a.m. Carl ushers Eden into a blast of wintry wind laden with snow. He settles her in the back seat with his hoodie balled beneath her head as a pillow and his new coat spread over her like a blanket. In his youth, Carl learned that it wasn't safe to let a person with a concussion fall asleep, but the ER doctors informed him that since Eden's pupils weren't dilated and her speech and motor functions were normal, sleep was fine, even beneficial. She slumbers all the way across the remainder of Iowa. Snow falls so heavily that it erases the world beyond the headlights. Carl has the illusion of traveling at light speed as the flakes whirl in a conical vortex around the car.

He has it all planned out. Sixteen hours in the car yesterday, including stops for meals. Today they'll drive even farther, but he hopes to be home before midnight, still enough time to collapse into bed and get enough sleep to hit the tables rested and refreshed tomorrow. He's looking forward to the tournament. For the past two years running, he's made it to the final table. He expects to this time as well.

After that, the real work will begin. He needs to look into local schools. He has no idea about the educational system in Vegas; he has never needed to consider it. A single father—that's what he is now. In the past, he has been the other parent, a part-time counterpoint to June. Carl squares his shoulders. He is about to get a crash course in dentist appointments and algebra homework and curfew, all the essential, relentless minutiae that have flown beneath his radar until now. The moment June landed her first punch, everything changed for Eden—and for him.

Last night, Carl spent hours scouring websites for parents of LGBTQ teens rather than getting much-needed sleep. He brushed up on the terminology and read lists of FAQs. Eventually he and Eden will talk, and he is determined to handle it well. His private bewilderment has not diminished; the mournful ache in his chest remains. His child is changing, changed, a changeling—but he knows better than to burden Eden with these thoughts. She has been through enough at the hands of her mother. Carl will box up his confusion and grief and hide them away at the back of his mind, storing them for some other season.

The sun rises as they cross into Nebraska. The car brims with light, triggering a stirring from the back seat. Eden sits up, her hair matted in the rearview mirror. Her bruises are even riper and more shocking. She looks like a boxer after a particularly savage match.

"I stink," she says, sniffing her armpit. "I don't have any clothes to change into, do I? We didn't think to pack anything. We're morons."

"My fault," Carl says. "I decided not to stop by the house on our way out. I just wanted to get you away from there. We'll buy you a whole new wardrobe in Vegas."

"And a phone." She climbs into the passenger seat, stepping on Carl's thigh.

"What happened to your phone?"

"Mom smashed it," Eden says in an expressionless voice, settling beside him. "She said it was how the devil got into me. Through my phone. And my friends."

Carl tightens his grip on the wheel. It is the closest Eden has come to discussing what happened. This is one of those moments, he knows. A milestone. A turning point. He has missed too many; he needs to handle this one right.

But before he can gather his wits, Eden turns on the radio, scrolling through stations with jarring rapidity. She settles on a tinkly pop song Carl has never heard before and begins to dance in her seat. She has always loved to dance, even as a baby.

"I need to pee," she sings along with the melody. "Please stop soon before I burst."

Carl takes the exit for Omaha, vowing to seize the opportunity more decisively next time.

Over the years, he has done his best to contravene June's

religious influence. Each summer, he and Eden would watch irreverent movies and discuss evolution and history. He made sure that his daughter was exposed to other viewpoints. Having been raised Taoist-Buddhist-spiritualist-agnostic, he could see with the clear-eyed perspective of an outsider how bizarre Christianity could be. An omnipotent deity impregnating a human woman? A faithful flock eating and drinking the simulated blood and flesh of a demigod? The absolute racket of tithing? Carl believed that the only difference between a cult and organized religion was scale.

Still, he never criticized June to Eden. Her religion, yes, but not June herself. That was the one ironclad rule of a well-behaved divorce—a rule he and June both agreed upon, despite their differences. She never spoke ill of him either. Even now, Eden remains unaware of his adultery and its role in the breakup of their marriage. June withheld the shameful truth, not for Carl's sake but for Eden's.

A good woman, a good mother, or so he thought. Until the events of the past few days, he would have trusted June's moral compass above his own, without question. How long has this hateful thing been coiled inside her? For a moment, navigating across a two-lane road patched with snow, Carl is almost too angry to breathe.

They get breakfast at a fast-food place and eat leaning against the side of the car in the parking lot. Despite the bitter wind, they both need to stretch their legs. The snow has stopped, though the roiling clouds look ready to unleash another torrent at any moment. Omaha appears to be one big strip mall. Eden points to the next parking lot, where an enormous Target stands behind a billboard for a strip club.

"Please?" she says. "Pretty please? Clean clothes? New phone?"

Carl checks his watch. “We can’t stay that long, honey.”

Eden sticks out her arms like a zombie in an old-timey film. “Newwww phone,” she drones, lurching toward the Target.

“Oh Jesus.” He laughs. “Fine, come on.”

Energetic music plays as they enter the monolithic store, the aisles stretching as far as the eye can see. People turn and gape as Eden passes by with her plethora of bruises. Then they look at Carl with suspicion and dislike.

It wasn’t me, it was her asshole mother, he wants to announce, but Eden seems intent on pretending that nothing out of the ordinary is happening, no gasps, no stares, no little kids pointing at her face. Carl does the same.

They visit the electronics section first, where things prove more difficult than anticipated. Eden is still on her mother’s cell phone plan. She’ll need a new number on Carl’s plan, which Target can’t do, according to the bored teenage boy behind the counter, scarcely older than Eden. She takes it fairly well, running her fingers over the locked cabinet where the phones glitter like jewels in a display case at a museum, then turning away.

“My friends probably think I’m dead,” she says. “It’s been a million jillion years since they’ve heard from me.”

On their way back out to the car, they pass the clothing section. Eden pauses to stroke a T-shirt with a picture of a robot on it. Carl notes that they’re in the boys’ area. He clears his throat, thinking quickly.

“It’s always bothered me that they separate the clothes into a binary,” he says, parroting the websites he googled the night before. “Boys on one side, girls on the other. I mean, what’s up with that? People come in all genders, you know?”

Eden freezes in place, as still as the mannequin behind her.

She does not appear to be breathing. Nearly a minute passes in agonizing silence.

At last, without looking at him, she says, "Mom told you?"

"She did."

Eden's hands begin to shake, still holding the T-shirt. But she maintains that poker face, saying in a casual tone, "You're the king of subtlety, Dad. I mean, that was a master class in segues."

"Smart ass," he says, matching her nonchalant manner. "Do you want to try anything on?"

"No, I don't need anything."

"Are you sure? You were just saying—"

"*No,*" she yells, hurrying toward the front doors with her head down.

◦

For the remainder of Nebraska, all six hours of it, Eden sits in the back seat, staring out the window. Carl tries not to glance too often in the rearview mirror, though she seems unaware of him, lost in some inner world. Shocks of wind pulse over the snow-tipped grass. An occasional butte rises lonely from the prairie.

Gradually Carl becomes aware of something moving up ahead. Dark shapes dot the plains at the edge of the horizon. He can't make out what they are—big as boulders, yet they keep shifting position. After another five miles, he realizes it's a buffalo herd. They are grazing along the south side of the highway, bulky creatures, larger than the rental car, with fur the color of burnt umber. Their cumbersome heads froth with curls. There are babies in the group, adorable and dangerous at the same time, like child-sized tanks. They skip gaily around the mountainous masses of their parents, all of whom are strolling in the same direction with their mouths in the grass.

Carl pulls over. There's no one on the road behind him or in front of him; he hasn't seen another car in twenty minutes. Thank goodness he thought to fill up the tank at the last oasis. Gas stations are few and far between in Nebraska.

Eden glances around curiously as the car comes to a halt. She hasn't noticed the buffalo. She hasn't been aware of anything outside herself.

"Look," Carl says, pointing.

Eden squeals and claps her hands. "Beautiful monsters!" she says. "I've never seen them in real life."

"A transcontinental drive brings many wonders."

One of the beasts lifts its head, crowned with horns, and stares in the direction of the car. Carl isn't certain whether it's male or female, since all the adults seem to have the same curved prongs. The creature snorts—Carl can't hear it at this distance, but he sees a puff of steam leave its nostrils—and resumes grazing.

"Are they buffalo or bison?" Eden asks. "Is there a difference? Can we get closer to them?"

"No, no," he says, answering her last question first. "We shouldn't even leave the car. They could crush you like a bug if they felt like it."

There is a click as Eden unbuckles her seat belt and climbs, once more, into the passenger seat.

"I like them," she says. "They're good buffaloes. Or bison."

Carl puts the car into drive again. The sign for Colorado appears up ahead, shadowed against the sky. Eden wins easily, lurching forward at the border with her arm outstretched; Carl does not even try to beat her.

"I'm the champion," she says.

"You've got skill, I admit."

At the next oasis, while Eden is in the bathroom, Carl takes his cell phone from his pocket and blocks June's number. She hasn't called since yesterday, but it's just a matter of time. She can contact his lawyer if she needs to get in touch. He doesn't want to hear her voice again.

Then, staring at the little screen, he googles the word *trans*. Last night, he packed his brain with information about gender identity and presentation and coming out and deadnaming. In this moment, however, he feels compelled to know exactly how *trans* is defined, not as a stand-in for *transgender* but in and of itself.

His phone informs him that it's a prefix meaning *across, beyond, through*. Carl grins, taken with this idea. *Across* the United States in a rental car. *Beyond* a simple understanding of who his child might be. *Through* this traumatic period together, side by side.

°

Back on the road, fortified by snacks and soda, Eden folds her hands in her lap. "When are we going to see mountains?" she asks.

"Soon," Carl says. "Watch the horizon."

She nods. Her hands twist, fingers white at the knuckles.

"So what *did* Mom tell you?" she asks.

He considers how to answer. June said a lot of things, most of them horrifying and unconscionable. Eventually he and Eden will unpack all that nonsense about God-given bodies and the devil, probably with a therapist. June's assault was as violent as an earthquake, and there will be aftershocks, fallout, and damage, both seen and unseen—marked on Eden's face and hidden beneath the surface.

For now, Carl decides that a simple answer is the way to go.

"Mom said you're a boy," he says. "You might be a boy," he corrects himself.

"She did?" Eden whispers.

"Not in those words. She said you've been using a binder and dressing in a more masculine way. She said you've mentioned not feeling like a girl. I didn't mean to put a label on you. Maybe you're feeling more nonbinary or agender. It's okay if you don't know right now. I know there are a lot of permutations of how a person's identity—"

"Dad. Stop." Eden shakes her head, her cheeks flushing pink. "I get it. You did some googling."

"Well, I might have scanned a few articles last night. What is the internet for if not to educate old fogies like me?"

"Porn," Eden says. "That's what the internet is for."

Carl groans. "Jesus, I'm not ready for that conversation. You've never seen porn, right? Not even one time?"

She draws an X on her chest with her forefinger. "Not even at Maddie Riley's birthday sleepover when I was ten. Definitely not then."

A few jagged chunks of stone jut up through the prairie, the first suggestion that the Rocky Mountains are approaching. Along the horizon, larger foothills stand in rows, purpling as they fade into the distance.

"Demiboy," Eden says. "That's what I am right now, anyway."

Carl doesn't know the term. It didn't come up in his research.

"It means sometimes boy, sometimes nonbinary," Eden says, correctly interpreting his silence.

"Got it," he says. "And your pronouns?"

"He/him mostly," Eden says, all business now. "I'll let you know if I'm ever feeling more like they/them, but I really like he/him at the moment. That's what all my friends call me. I *really* like it." The words are coming out in a rush, a dam breaking. "Eventually I might be male. Not demiboy, but fully male. I felt like I was agender for most of the fall, but things seem to be changing lately. Like with the binder. And the boxers. My friends have been great about all of it. Really great."

They are not looking at each other. That seems to be what Eden wants, both of them staring straight at the horizon. Matching poker faces.

"Do you have another name I should know?" Carl asks.

"Eden's fine. For now. Maybe eventually Ethan. It means 'strong and safe' in Hebrew. And it's close enough to Eden that I'll respond to it sort of naturally, you know?"

Grief swells inside Carl, but he crushes it back down. There is no room for it here. He remembers flipping through a book of baby names with June, nestled on the couch, their foreheads touching. They argued playfully and vetoed one another's suggestions until they came upon *Eden*, which both of them loved—June for its meaning, Carl for its sound.

"Ethan is a great name," he says softly. "If you end up choosing it."

The websites all said to celebrate a child's coming out. Cakes and balloons and congratulations. But Carl isn't sure how to summon that kind of jubilation. Besides, Eden's first attempt was met by such savagery that it doesn't seem right to cheer and clap now, while the bruises and concussion are still fresh.

He/him. Carl will start there. He glances across the passenger seat at this demiboy, his son, his sometimes-son, sometimes-nonbinary child.

Eden wipes his eyes with the back of his hand. “Are you mad?” he asks. “It’s okay if you’re disappointed. Mom was so . . .” His voice hitches in his throat, and a strangled sound escapes him as he tries to hold back tears.

“Oh, honey.” Carl begins to reach across the space between them, then thinks better of it and withdraws his hand. He will let Eden decide when they next make physical contact. “I couldn’t be prouder,” he says. It’s a line borrowed from one of the websites, but in this moment, Carl means every word.

Eden begins to shake again, his whole body juddering. Carl worries for a second that his son is having a seizure, but then the sobs come, wrenching and wracking, torn from his throat. Eden leans forward in his seat, arms wrapped around his head, screaming as each sob leaves him. Tears spatter the floor mat and the dashboard. Carl has never seen anyone cry like this. He parks on the shoulder, letting the storm pass through his son’s body. He wants to pull Eden into his lap—he would have done it before without a second thought.

“I’m here,” he repeats instead. “I’m right here.”

Eden throws open the car door and vomits onto the packed earth. Carl hurries around the vehicle to gather his son’s hair off his nape. Eden voids the contents of his stomach and keeps gagging after there’s nothing left to come up. He collapses into a crouch, leaning against the front wheel, his face a mess of snot and tears and blood from his split lip, which has reopened into a raw gash.

Carl sits on the ground beside him. The sun is high, and a cold wind stirs the prairie into silken waves. Eden’s breathing slows to a normal rhythm. Carl fishes in his pocket and finds a handkerchief, passing it over. Eden dabs his eyes and nose and mouth, staining the fabric crimson.

"Wow, I'm hemorrhaging," he says.

"Head wounds bleed," Carl says. "Put pressure on it."

"I know."

A high, crystalline call shivers the air. A hawk soars overhead, flicking its shadow across their bodies.

"I feel dizzy," Eden says. "Everything's kind of spinning."

Carl leans forward to examine his son's pupils. No dilation. No slurred speech. None of the dangerous concussion symptoms the doctors mentioned.

"It's your ear, I bet," Carl says. "That was a big cry. Your sinuses are inflamed. Come on, let's get you into the back seat."

He tucks his son in, hoodie balled under the head, coat over the body. Eden mumbles something as he dozes off, but Carl can't catch what it is.

◦

Eden is asleep when the mountains appear. First they are faint, edgeless shadows, then cloudlike blobs, and finally solid peaks glinting with snow.

Carl has not been looking forward to this part of the trip. The road zigzags up steep slopes. So many narrow switchbacks. The engine whines, complaining about the angle of the incline. Then comes a ridge with a sharp drop-off on one side. There are no barricades to stop the car from careening right into the valley. Carl knows that the lack of a guardrail is an intentional choice by the highway administration to keep drivers from feeling overconfident and pushing their luck. But still, the inky shadows in the chasm below make his extremities tingle.

A pronghorn bounds across the road thirty feet in front of the vehicle, moving with such swiftness and surety that it is gone almost before Carl registers its presence. A flash of auburn fur. A lattice of horns. He grips the steering wheel at ten and two, as he was taught in driving school. A cliff on the left side, then a cliff on the right. For a short stretch the road is bordered by empty space. The mountains are beautiful, but Carl can't take his eyes off the road long enough to enjoy the view, and Eden is still asleep. The air seems rarified as they ascend into higher altitudes.

He wants to wake Eden when they reach the continental divide, then thinks better of it. Rest is essential to recovery. The body heals only during REM sleep, he once read. Still, Carl stops the car and climbs out to look at the big yellow sign marking the moment of transition. They have been climbing toward this point for hours. Now they will begin to descend on the other side.

Darkness comes earlier here, the sun setting behind the mountains long before it reaches the horizon. In the back seat, Eden has begun to snore like a pack-a-day smoker. A natural aftereffect of such powerful weeping.

They cross into Utah without fanfare. As the miles pass, the peaks shrink back into foothills. Carl drives between arches and towers of stone. The last of the sunlight drains from the air, and stars appear, more stars than he has ever seen. There is no light pollution here. So few people live in Utah. Carl is elated by the wealth of constellations, the splash of the Milky Way across the great bowl of the sky.

A rustle from the back seat. Eden yawns, then groans. "Shit, my mouth hurts," he says.

"No swearing."

"Really?"

"Well, only do it when we're alone."

There is no moon tonight. The car's headlights, sweeping

across shrubbery and stone, might be the last lights in the whole world.

"Dad?" Eden says.

"Uh-huh."

A small silence. Carl wishes he could see his son's face in the rearview mirror, but Eden is still lying down, and anyway the interior of the car is black as pitch.

"Is Mom going to prison?" Eden asks.

"I don't know. I've been thinking about that too. She might. But she's white and middle-aged and fairly well-off, so I don't know what'll happen." He pauses, then asks, "Do you want her to go to prison?"

"I don't ever want to see her again."

"That's fair."

"I don't give a shit what happens to her. She can die for all I care."

Carl knows this isn't true, but he only says, "How's the dizziness?"

"Better."

For a moment there is only the thrum of the engine and the murmur of wheels on pavement. Then Eden says in a tone of wonder, "Look at the stars."

°

It's after midnight when Carl parks in the garage beneath his building. He'll return the rental car on his way to the tournament later. In the elevator, Eden slumps against the wall. His mouth is no longer bleeding, but the scab is fresh and painful-looking once more. Carl leads the way down the hall to his apartment. He hurries to hide his one-hitter and stash while Eden is in the bathroom. Then he wipes the kitchen counter down with a sponge and frowns into the fridge, empty except for condiments and moldering takeout boxes.

Eden enters the room with a strange look on his face. Carl can't quite interpret it.

"Straight to bed with you, young man," he says. "Your room is pretty much the way you left it. Might be a little dusty. I'll vacuum in the morning."

Eden sits at the kitchen table. "Actually, can we do something first?"

"Sure, I guess."

He looks at his lap. "I asked Mom. She said no."

"Well, your mom is a jerk. Fuck her." The words are in the open air before Carl has the presence of mind to stop himself. Normally he would never say such a thing.

"Fuck her," Eden echoes fiercely.

"What do you want to do?"

He cuts his son's hair right at the table. Eden holds a shaving mirror to watch as Carl lifts each lock, grown to an impressive length over months and years, and snips it away. Red-brown coils fall to the floor like autumn leaves. Eden's face is aglow with happiness, unmistakable even beneath his mask of wounds.

Nothing around Carl seems entirely real. Too much has happened in the past couple of days. He feels caught between waking and dreaming, unsure which state he currently inhabits, but he keeps cutting. Soon Eden sports a mop top of uneven tufts. He tips his face this way and that, investigating his own reflection with his mouth open.

"Ready?" Carl asks, reaching for his beard trimmer.

"Born ready."

The oddest things whirl through Carl's head as he shears his son like a sheep, leaving only a quarter inch of ruddy fur. *Murder,* June said, but she couldn't have been more wrong. What is the inverse of death? What is the opposite of grief? Carl's heartache has burned away like morning mist beneath the rising sun. Nape to crown, he works the trimmer with a confident hand. There is no stranger here, no changeling, only Eden, always Eden, his own same Eden. A concentrated version, stripped of superficialities, distilled to pure essence. More Eden than ever before. His lip has begun to bleed again from too much smiling.

Carl finishes the buzz cut with a flourish, meeting his son's eyes in the hand mirror. Eden's jaw seems more pronounced without the frame of his curly mane. His long-lobed ears are visible now. Has he always had those sharp cheekbones? He looks so much like Carl at fourteen that Carl finds himself groping for the back of the chair to keep his balance.

Silence falls. Eden pushes back his chair and rises to his feet. He wears that same new expression, which Carl can now identify as relief. Eden spins in the glow of the bare bulb hanging from the ceiling fan, and Carl finds himself laughing, and maybe crying too, for the first time since getting his son's midnight call.

Across, beyond, through—that was the first definition for *trans*, but there were others beneath it. The second was *a state change, as in liquid to solid*, or, Carl thinks now, a literal change of states, New York to Nevada. The final definition was *on or to the other side of*, as in a transcontinental road trip or, perhaps, the process of healing from a wound. One day Eden will emerge on the other side of this suffering recovered and renewed. That's the hope, anyway.

Carl was not present when Eden was born, and he has missed any number of moments along the way, but he is here, now, for what may prove to be the most crucial milestone of them all.

Eden strikes a proud pose. Carl wipes his eyes with the heel of his palm. Through chance and calamity and wild good fortune, he will bear witness to whatever this transition is: experimentation or affirmation, rebirth or revelation, homecoming or becoming. He will see who this miraculous child turns out to be.

The First Rule of Natalie

My sister was found as a newborn at the edge of the ocean, washed up on the beach by the tide. She lay on her back with her sea-colored eyes open. She did not cry as the waves surged around her, carrying her little body farther up the sand with each foamy swell. Strands of seaweed coiled around her plump belly. In lieu of a parent's finger, she clutched a shell in her fist—a coiled mollusk spiral, thumb-sized and tapered, as brown as flesh, plucked from the bottom of the ocean.

My parents insisted that Natalie was not found that way at all. They said she'd been born in a hospital, just as I was. My sister was two years older, so I had not been there and could not be certain, but I did not believe them.

°

I first formed my hypothesis at the age of eight. We lived in Annapolis then, my father, mother, Natalie, and me. Our house was squat but cozy, and I could see Chesapeake Bay from my bedroom window. Mama and Papa were both psychiatrists, and the similarities did not end there: they were both slight of frame with limp mouse-brown hair, they both wore glasses, and they both routinely left half-empty coffee cups and half-finished books all around the house. When presented with new information, they both responded identically: a pause, a head tilt, and then: "Interesting." They were so alike I sometimes forgot they weren't related by blood.

I was a carbon copy and a combination. Like Mama, I'd developed astigmatism in kindergarten. Like Papa, I was allergic to dogs. Like both of them, I had dark eyes and freckles on every square inch of skin.

And then there was Natalie. At ten years old, she towered over me, nearly our father's height already. Her shoulders were broad, her hair as straight and blond as straw. A prominent brow. Webbed hands and feet. In family photographs, she looked like a gangly stork accidentally hatched in the nest of stubby sandpipers.

I always knew Natalie was not like other children. She did not speak. She had no language at all, in fact, neither active nor passive. She did not even know her own name. She spent her days in the playroom, drawing, working with modeling clay, or adhering stickers to her face. She wore diapers to sleep. Though she knew how to use the toilet, she refused to get out of bed to do so.

Natalie was prone to rages, and we never knew what might set them off. A car horn. A stomachache. Nothing at all. Mama had a scar above her left eye from the time my sister hurled a mug across the kitchen. Papa needed stitches when Natalie slammed a door on his hand. I bore so many scratches up and down my arms—always in the process of scabbing and healing—that the kids at school assumed I had cats.

No pets. They would not have been safe with Natalie.

My sister functioned best with a strict routine, which Papa, Mama, and I knew by heart. Always the same breakfast: plain oatmeal and a cup of orange juice. Morning in the playroom with her art supplies. Lunch of peanut butter and jelly and applesauce. Afternoon in the backyard in good weather, or a Disney movie in the living room if it was raining or cold. Dinner of chicken fingers and broccoli. Bedtime at seven on the dot, her star nightlight projecting a whirling galaxy on the ceiling and New Age music playing on a loop.

Baths were a hassle. That was my first clue. Natalie had a thing about water; she did not even like the sound of the kitchen faucet running and would press her palms over her ears. My parents had taught her to tolerate being wiped down by a damp washcloth every evening, but Sunday was bath day, a weekly trauma. Mama always sent me to my room, but the screams and splashing carried down the hall. Whatever happened in the bathroom often resulted in injuries—black eye, fat lip.

Once Natalie came crashing into my room on Sunday night, naked and dripping, with suds in her hair. She appeared to have fled in the middle of things, evading the final rinse and the towel. I looked up from my book as she climbed into bed beside me and squirmed under my blanket, soaking the mattress. Her pupils were pinpoints. She rocked back and forth, making the humming monotone that served as her distress call.

Mama poked her head into the room, her hair disheveled. When she saw that I was not in danger, she left again, her back bowed.

Natalie shivered and snuggled close to borrow my warmth. I

was used to her nakedness; she often decided that clothes were a nuisance and would strip without embarrassment wherever she was, even in the backyard in clear view of the neighbors' houses.

I wondered why she was so afraid of the water. I wondered why God had gifted her webbed fingers if she was never going to swim.

"Natalie," I said, and she darted her blue eyes at me, then away. Words were not words to her—they were music, a sequence of notes without meaning. She communicated best through touch, though you had to let her initiate. If you patted her shoulder or stroked her hair when she wasn't ready, she often bit.

She continued to rock gently against the mattress. The steady, repetitive movement reminded me of the buffeting of waves in deep water. After I'd spent a long day swimming in Chesapeake Bay, I would feel a phantom echo of the surf's constant motion for hours afterward. Natalie hummed, and this, too, reminded me of the sea: a muffled monotone, the way human voices sounded underwater.

She reached for my hand and laced her fingers through mine. I felt the webs between her fingers stretch against my knuckles, and that's when I got my idea.

°

At school, I researched mermaids. The library was the best part of the pricey private academy my parents had chosen for me. Heavy mahogany bookshelves stood interspersed with stained-glass windows. The light was diffuse and marbled. A reverent hush filled the air, broken only by the scratch of students taking notes.

I hefted a stack of books into the seclusion of a carrel. Turning the pages, I read that nearly every culture had developed legends about mermaids. Some people saw them as good omens or benevolent spirits, while others believed they were dangerous. In China there were stories of mermaids who wept pearls instead of tears. In Zimbabwe they were called *njuzu* and got blamed for foul weather. The Greeks pictured them as malicious sirens, luring sailors to their deaths for sport.

Scientists theorized that manatees were the root of the myth of the mermaid, though the photos on the glossy pages—lumbering gray beasts with whiskers—looked nothing like women to me. But then, I was not a sailor who had been at sea for forty days on a ship crewed entirely by men.

According to the books, mermaids never appeared in human form. They always had long fish tails, sometimes gills. The only story I could find of a complete transformation was *The Little Mermaid*, a horrifying cautionary tale in which a mermaid traded her voice and tail for human legs and feet that felt with every step as though she were walking on broken glass.

None of this sounded like Natalie. Discouraged, I put the books back on the shelf and went to lunch.

I had known most of my classmates since kindergarten. The school was a small, intimate affair. Patsy, Ellie, Aliyah, and I always sat together, proud third graders, no longer relegated to the little-kid area of the lunchroom with its rainbow chairs and constant supervision.

My friends often had playdates at one another's houses after school. I was sometimes invited but rarely accepted, since it would have meant leaving my parents with Natalie for an extra few hours without the relief of my presence, rendering them irritable and spent. Besides, I could never reciprocate by asking Patsy, Ellie, or Aliyah over in return. No one but my parents and me ever crossed the threshold of our house; we did not know how Natalie would react.

I did not particularly mind this. I found my school friends nice but overwhelming. They laughed so easily, so loudly. Their movements were unguarded and uncontrolled; Natalie would have smacked me if I ever gestured as freely as Patsy did. Aliyah and Ellie were criers, bursting into sobs while describing a sibling who would not share or a parent who had punished them by taking away their video games. I often failed to react to the crowning climax of this kind of sob story, expecting there had to be more to come. Such minor things—big sisters who hoarded cookies, little brothers who wore diapers and stank—did not merit tears.

I was the quiet one. There was no point in talking about my home life. My friends would not have known what to do with stories about Natalie rocking and humming for hours on end or gouging her fingernails through the flesh of my forearms because I dared to leave the room before she was ready to be parted from me.

°

Every Sunday morning, my mother and I walked the two and a half blocks down the hill to the beach. It was our special time together. There was never enough to go around in our house—Natalie was a whirlpool that sucked up all the light and energy and love. But for two hours on Sunday morning, Mama belonged only to me.

It was March, too cold to swim. The summer tourists, thankfully, were not yet present. Mama and I took our shoes off and strolled side by side on the chilly sand, not saying much. I picked up sea glass and showed it to her. The beach was bordered at both ends by a pile of stones, each rock bigger than I was. Sometimes seals gathered there, sunning themselves.

"Do you believe in mermaids?" I asked my mother. The wind was icy, whipping my hair against my face and buffing Mama's cheeks rosy.

She considered my question. "As symbols of men's idealization of the feminine, yes. Mermaids might also represent a fear of women."

"Okay."

"I suppose they could be seen as emblems of female empowerment. It depends on which myth you're thinking of."

I nodded, feigning comprehension. My parents did not childproof their conversation for me, which gratified me even when I struggled to understand. They treated me as though I, too, were a trained psychiatrist.

And then my mother grinned. "I always liked selkies better, though," she said. "They make a much more interesting story."

"Selkies?" I did not know the word.

"I'll tell you on the walk home," Mama said. "Your father has been on Natalie duty for almost three hours. I'm betting he's at the end of his rope."

°

That night I lay awake, blazing with new ideas. My sister was a selkie. I'd come close with my hypothesis—I had just chosen the wrong mythical creature.

Mama's people were Irish, and in her childhood she'd been told about selkies by her grandfather, who died before I was born. Selkies were chimerical beings, part human, part seal, morphing their biology when they crossed from water to land. In the ocean, they swam and frolicked with other pinnipeds. On the shore, they shed their pelts, peeling off the heavy fur and tucking it somewhere safe, out of sight. They looked like people then, moving through the human world unnoticed.

Selkies were neither one thing nor another, living a halfway existence, always yearning for their other state of being. You could befriend them in their human shape, even love them, but you could not keep them. One day the call of the sea would overpower them, and they would return to the beach where they first had come ashore, find their hidden sealskin, change their form, and swim away.

Mama had never seen a selkie herself, but she told me that her grandfather had. It was a brief encounter, a distant glimpse along the Irish coast. My great-grandfather was a young boy, watching from a cliff top as a woman picked her way over the rocky shoreline far below him. He saw her stoop and gather something up off the ground—he couldn't tell what it was. A moment later, a seal lolloped over the stones and dove jubilantly into the waves.

°

On a sunny afternoon, my sister and I sat at the playroom table, drawing together. The first rule of Natalie was that she could never be alone. In part this was her own choice—she became distressed without one of us in sight—but it was also a matter of safety. What if she marked up the walls with her crayons? What if she figured out how to open the window and climbed out?

So I was on Natalie duty while Mama saw clients and Papa prepared dinner. My parents shared an office on the east side of the house and took turns meeting their patients there. I'd visited their workspace only a few times—plush leather chairs, a spidery fern, ochre light, soundproofing, and a white noise machine for good measure. The room had its own entrance where clients could ring a private doorbell and go in and out unseen by Natalie and me.

I was teaching myself to draw seals out of a book. The tricky part was the snout—I kept giving them dog faces. Natalie drew spirals, her favorite shape, swiveling her whole torso with each rotation of the crayon. The walls of the playroom were papered with her artwork. Mama and Papa wanted her to feel that her efforts were as valued as mine—my A-plus essays on the fridge, my chess trophies on the mantel—though I knew Natalie did not care. Drawing was an experiential need for her, and as soon as she finished each page we might as well have lit it on fire.

After a while she became interested in what I was making. I'd mastered the seals now, getting the faces right, as well as the low frontal placement of the flippers, which initially I'd drawn too high, mid-torso, like fish fins. Natalie leaned close to me, breathing sticky breath on my shoulder. She could draw with great precision when she chose; she'd gone through phases of sketching crisp five-pointed stars and multicolored flowers in the past. I'd taught her how to do both.

Now she held out her hand, asking me to teach her this too. We had our own method. She placed the tip of her crayon against the paper, and I grasped her wrist and guided her through the bulbous outline, the strong tail. Again and again I rendered the shape, using Natalie's whole hand as my drawing instrument.

Gradually she began to take charge of the easy parts. She would make the curve of the belly herself, then let her arm go slack so I could do the complicated face. Each time we sketched another seal, Natalie did more of it on her own. At the end, my fingers lay lightly on her wrist as she drew the animal without any help.

It occurred to me that no one watching us would have been

able to tell who was in control of the work at any one moment. In silence, through my sister's language of touch, we communicated perfectly.

°

That night over dinner, I asked Mama and Papa for details about Natalie's birth. They were tired, distracted. A vaginal delivery. Unmedicated. No, she wasn't adopted, why on earth would I ask that? Natalie gobbled her food and pushed my father's hand away when he attempted to wipe her face clean with a napkin.

As Mama washed the dishes and Natalie sat with her palms against her ears to block out the sound of the water, I pulled my father aside and probed for more specifics. Was there anything he and Mama had not told me about my sister? Anything mind-blowing or life-changing? A walk along the beach one day, perhaps, back when they were a childless couple yearning for a baby? An unexpected gift on the sand?

Papa seemed to focus fully on me at last, pushing his glasses farther up his nose. I thought he was about to admit the truth—a foundling child, a seal pup missing its fur.

But instead, he began to explain the mechanics of human reproduction, something he had covered in excruciating detail years before. Menstruation. Sperm and egg. The placenta. Apparently he thought I was hinting that I wanted a refresher course.

"That's not what I meant," I said, but my father had already gone to get a notepad to draw some diagrams, and there was no stopping him now.

°

The school library possessed scant information on selkies—this was Maryland, not Ireland—but a dusty encyclopedia on a back shelf offered a few details I hadn't yet heard. There were legends of selkies who lost their sealskins and could never return to the water. Bereft, they would wander the shore, unable to change back into their oceanic form.

Sometimes it was their own fault; they had been careless in hiding their pelts, which were then taken by unwitting trappers or eaten by animals. Sometimes they stayed too long in the world of humans and forgot where they'd come ashore. There were even stories of men and women (usually the former) who found a selkie skin and hid it on purpose, then married the poor landlocked creature.

I slammed the book shut in alarm. Something like this must have happened to Natalie. Mama and Papa would never have hidden her sealskin intentionally, but they might not have known what it was. I imagined them plucking the infant from the surf. I imagined them wrapping my sister's damp body in one of Mama's fine silk scarves. Perhaps, off to the side, a dark shape lay on the sand, rumpled fur and a gleam of blubber. Mama and Papa would not even have noticed it. They would have hurried home with the child in their arms, never realizing what they had left behind.

°

My parents often talked late at night. This was something I knew without entirely knowing it, the way children do with information that is too difficult to absorb. I half-woke often to hear raised voices in the kitchen. They cried—sometimes Mama, sometimes Papa—and said Natalie's name. Never mine.

○

The weather warmed. When Mama and I walked to the beach on Sundays, I splashed through the shallows, wondering exactly where Natalie had floated ashore. Did my sister have another family out there in the deep water? Had her selkie parents lost track of their little seal pup, not noticing as she swam too close to the land and transformed without meaning to, shedding her precious pelt? I imagined her parents—her real parents—crying for her all around Chesapeake Bay. Maybe she even had siblings.

Natalie never came with us to the beach. Mama had told me that she'd brought my sister here when she was younger, but Natalie screeched if even a crumb of sand clung to her skin. She refused to look at the ocean, much less approach the water. Eventually Mama gave up.

In truth, Natalie hardly ever went anywhere anymore. My parents used to take her to the park or the nature preserve, back when she was little enough to be caught and physically restrained if she ran off or attacked another child. Now, though, she was too big, too strong. Besides, any deviation in her routine caused disruptions to her nervous system; she could become more violent. It was best for everyone if she remained confined at home.

Sometimes I tried to approach the seals that lay heaped on the stones at the edge of the beach, basking in the sun. Mama did not pay much attention to what I did. Her dark eyes sought the horizon, and her gait often faltered. She would stop and let the waves wash over her feet as though she did not have the wherewithal to move on.

The seals ignored me when I spoke to them, just as my sister always did. I asked them about Natalie, about her lost family, but they only slumbered and snorted. I knew better than to get too close; the seals would not like it any more than Natalie, and they had razor-sharp teeth.

°

Back home, I found the shelf where Mama stored the photo albums. The first snapshot in my baby book showed me in a hospital basinet, swaddled in a standard-issue green-striped warming blanket. The first photo in Natalie's baby book, however, showed a damp newborn curled on Mama's chest against the backdrop of our front porch. In the picture, Mama's expression was not proud or exhausted but startled, staring down at the child in her arms as though she had never seen such a thing before. My sister's eyes were open, white-blue, unfocused. Her fingertips were pruney—from the amniotic fluid in the womb, Papa would have told me, but I knew it was really from the sea.

My theory was faultless. Everything about my sister made sense when viewed through this lens. Her rocking, which baffled strangers, was an attempt to replicate the surging of the current. She preferred to be naked because seals were naked. She did not speak because seals did not speak. Her nonverbal vocalizations—humming, gurgling, a high-pitched squeal—would no doubt have been perfectly understood underwater by others of her own kind. She threw tantrums because she had misplaced part of her essence; she must have constantly ached for what she had lost. Her webbed fingers and toes explained themselves.

Her dislike of baths and faucets, too, was as natural as could be. Without her sealskin, she could not transform. Water surely felt odd against her human skin, unpleasant and unfamiliar. It must have evoked the enormity of her deprivation. The hiss of the kitchen sink, the meager trough of our little tub—these things were paltry echoes of the wide ocean, a perpetual reminder of Natalie's imprisonment in our realm. Trapped, marooned, and halved.

°

Everything changed on an ordinary day in April. It was snowing, I remember, the last snowfall of the season. Natalie and I sat in the playroom as Papa saw clients and Mama nursed a migraine, lying in bed with a wet cloth over her eyes.

Natalie was in one of her moods. She kept growling as she drew angry spirals, wearing her red crayon down to a nub. She crumpled up each page when she was done and hurled it to the floor. I got to my feet, thinking about my homework. Aliyah and I were partners in a presentation about bats. I was in charge of research, while Aliyah, a natural performer, would do the talking in front of the class.

Natalie screeched at me, forbidding me to leave the room. I told her I was just going to get my science folder; I would be right back. We all did that, Mama and Papa and me, telling Natalie things even though we knew she did not understand.

The next part is hazy in my memory, permanently blurred by the concussion. I hurried past Mama's closed door toward my bedroom at the end of the hall. As I passed the top of the staircase, there were footsteps behind me. Something slammed against the side of my head, and I woke in an unfamiliar white room.

°

I remember pieces of my recovery. Either Mama or Papa was always at my bedside, helping me to the bathroom or paging the nurses to get me more medicine for the pain. They both stared at me with the same haunted expression, their faces etched with lines that appeared to have formed since my hospitalization. They looked more alike than ever before, twinned by their remorse and misery.

Gradually I learned what had happened. Natalie hit me while I was off-balance, walking past the stairs, and I fell all the way down to the first floor. Mama woke from her nap to my sister's wails and found me unconscious. She thought at first that I was dead. She interrupted my father's session—an unprecedented event—so that he could deal with Natalie's hysterics. Mama rode with me in the ambulance. I spent three days in a medicated coma as the swelling in my brain went down.

Natalie did not visit me in the hospital, of course. When I asked about her, my parents patted my hand and changed the subject. I remember a series of tests: naming colors, pointing out shapes. I remember that my head ached all the time. The concussion had worsened my already-poor vision, and I needed a stronger prescription for my glasses now. I got winded just walking down the tiled corridor of the hospital wing. The doctors explained that I'd lost a startling amount of muscle mass in the brief span of my inactivity.

My friends from school sent a get-well card that sang a tinny message. The nurses rumpled my hair and told me I was a wonderful patient. It was strange to be the center of everyone's attention. I felt a little guilty about the stares and smiles, as though I was using up a finite, precious resource that must be needed elsewhere.

I left the hospital on a warm day in April and stepped into a world alive with spring, every flower blooming, the air scented with pollen. The season had changed while I recovered. I came home to find a celebratory banner hung in the living room, a bouquet of flowers from my teachers on the kitchen table, and all my sister's things packed into boxes.

◦

Children accept the world they know. At the age of eight, I was accustomed to a state of being in which my parents never went out or had a night to themselves. My friends had babysitters; I did not. I was used to dabbing my wounds from Natalie with hydrogen peroxide and applying bandages on my own, without complaint. It was my job to love my sister and care for her, no matter what it cost me. I never questioned that. It was my job, too, to help my overburdened parents in any way I could, supervising Natalie so they could shower or cook a meal, accepting her violence without blame, and never asking them for anything myself. I understood without ever being told that I needed to be smart and successful, a source of pride for my parents and a counterpoint to my sister. I needed to be easygoing and agreeable, too, showing my parents that Natalie was not too much for me, that I could handle it, all of it. It never occurred to me that there was any other option—for my sister, for my parents, or for me.

Now, of course, I know better. Even before my fall down the stairs, my parents had often discussed putting my sister in an institution. That was the subject of their anguished late-night conversations, debating both sides of the issue, my mother reversing her stance, my father playing devil's advocate, going back and forth until one or both of them wept. They'd made calls and done research, once going so far as to tour a facility in western Maryland before changing their minds. Now, looking back, I understand the terrible math they could not solve: black eyes for them, a real home for Natalie, no vacations or trips or even a night alone together, security for Natalie, scratches on my arms, comfort for Natalie, my childhood constricted and curtailed and diminished, a sibling for Natalie.

My stay in the hospital tipped the scales. I don't remember how my parents explained it to me; my head was still fuzzy then. I do remember crying and begging them not to send Natalie away. I could not imagine my life without her, I said. At this, my parents exchanged a glance, one of those knowing looks that communicated a great deal.

"It's best for both of you to forge a separate identity now," Mama said.

"We don't want you to become an undifferentiated ego mass," Papa said.

"That's right," Mama said. "Codependency isn't a panacea."

My temples throbbed. All I could do was nod.

°

I did not sleep for most of Natalie's last night at home. Partly this was the fault of the hospital—I was still readjusting to a normal circadian schedule and an unmedicated brain. But mostly it was grief. Natalie did not know what was about to happen. We could not explain it. She was irritated by the presence of the boxes and her inability to find her toys and art supplies, but Mama and Papa were letting her watch TV as much as she wanted, so she was happy enough.

In the morning, Papa would drive her across the state, and I would see her on holidays, maybe. Tears welled in my eyes. Mama had shown me the website for the facility. Smiling children waved in front of a brick building, dressed in tie-dyed T-shirts they'd presumably made themselves. They were all different ages and races and sizes, yet they all had faces like my sister's, though I couldn't pinpoint exactly what in their disparate features overlapped. In Natalie's darting eyes and wide mouth, there was the suggestion of her pinniped lineage, some vestige of her oceanic form glimmering under the surface. I could see it in these children too. Selkie faces.

Before dawn, before the robins even began to sing, I crept into my sister's room. Natalie was awake too, sitting up in bed with both arms raised as her nightlight spun on the bookshelf, projecting stars across the wall and her skin.

"Come on," I said. "Let's go."

She did not want to put on her coat. She kicked me as I laced up her shoes. She stepped through the front door as though it were a portal to another world, stroking the knob and the dead bolt curiously with her fingers. When was the last time she'd left the house? I could not remember.

I held her hand as we walked down the hill to the beach. Natalie let me, though usually she hated persistent skin contact. The sun was rising on the other side of the ocean. I expected my sister to throw a tantrum over the change in her routine or to balk at the overstimulation—seagulls crying overhead, a motorcycle whizzing down the road, airplanes crisscrossing the sky. But Natalie was surprisingly docile, clinging to my fingers and gazing around in evident awe, her azure eyes wide.

She stopped dead at the edge of the sand. A cool breeze blew off the water, lifting the greasy strands of her hair away from her face. Mama and Papa appeared to have given up on Sunday baths. A few seals lolled on the distant rocks, soaking up the morning rays. Their bodies were as round as eggs, dappled with spots. One of them lay on its side with a single flipper sticking straight up in the air.

I pointed to the seals. "Those are your sisters," I told Natalie. "Your other sisters."

She let me lead her onto the beach, step by cautious step. Her lips parted in amazement at the squish and slide of the sand beneath her shoes. The sun rose, bejeweling the water's surface with light. I guided my sister toward the waves without pulling or insisting. I touched her as gently as I did when she had mastered a new drawing on her own but had not yet removed her hand from mine. Together we crossed the midline of the beach. High tide had come and gone, leaving shells and whorls of seaweed on the compact brown sand.

"Do you remember where you left your sealskin?" I said. "They're taking you away today. Away from the ocean. This is your last chance."

Natalie took another step toward the water. In the distance, one of the seals broke away from the others and galumphed noisily into the surf. My sister did not appear to notice. Her gaze was fixed on the shimmery shallows ahead of her. The waves glided up the beach with a delicate hiss, and a bubbly spume skimmed the toes of Natalie's sneakers. I expected her to scream or bolt, but instead she smiled.

I had rarely ever seen my sister smile. I'd never heard her laugh.

I glanced back up the hill toward the house. We didn't have long. Any minute now, my parents would wake and find us missing. Maybe they would call the police. Maybe I would be punished for the first time in my life. Would my parents even know how to do that? I'd never broken a rule before, never said no to anything they asked of me, not once.

Natalie knelt and spread out her hands, the webs between her fingers catching the light. She laid her palms on the surface of the water, making tiny ripples, feeling the heave and swell of each new wave. Soon she would be taken from me, packed along with her boxes into the back of our minivan and driven out of sight. I could not imagine what would happen after that. There was only a strange void when I looked ahead to a life without her—wild, sharp, unwanted freedom.

"We need to find your sealskin," I said. "Did it wash up here on the sand with you? Or over there by the rocks? Think, Natalie. This is important."

She was still smiling. The expression sat oddly on her angular face. Her palms dimpled the silver veneer of the sea.

I left her there and darted down the beach. I was certain that my sister's lost pelt had not decayed during her ten years on land. In the stories, selkies sometimes hid their skins for decades before retrieving them unharmed. I poked into the crevasses between the rocks with a stick. I dissected a clump of seaweed, glancing over my shoulder to check that Natalie was all right. She was.

It had to be here somewhere—a charcoal-colored scrap of fur just big enough to swaddle an infant's body. The tourists wouldn't have taken such a strange item; they were like magpies, attracted by shells and pretty stones. No animal would have eaten it either. There were only seals here, and they would understand the significance of that precious object. I checked under rocks and uprooted half-buried driftwood. I investigated the gaps between the rusted beams of the pier.

I did not find Natalie's sealskin before a scream broke the air and my parents came running down the hill, red-faced and breathless. I did not find it before my sister was forced into the car, yowling, leaving scratches on my arms, her final good-bye. I did not find it that summer, though I searched the beach every time Mama and I continued our Sunday tradition, Papa joining us now, no longer tethered to home, the two of them strolling hand in hand. I looked for my sister's skin when my friends and I played at the shore together, Aliyah and I each wearing one half of a heart around our necks, Patsy showing off her handstands. I looked for it the day I asked Papa when I could visit Natalie and learned that it would be a while; my sister needed time to adjust to her new routine, her new surroundings, and my presence would only destabilize her. In the fall, maybe. Or next year. I looked for her sealskin after my first real birthday party with friends, nine years old, and we actually lit the candles because there was no danger of Natalie tipping the cake over and setting the house on fire. I looked for it after a photograph of my sister bloomed overnight on the institution's website, her flaxen head bent over a sheet of paper, drawing a seal with a rotund belly and perfectly placed flippers. I took my first-ever babysitter, a high school student with pink hair, to the beach to help me search after Mama and Papa went out on a date, him freshly shaven, her unrecognizable in lipstick and a low-cut dress. We scoured the sand for an hour, and then I came home and sat cross-legged in Natalie's empty room, the walls bare and washed in sunlight.

I have not found it yet, but I keep looking.

Love in Florida

The letter said only: *Come see me.*

She didn't have to sign it. I would have known Betty Sue's handwriting anywhere. Sitting in my living room, floating on the humid tide of summer air, sweat in my beard, sweat sticking my clothes to the chair, I turned the envelope over in my hands. I ran my fingers over the crinkled line of her cursive, then sniffed the paper. A faint antiseptic tang.

Betty Sue had mailed it to me from the Homestead Correctional Institution, a women's prison at the southernmost tip of Florida. I knew she had been incarcerated there for a few years now. I hadn't talked to her in a decade, but I kept up with the local gossip back home. The fact of Betty Sue's imprisonment had taken our small town by storm. Everyone was shocked; nobody was surprised. Hadn't she always been a brat? Remember the plate-smashing tantrum she threw as a five-year-old in Millie's Diner? Remember her penchant for shoplifting in middle school?

I could not picture Betty Sue as a full-grown woman, let alone an inmate, behind bars. I had not seen her since the age of thirteen. That was when I loved her.

°

Picture this:

Two scrawny kids fighting on the lawn. Betty Sue and I grew up in the muddiest, ripest corner of the armpit state of Florida. In my memory, I wear denim overalls with a rip in the knee. My hair is a mess, dirt on my neck; I probably haven't showered in a week and a half. I remember Betty Sue's pigtails, as skinny as garter snakes, lashing around her shoulders. Her cheeks are flushed. She scoops up a handful of mud and flings it into my face. Direct hit. Two figures catapult sideways, into the bushes.

If you look past this image, you will see the house where I was raised. A mildewed porch. A blue-painted door. The walls hold one another up like a group of drunks heading home from the bar. The roof is beaten in. A tree branch fell years ago, and the breach has been patched inexpertly. It drips in the rain. My family is used to navigating around the rotten, mossy floorboards and stagnant pools of water.

No one is home. My older sister clerks at the drugstore during the day and waitresses at night. I scarcely ever see her—a thin figure slipping past my room before dawn, hair drawn back in a severe ponytail. She's working her way out of here. My mother cleans houses for rich people. My father is a track laborer on the railways, making it home for one week out of every five or six.

And I—Silas Warner, off school for the summer—tackle Betty Sue Sullivan, the only child my age within a three-mile radius, into the dirt and pin her down with both hands.

"Say uncle."

She narrows her eyes. "Screw you."

Her breath is short. I'm sitting on her solar plexus. A crimson blush spreads up her freckled throat like the stain of sunset. I can feel her heart whanging against the cage of my thighs. Suddenly concerned—she could die there, her eyes fluttering, her lips going blue—I slither off her torso. Betty Sue rolls away, holding her gut and coughing.

"I won," she gasps. "*I* won."

Even now, all these years later, the smell of a coming storm still does it to me. The heaviness in the air before it rains. The rank musk of adolescent sweat. Pearly skin spattered with freckles. Green eyes wide beneath the thunder.

°

After a week of thinking, I wrote her back. I told her no.

I had my reasons. Work obligations. A brand-new baby. The pregnancy had been hard on Jasmine. She had always been an elegant woman, pale and self-possessed, like a lily rising from still water. She wanted children—we both did—but she was not prepared for what would be required of her to gestate and birth one. She would have preferred to do it like Zeus, knocking a hole in her skull to bring forth a fully formed, adult offspring.

Instead, she vomited into the toilet every morning for the full nine months. Her feet and ankles swelled. Her belly became a glistening globe, striped with stretch marks. I still found her beautiful, but when she looked in the mirror, she seemed to see something less than human, a fecund, slobby animal. Giving birth—the pain, the blood, the indignity of her own nudity, the touch of strangers' hands on her skin—left her raw and bewildered. Even breastfeeding went against her nature. These days, she tended to trail around the house in a shapeless robe, the baby on her hip, her face blank. She still used animal terms to refer to herself. *Fat as a whale. Milked like a cow.*

And so I replied to Betty Sue with a no. A gentle no. Not just now, maybe one day, if only. At the mailbox, I dusted off my hands.

°

That same night, the baby woke me with his gut-wrenching screams. I kicked out and muttered, "Betty Sue." The image was hot and blurred: a yellow bathing suit, wet pigtails, the splash of a river. I had not dreamed about her in years.

Then came the incident at Danny's Rental. My job required me to be personable, curious, and unflappable. Your child peed in the back seat? No problem, we have a protocol for that. Your dog jumped up on the side door and left scratches in the paint? No problem, I'll refer you to my manager. The engine won't start? The oil light's on? No problem, no problem at all.

Beneath the buzz of fluorescent lights, I stood sweating through my shirt, the phone cupped against my ear.

"Yes," I was saying. "Thursday. A minivan." I looked down, and there, in my notepad, I had printed in emphatic letters: *Betty Sue. Betty Sue. Betty Sue.*

She haunted me. Later that week I sat alone at the kitchen

table, a beer at my elbow. It was a Saturday night, and the house was blessedly silent for once. Jasmine had taken herself and the baby off to her mother's for the evening.

Then I heard a light footfall on the stairs. I got up to check, but I was alone in the house, only my own shadow moving. As soon as I sat back down at the table, though, I heard it again. Trip-trip-swish. No one walked that way but Betty Sue in a mood.

She haunted me in the garden when I dug up weeds to suit my wife's taste. During her pregnancy, Jasmine had become enamored with tomatoes, and our backyard was a minefield of swollen orbs. I crouched in the dirt, my body gritty and fly-bitten, broiling red in the Florida sun. Jasmine knelt beside me, worrying away with her spade. The baby lay in his basinet. His eyes were open, staring up at the toss of tree branches. I sat back, removed my hat, and felt a wind touch my nape. A teasing breath. Betty Sue blowing sharp between her teeth.

She haunted me in the slow drift toward sleep. She haunted me when I leaned my forehead against the window of a pickup in the parking lot of Danny's Rental. She haunted me at the seashore, where Jasmine stood on the sand, laughing and clapping, as I, waist-deep, spun my bubble-bright, hilarious son in a circle above my head. Wallace had only recently begun to laugh. His mouth was as wide as it could go.

Betty Sue haunted me when my wife brushed her sugar-soft hands over my back. She haunted me as I met Jasmine's eyes in the dark bedroom. She haunted me as I made love to my wife for the first time in months, as I entered her dry and delicate body and felt her arch underneath me, a cry caught in her throat.

°

In childhood, Betty Sue and I lived at the edge of a swamp, not far from the Everglades. Her house and mine were separated by vines, creepers, and mud. There were tree trunks slimy with moss, quicksand pools, and turtles the size of your stomach. There were bobcats in the underbrush—noiseless, watchful creatures that melted away between the leaves but left their fish-smell on the wind.

My house was situated in an uncertain clearing that my father always intended to mow when he was home but rarely did. Betty Sue's house, half a mile away as the crow flies, could have been on the far side of the moon. There was no safe passage through the marsh. You had to walk the long way: three miles across the parched curves of the country road.

And we did, Betty Sue and me. During the sweltering summer days, she would wander into my yard with her hands in her pockets, feigning casualness, as though she had stumbled upon the place by accident. I never knew when she would appear, so I kept one eye on the road, pretending even to myself that I did not care if she came. Eventually, if she did not turn up, I would walk the miles to her house instead, grumbling all the way.

Things were never amicable between us. We argued about everything from her overuse of the word *like* to my obsession with baseball stats to her father's drinking to the future of the great state of Florida when the oceans inevitably rose. We dared each other to dangerous feats, walking the eaves of the roof or teasing the alligators. Often we came to blows. Even when we were really too old to be rolling in the mud, we needed to make contact and it was the only way we knew. We snapped and sparred until we grew tired. Then she would leave, or I would, striding away as though this time were the last time, never acknowledging that we would meet again the next day, and the day after that, seeking each other out unerringly and unwillingly, driven by loneliness and yearning and the strange, prickly electricity of our bond.

Alone in my bedroom at night, I would hear her. As I lay on the bare mattress on the floor, I gazed at my treasures: a jar of sea glass, a four-foot snakeskin, an alligator tooth, and the dirty magazines I'd stolen from my father. All of these things—and me—were transformed by the moon, made fantastic, blue-tinged, deeply shadowed. I listened to the snores of my mother in her room next door. I listened to the restless shuffle of my sister on the other side as she doffed one work uniform and donned another. I listened to the patter of mice inside the wall.

From across the forest, between the dark tufts of reeds, beneath the creak of branches and the gusting of the wind, I listened to Betty Sue. Her sniffle and sigh. Her fingers tangling in the blanket. The blink of her eyes. Her cough. The expansion and contraction of her rib cage. The flutter of her dreaming brain.

°

After sending my letter, I intended to return to the state of poignant nostalgia that had characterized my relationship with Betty Sue for so many years. My childhood crush. My first love. A fond memory.

But I couldn't help myself. Every day, as soon as I returned from Danny's Rental, I would shuffle the mail like a deck of cards. Jasmine, shambling by in her dressing gown, tugging a used Kleenex from her sleeve to blow her nose, did not notice my agitation. Each day that passed without a letter from Betty Sue wound my nerves a little tighter. I had told her not to write back, but surely she wouldn't take me at my word. She never had before.

Two years earlier, I had heard about her incarceration during one of my visits home. My mother was the one to tell me, dropping this bit of news as a casual aside in the middle of dinner. I sat stunned, feeling the blood in my ears, not hearing a word of the rest of the conversation.

Jasmine was with me. Before Wallace was born, we traveled to my hometown every few months, driving four hours across Florida, north to south. My wife always handled these trips well. She was skilled at adjusting her conversation to meet people at their own level. She would sit beside my father in his recliner, ignoring the miasma of cigar smoke, listening as he rambled on about the technical elements of a piston engine. She would watch soap operas with my mother, exhibiting every sign of enjoyment. She would gaze at pictures of my sister, now a flight attendant, groomed and immaculate in her blue uniform, the family's success story. Jasmine would comment on her poise, one hand fumbling for mine to give me a reassuring squeeze.

But that visit was different. I spent most of it in a state of shock. Whenever Jasmine was out of earshot, I would draw my mother aside and try to extract more information. What else had she heard about Betty Sue? What exactly was the word on the street? Could she repeat the whole thing from the beginning?

My mother was frustratingly short on specifics. In her customary manner, hesitant and uncertain, she nattered and apologized. She had heard something about it from a neighbor, who had heard something from the postman, who knew Betty Sue's mother's cousin. Actual details were few and far between.

During the remainder of my visit home, I tried to ask around. The gas station attendant said grand theft auto. The clerk at the grocery store informed me it was possession with intent to sell. The librarian murmured it was murder, cold-blooded murder.

Nobody knew for sure. The consensus around town seemed to be that Betty Sue was a bad seed, and it had just been a matter of time until she found her way to a sorry end.

But I knew better. That was the distortion of hindsight—people shaping events in retrospect to fit a particular narrative. Hadn't we both been feral children, dirt-poor, raising ourselves at the edge of a swamp? I could easily have been the one who went astray, and everyone would have said the same about me, as though they'd known all along that I was no good.

In retrospect, I could have done more to find out what crime Betty Sue actually committed. The full story was doubtless a matter of public record. I suppose that when push came to shove, I didn't really want to know.

°

Two weeks after I mailed my letter, the phone rang in the middle of a Saturday afternoon. Jasmine and I were drowsing in bed, taking the advice of every parenting book and sleeping when the baby slept.

"You get it," my wife snorted into her pillow. It was the landline, which we kept only for emergencies; Jasmine's parents, in particular, had trouble with the whole concept of cellular technology. The night table was on her side. I lunged across her body, took up the phone, and fell back against my pillow.

Someone was already speaking, an electronic voice: "—a collect call from the Homestead Correctional Institution. Will you accept—"

"Yes, yes," I said.

The air changed, charged with tension. Sunlight played

through the curtains, casting shifting patterns of glow and shadow on the wall.

"Silas," a voice whispered.

Jasmine seemed to have gone back to sleep, snoring beneath her cloud of dark hair. Perhaps she had never really woken up.

"Betty Sue," I said.

She laughed. "You recognized my voice!"

"Oh, honey," I said. "Oh, kid. You calling me from prison?"

"That I am."

I laid a hand on the plane of Jasmine's shoulder blades to steady myself.

"How'd you end up there?" I said. "I never heard."

"It's none of your beeswax."

"Did you steal something? Remember that time in the Five and Dime, with the lipstick? I always told you—"

"I don't want to talk about it. We don't talk about it here."

I bit my lip, deciding not to push. Betty Sue inhaled, a familiar sound, quick and impatient.

"Is your wife there?" she said. "Right there?"

"She's napping."

"Married man," she said.

"And a kid. Wallace. My baby boy."

"Oh, hush."

A silence fell between us. I could feel her—lithe limbs, hard knees, clambering into my lap.

"I'm in this ugly room," she said. "The wall is an awful color. Beige. Not really a color at all. There's another inmate with me. She's waiting to use the phone. She's got her eyes on me but she isn't really listening." Betty Sue's voice dropped to a whisper. "Nobody's really listening, Silas."

"I'm listening. I wish I could take you away from there."

She laughed. "Oh no. They ain't never gonna let me out."

There was a moment of stillness. When her voice returned, it was so low and urgent that I flinched. Her breath touched my ear.

"You've got to visit me," she said.

"What?"

"You get yourself here. You have to—"

I lost her again. The line clattered with static.

"What's happening?" I said desperately, forgetting to keep my voice low. Jasmine jerked in bed, kicking a foot clear of the sheets.

"—got to go," Betty Sue said. "They're making me—"

"What?" I gripped the phone in both hands. "Are you there?"

She was gone. I could tell by the quality of the silence, but still, I waited for a good long stretch with the phone to my ear, listening to nothing.

°

The drive seemed endless. Wallace, colicky, squirmed in his car seat. His face was red, mouth distended, hands working like sea anemones. I watched him in the rearview mirror.

Jasmine sat beside me, radiating a kind of martyred grace. The night before, I had told her about Betty Sue. I told her everything, and Jasmine listened with her head cocked to the side. In a strange way, her reaction reassured me. Yes, she was angry about my deception, suspicious of my motives. But she told me she would come along, and I said thank you, yes, I needed her there.

The drive took nearly six hours. We lived near the Georgia border, as far from the Homestead Correctional Institution as you could get without leaving the state. The highway shimmered with mirages, the broiling asphalt casting up warped reflections of the cloudless sky. The car's air conditioner whined and sputtered in a feeble protest. Beneath my wife's honey scent and the diaper-and-flour odor of the baby, I caught the sting of cigarettes, fused deep into the seat fabric, from the days before I'd quit. Jasmine had done that, weaning me off the smokes with her patented brand of reasoned argument. It was one of many painful gifts she had given me.

Florida rolled out before us, hot and forsaken. Roadkill lay crushed on the melting tar. Clumps of identical houses were clustered like patches of mushrooms. Children with dirty legs played by the side of the highway. As the merciless sun climbed the sky, the moon followed us, refusing to set on schedule. A ghostly silhouette against the blue, it hung in my window like a stopwatch, counting how many years, days, and hours it would take me to finally quit betraying Betty Sue.

°

We made love only once, Betty Sue and me, at the tender age of thirteen. We were both too young for it, but when we learned that she would be moving away—when her father took a new job in Grand Landing—we met in the forest one last time. We were both angry at the situation, scuffing our feet, hands jammed into our pockets. We did not know how to end our difficult relationship. There wasn't a word for what we were to each other.

I kissed her first. It was a strange little bump, our mouths colliding. She stepped back and stared at me, astonished. I waited for a slap, for her to turn to the side and spit on the ground.

Instead she flew into my arms, weightless and glimmering. It didn't last long. We peeled off half our clothes and lay down among the weeds, my hands shaking as she buried her cry of pain in my shoulder.

Even now, I remember every moment of it, every shift, every inhalation. The line of her jaw. The way her fingers dug into my forearm, marking five perfectly round bruises that lingered for days. When it was over, we rolled apart, wide-eyed and scared. Betty Sue had leaves in her hair. There was a streak of blood on her inner thigh. I could not move. I lay in the grass, feeling as though God himself had reached down and pinned me to the earth, like a butterfly stuck to a corkboard backing.

°

Picture this:

I am standing in a room that is not exactly a color. Tables dot the space, the air charred fluorescent. There are women in orange clothing strewn in plastic chairs, conversing in low voices with friends and family.

Jasmine stands outside the door, the baby on her hip. In the lobby. In safety. Through the square, scratched window in the door, her gaze is fixed on me like a laser, her expression unforgiving. The glass frames her and Wallace like a portrait in a museum: *Madonna and Child, Plagued by Lunatic Husband.*

Trip-trip-swish. A woman in orange dashes toward me. She still wears pigtails, now threaded with gray. I stumble at the sight of her. She sprints to the nearest table and stops on the other side, panting. We are not allowed to touch. Her grin is as bright as ever, though one tooth has yellowed, beginning to rot. She is giggling and crying at the same time, no tears, only breath too big for her little torso, rocking in her chest like wings.

Overlaid with this, I can still see the child I knew. Same height, same build. Same face, though the skin is weathered now. Same glittering eyes.

I sit down, keeping to my side of the table. I do not allow my fingers to wander. Betty Sue mirrors me. I send a reassuring glance to Jasmine, noting that her shoulders have relaxed. I understand: it is a relief for her to see the reality of things, a human being, flesh and blood, no siren with magical powers, no seductive minx, no rival. Jasmine bounces the baby, who has begun to fuss, and turns away.

Betty Sue begins to talk a mile a minute, just as she always did. She tells me about her father, who recently passed from cirrhosis. She tells me about learning to play basketball in the prison yard. I tell her about my mother's increasing addiction to soap operas. I tell her about my father's promotion on the railways. Betty Sue knots her hands together. Her fingers are chapped, her nails bitten down to the quick. This is small talk, breezy conversation, yet somehow it makes my head swim. Her brother. My sister. Her memories of our old neighborhood. I tell her how the place has changed. We can't shut up long enough to draw breath. She waits until the guard is looking away, then strikes my shoulder to make a point. I'm gesturing with both hands, trying to shape my life in front of her. Here, the house. Here, the big tree in the yard. Here, my family. Her whole face follows every movement, drinking me in with affection and hunger, a lover who has missed me with every breath, a bird eyeing a worm.

Underneath all these things, another conversation takes place in silence. I tell her I always loved her. I tell her good-bye. With her eyes, she says the same back to me. We never got to say these things when we were kids. We didn't know how.

°

That was the last time I saw her. We did sustain a written correspondence for a while; we gave it our best shot. Every few weeks, an envelope would turn up in the mailbox. By that time, Jasmine found the whole thing amusing. "Another letter from your girlfriend in prison!" she would cry. A page or two of misspellings and cross-outs. Nothing intimate or revelatory. The epistolary equivalent of chitchat. It would take me a few weeks to accumulate enough words for a reply. The span of time between call and response got longer and longer on both sides.

I had other things on my mind. Jasmine was herself again. She read late into the evening, cooked her special pasta, and listened to jazz. She gazed at the baby with a satisfied glow in her cheeks. I had missed her. I took her out to fancy dinners so she could dress up. I fixed the crooked kitchen cabinet. I brought home a stuffed bunny for Wallace, one that squeaked when you squeezed it.

In the end, Betty Sue and I stopped trying. I stored her letters in a shoebox at the back of the closet, gathering dust. I sweated her out of my system like the last remnants of a bad flu. Perhaps she had been in my bloodstream since childhood.

On that fateful day—when I took her virginity, or she took mine, or we both gave them away, or maybe that's the wrong way to think about it altogether, because really what we did was cross a threshold, both of us, staring into each other's eyes—Betty Sue climbed to her feet right away and tugged on her jeans. I remember her standing over me. A chortle rose out of her throat. I smiled up at her, at the sunlight crowning her brow. She laughed until she had to clutch at her stomach.

"I got you," she told me, in between shuddering bursts. "I got you *good.* Nobody else can ever be your first. It's always going to be me."

I opened my mouth to answer, but she turned on her heel and ran away. I watched her flash between the trees and disappear.

Porcupines in Trees

At midnight, she is still awake. The cabin is a noisy place, filled with the bang of a shutter, the groan of ancient plumbing. Lila wanders the rooms, unnerved by the density of the darkness. There are no streetlamps here. No ambient city glow, soaking up the stars. Trees clack in the wind outside. Lila shivers inside her robe.

Most of the day was spent driving. Two hours to make it out of Brooklyn. Another six, heading north through rolling hills, to reach the Adirondacks. The GPS gave instructions in clipped, clinical tones. Lila did not like being directed this way. Born and raised in New York, she was branded with a mental map of the city. She was never lost there. Now the silence presses against her ears. She misses the wail of sirens and the subterranean thunder of the train.

Simone, impervious, is sound asleep, taking up more than

her half of the bed, as usual. Her droning snores carry all the way down the hall to the living room. Lila goes to the window and pulls the curtain aside. The lake is a smear of gray, and the mountains rise beyond that, black and two-dimensional, as though painted on the sky.

When the porcupine first appears, Lila assumes it is a monster. Her experience with the forest begins and ends with horror films. Something is snuffling among the bushes, cracking twigs and overturning leaves. Then the animal barges into the clearing, and, with a gasp, Lila takes in the quiver of quills.

The porcupine has a lazy, lumbering gait. As it moves, its armament clatters—an obvious warning, like a snake's rattle. It noses through the grass, scratching at the ground with a paw in search of food. The creature's head lifts, and it glances in the direction of Lila's window. She wonders if it has sensed her there, watching. Despite the darkness both inside the cabin and out, she experiences a jolt as the animal's gaze brushes her body.

The porcupine grows still, eyes unblinking, quills bristling like an eave hung with icicles. Lila lifts a hand in greeting, an automatic wave. In reply, the animal turns and shuffles back into the woods.

○

In the morning, Lila takes six pills, swallowing them with water. Simone stands next to her at the bathroom sink, brushing her teeth and watching Lila in the mirror. Two red. One yellow. Two blue. One purple. Lila chokes them all down. The water has a sulfurous aftertaste—or perhaps it is the residue of her medication.

At her side, Simone gargles noisily. Her white hair is bed-crumpled, her mouth chapped, her eyes heavy. Lila does not meet her wife's reflected gaze. She keeps her attention focused on the furnishings of their rented cabin. The place is quaint in every particular, from the knotted pine walls to the leaf-shaped sconces to the cheery toothbrush holder. Sunlight filters through gingham curtains. Lila lines up her pill bottles on the counter, then begins to stack them into a tower.

"We have to check your stitches," Simone says.

Lila examines herself in the mirror. Frizzy gray hair. Eyes as flat and dull as old dimes. Skin like dry clouds. She is sixty-one. In the last few months, her aging has seemed to accelerate. She is becoming less human, more papier-mâché.

"Lila," Simone says sharply.

"I heard you."

She holds out her wrists. The ritual is familiar to them both now. Simone has all the equipment ready—gauze pads, rolls of medical tape, antibiotic ointment. She removes the bandages, her fingers clumsy but gentle. Lila does not wince, even as the tape pulls at her wounds. Simone bends down, adjusting her reading glasses. Lila holds still.

The sight of her own injuries is still a shock to her. It induces a kind of distance in her mind, as though she is observing herself on television—a crime show, the gore sealed off behind a screen. Her forearms are marked by jagged red scars. Three cuts on one side. Four on the other. The wounds on her right arm are much more pronounced. This is to be expected, apparently, since she is left-handed.

Simone presses on the inflamed skin, checking for infection. Lila sucks in a breath. It helps to think of the injuries as something else. A drawing. A map. The crimson scars run like rivers. The stitches, bold and black, look like bridges. Her wrists could be the topographical representations of a faraway country.

"Seems to be healing fine," Simone says. "Remember, no heavy lifting. Nothing over ten pounds."

"I know."

Simone reaches for the gauze, her expression weary.

"I saw a porcupine last night," Lila says.

Simone says nothing, wrapping her wrists in white.

°

The trip was Simone's idea. She first broached it on the way home from the hospital. This was a week ago, though it feels much longer to Lila. At the time, she was too heavily drugged to attend. She lolled in the passenger seat. The doctors had put her on a cocktail of mood stabilizers and pain pills. Simone's question—a cabin, the mountains—flitted past her like a flock of butterflies.

But Simone persisted. She raised the matter again in the psychiatrist's office, several days later, as she and Lila sat in plastic chairs, not touching. The room was dim, perfumed by cinnamon candles and illuminated by lamps with heavy orange shades. The hospital had referred Lila to Dr. Conroe. She was not sure what to make of him. She had never been to a therapist before, and Dr. Conroe had an odd manner. Bearded. Heavy glasses. Soft voice. He ruminated, interrupting himself and stepping on his own sentences. He seemed distracted, but Lila knew better. As they chatted about the weather, as Simone nibbled her fingernails, as Lila did her best not to fiddle with the dressing on her wounds, Dr. Conroe looked her over with shrewd eyes. He threw out the occasional question, as sharp as a slap. How was her mood? Was the medication making her nauseous? Was she still fixated on the kitchen knives?

Lila answered in monosyllables: *Fine. Yes. No.*

Simone had talked about her plan. A forest getaway. The natural world. It would give Lila a chance to heal, away from the noise and bustle of New York, away from their friends and prying questions, away from the apartment where Simone had not been able to remove the bloodstains entirely from the floor.

Dr. Conroe gave the trip his blessing. Lila was not in danger now, he said. The fresh air might do her good.

°

In the afternoon, Simone goes for a hike. Lila watches her banging around the cabin, strapping on her fanny pack and filling her water bottle. She knows better than to ask Lila to accompany her; the pills have left her too dopey for this kind of exertion. Before leaving, Simone fusses around her, helping her onto the porch swing. The air is both cold and humid, that peculiar mix of early spring. At last, Simone crunches off down the path. The trees reduce her to flashes of color—blue coat, red cap—before swallowing her up.

Lila breathes quietly. Her mind is empty. She has no thoughts, her head filled with cotton. It has been years since she has sat like this, without music, without NPR, without conversation. New leaves coat the trees. The whole forest is an almost indecent shade of raw, pale, hopeful green. In the distance, little waves dance at the edge of the lake, while the deep water remains serene and motionless.

It was Simone who chose this place. Lila has never been to the Adirondacks before. She is aware, however, that the mountains hold good memories for her wife. Simone used to visit the area as a child. She has often shared stories about cookouts and singalongs. Her parents, raising six children in Queens, were too poor to rent a cabin, as Simone and Lila have done. Instead, the family would camp in mildewed tents. They made fires for warmth, peed in the woods, boiled lake water to purify it, and subsisted on trail mix. Simone has spoken fondly of all these things. Building ineffective rabbit snares. Skipping rocks on the lake. Fishing with makeshift poles. The mountains were a haven for her. They were a respite from her family's cramped apartment, the bedroom she shared with five brothers and sisters, the crush of the city, the indignity of school, and reality in general.

In her current state, Lila does not care where she is. Awash in medication, she is unattached to the physical realm. But she understands Simone's desire to return to the mountains now, after the recent shock and trauma. It is instinct, rather than logic. It is a primal, ancient pull, like a salmon's desire to swim upstream to a half-remembered, sunlit home.

Lila hears something moving. The bushes toss on the hillside. Her mouth goes dry. It might be a bear. There are black bears in these woods; Simone has told her so. Lila rises to her feet, shading her eyes with a hand. She takes a cautious step toward the cabin. If it is a bear, she must not bolt, since the action of flight might trigger a predatory response. Is she supposed to play dead? Or should she make herself look bigger? Why can't she remember? The bushes rustle, the leaves dancing ominously. A twig snaps. A bird rises with a clatter of wings, startled into flight.

Then Lila sees it. A porcupine. She lets out a relieved breath.

The animal's face is bemused and benign. It might be the same one from the previous night; there is no way to tell. Lila considers yelling for Simone, but she does not want to spook the creature. It bustles between the trees, its manner businesslike, like a commuter on a Manhattan sidewalk. The porcupine is bigger than a breadbox, but not by much. In the daylight, its mess of fur and quills seems rumpled, like a bad case of bed head. Clearly it has some ancestry in common with mice and squirrels, but the porcupine does not pause, in the manner of prey, to look around for predators. It does not notice Lila this time. It shoulders through a thicket of dense bushes. Stamping and grunting, the animal vanishes into the lattice of green.

°

Lila does not like the word *depression.* It has a geological sound, a fitting descriptor for a sunken patch of earth, not an emotional state. Not a form of mental illness. Not something that could claim a person's life if left unchecked.

Still, it is her word. It is the name for her condition. Over the past week, she has found herself whispering it aloud. She has scribbled it on notepads like a reminder. The word has even cropped up in her dreams.

Until recently, she did not know she was sick. Dr. Conroe believes that she has been dealing with depression—undiagnosed and unacknowledged—for ten years. Maybe more. Probably more.

This is the nature of the disease, apparently. Depression is gradual, as subtle as nightfall. The sky dims by degrees. The shadows pool together. It is impossible to pinpoint the moment when the light is gone completely.

Now, looking back, Lila can chart her descent in terms of what she has lost. So many things have slipped into the gloaming, the air darkening, the horizon blurred. She has lost her brisk walk and her enjoyment of practical jokes. She has lost her love of knitting—an act that used to be both meditative and productive, good for her soul and her collection of hats. She has lost the desire to water her plants, which withered and died.

She has lost her ability to read for pleasure. The words on the page have become a barrier, not a window; she cannot find her way inside. She has lost her love of fine cuisine, subsisting instead on bread and chocolate. Occasionally, upon trying healthier fare, a salad or piece of fruit, she has found herself gagging, unable to get it down. She has lost weight. She has lost friends. Social outings are something to be endured or avoided. She has lost her wit and sparkle.

She never used to be aware of the passage of time, but now she feels every tick of the clock. She checks her watch throughout the day, tallying up exactly how many hours and minutes remain before she can go back to bed. She has lost her joy in her wife. She has lost her carnal desire for Simone, her lean torso and long hands. Lila no longer feels a rush of glad warmth upon seeing her wife for the first time after a day apart. She no longer feels much of anything on the positive end of the emotional spectrum. She has lost her capacity to make decisions, both large and little. Whether to brush her hair. Whether she and Simone should move to a smaller apartment. Whether the knives in the kitchen might be a reasonable solution to her problems.

Each loss, on its own, has been manageable. But together, they have amounted to nightfall. The sun dipping beneath the horizon. The blue wrung from the sky like paint from a rag.

°

At three in the morning, Lila is still awake. Beside her, Simone snores, one of her lanky legs crisscrossing Lila's side of the bed. Lila gazes at the ceiling. Her medicine is a blender, whipping day and night into a frothy, undistinguished concoction. She has no semblance of a schedule at the moment. At last she hefts herself out of bed. Trailing a blanket over her shoulders, she shuffles down the hall. She will find something to read. Maybe she is medicated enough now to reclaim her love of literature.

The cabin is stocked with nature books about the local flora and fauna. As Lila touches the dusty spines, her wrists ache. She ignores this. She tugs a book about mammals off the shelf and settles in an armchair. Outside the window, the trees surge like kelp in a current, the sound of leaves as rhythmic as the sea.

Lila flips to a page about porcupines. With interest, she scans the image of the animal: *Erethizon dorsatum*. It is the second-largest rodent in North America. Only beavers are bigger. There is a drawing of a quill, scaly and sharp. The porcupine cannot throw these darts—as Lila feared—but they are deadly nonetheless, tipped with minuscule barbs to lodge in an enemy's flesh.

From there, it only gets worse. The quills are designed to work their way into the body. Each contraction of the muscles tugs the weapon deeper. A coyote might try its luck with a porcupine, take a few quills in the shoulder, and die days later, its heart pierced by tiny swords. According to the book, a hunter in Idaho once cooked and ate a porcupine. Two weeks later, he perished in the hospital. One lone quill had perforated his large intestine, with slow but inexorable malice, from the inside out.

°

Lila wakes to the sound of Simone's voice. There is a crick in her neck. She appears to have dropped off while reading about porcupines. The room brims with the ochre glow of sunrise.

Simone is in the kitchen, pacing and yelling into her cell phone. It is a work call; Lila can tell by her wife's stentorian tone. Simone is an accountant, specializing in numbers and irritability.

Lila pushes the hair out of her eyes, watching as Simone gestures to no one, her footsteps unceasing. She cannot talk on the phone without motion. The person on the other end of the line would never know that she is wearing flannel pajama pants, a ratty tank top, and an open robe that flaps with each stride.

Lila herself is retired. She spent forty years as a court reporter, lugging around a stenotype, sitting in overheated rooms, and warping her spine into an achy coil. On her last day, she left the office with a skip in her step, feeling like she'd shed fifty pounds. Simone could have retired too but chose not to. She claims to need her work. As much as it aggravates her, it organizes her life.

Lila gets to her feet. At the counter, she reaches for her pills, the bottles lined up in order, waiting. She is aware of her wife's gaze on her back. Simone has stopped in her tracks, counting silently but palpably as Lila swallows. Two red. One yellow. Two blue. One purple. As soon as she is done, Simone resumes pacing again, bellowing into the phone.

Lila brews herself a cup of tea, thinking about Dr. Conroe. Since her hospitalization, she has spoken with him every day. He explained that she has been through a major depressive episode. He explained that the disease is part biological, part environmental. The likelihood of pain was coded into Lila's genetic makeup, present from birth. All that was needed was the right trigger. The wrong trigger. Dr. Conroe has talked about catalysts and causes. So many things might have contributed to Lila's downward spiral. Her retirement, one year ago. The illness of a good friend, five years ago. The onset of her menopause, ten years ago. The death of her mother, fifteen years ago. The fact that she and Simone decided not to have children, thirty years ago. All change is stressful, according to Dr. Conroe. Even events that seem positive in the moment can have a negative impact on brain chemistry.

Depression is cumulative. It builds over time. It hides inside its slowness.

Lila returns to the couch and picks up the book she began reading last night, still open to the page about porcupines. She glances through it idly, sipping her tea. These animals, it seems, rely completely on their arsenal of quills. They do not have a potent sense of smell or hearing. They are not nocturnal, like other rodents, moving under the cover of darkness. Porcupines have put all their eggs in one basket—all their arrows in one quiver. Many inexperienced predators find themselves drawn to that plump, vulnerable shape, the slow shuffle. The porcupine looks like it couldn't run more than a few feet without stopping to catch its breath. They are routinely stalked by young foxes, coyotes, and mountain lions. One bite, however, is all it takes. If the predator is lucky enough to survive those quills, it will never risk another encounter.

There is more, but Lila is already yawning. *Endothermic. Bilateral symmetry. Sexual dimorphism. Omnivorous diet.* She lays the book aside and curls up beneath her blanket, sedated, lulled, belly full of warm tea, eyes closed.

°

That afternoon, she calls Dr. Conroe. She has promised to call him every day without fail. He might as well be her parole officer.

"How are you feeling?" he asks.

Lila sighs, sitting at the kitchen counter, swiveling her stool back and forth. This question is too complicated to answer. "Fine," she says.

"I'm not asking as a formality, Lila. I want details. How's the pain?"

"Mental or physical?"

He laughs, a genuine chuckle, ripe and warm. Lila finds herself grinning in response. It has been a while since she smiled.

"Let's start with physical," he says. "How are the cuts? The stitches should be coming out in two days, is that right?"

"Yes."

Simone enters the kitchen and pours herself a bowl of cereal as a snack. Her pigtails seem unfinished, one side sleek, the other unkempt and crooked. She must have heard Lila's voice and rushed out of the bathroom in the middle of doing her hair to snoop.

Dr. Conroe, meanwhile, is talking about dosage and milligrams.

"You're at a hundred now," he says. "That's what's making you feel sleepy. I might drop you down to seventy-five or even fifty, in time. But not yet. I want to make sure those compulsions keep their distance."

"I see," Lila says.

"How are you feeling about the kitchen knives?"

She glances at Simone again, standing at the sink to eat, facing the window, as though unaware that Lila is on the phone. On the kitchen counter sits a wooden knife holder. It is empty. The first thing Simone did upon their arrival was to gather up all the sharp objects in the cabin and hide them. Lila wonders how her wife managed this. Perhaps she dunked them in the tank of the toilet. Perhaps she buried them outside in the cold ground.

"Lila?" Dr. Conroe says.

She shivers a little. "Simone hid the knives."

"Ah," he says. "Good woman. Out of sight, out of mind."

Lila runs her fingers down the line of her stitches. They are arranged like braille, a message printed on her flesh in a language she cannot understand. Soon they will be gone. In two days, she will return to the hospital. The doctors will inspect her wounds one last time, and then her recovery will begin in earnest. She will no longer have to wear uncomfortable splints at night to keep her wrists from bending. She will be able to type again. She will be able to carry grocery bags. She will be able to wash her own hair, instead of being shampooed like a child by Simone.

Eventually her mind will recover too. Dr. Conroe has promised this. The medication will take effect. The depression will subside.

But Lila cannot imagine it. She has been in the darkness too long. She pictures herself as a fish in a cave, sealed away from the sun. Over the years, the absence of light has altered her physiology. Her vibrant color has paled to an apathetic white. Her eyes have atrophied, leaving her bewildered and slow. Her skin has cooled. Her senses have dulled. She has become a still, pale shape, floating in the black.

On cue, Dr. Conroe says, "You should be feeling better any day now. Mentally, I mean. It'll happen gradually. Mood is a funny thing."

For a moment, Lila is almost too tired to breathe.

"I don't believe you," she says.

"It's medicine," he says. "It works whether you believe in it or not."

°

Even now, she does not know why it was the kitchen knives. The steak knives, in particular. Some people choose poison, some jump off bridges, and some prefer a noose. But Lila never considered any other options. There was something so homey about the kitchen knives. Almost friendly. They had served her well, slicing cucumbers and opening recalcitrant packages of lunch meat. She was intimately familiar with their sculpted handles. They had been with her for years.

At first, the thought of suicide was vague. It came every so often, usually late at night—a gleam at the end of a long, dim tunnel. A sweet release. She would picture the knives, consider the idea, argue with it, and ultimately dismiss it. No, she could not do that to Simone. No, she did not want to die; she only wanted a measure of relief. Surely she would feel better in the morning.

But the notion was like a mosquito. It would drift off, only to return a while later. Buzzing in her ear. Irritating and persistent. Not worrisome—not yet. She would brush it away, and it would come back, away and back, over and over.

Then something changed. One morning, perhaps a month ago, she was doing the dishes. Simone was at work. The radio played as sunlight trickled through the curtains. Lila was washing the silverware, elbow-deep in foam, when she felt a shift in her perception. The air seemed to thicken. She lifted a knife and ran it down her wrist. A light tickle. She did not open the skin. She did not even leave a mark.

As soon as she had done it, her head cleared. She came back to herself as though waking from a dream. Shaken, she set the knife aside. She backed away from the sink. She left the apartment and did not return for hours.

After that, the knives were often on her mind. She visited them regularly in the kitchen. She picked them up and played with them. The compulsions came in surges. If she ran a blade down her wrist—tenderly, softly—it would relieve the desire. Afterward, she could detach. She could walk down to the bagel place. She could watch TV. She could think of something other than the knives.

She did not tell Simone. She did not tell anyone.

She was aware, even at the time, that she was in danger. But it was hard to see the situation clearly. Perhaps if she just waited, the ship would right itself on its own. Perhaps, if she did not speak of it, the whole thing would go away as mysteriously as it had come. Intellectually she knew that knives were not a pleasant thing, a joyful thing. Yet the compulsion itself was delicious, like the urge to eat an entire birthday cake or run outside in a thunderstorm. Wicked and wonderful.

As the days passed, she began to leave lines on her wrists, puffy and pink, like the innocent scratch of a fingernail. Sometimes there were scabs, flashes of festive red. The yearning increased. Lila grew weary of resisting it. She had never before needed to sift through her own urges, discerning which were rational and which were not. She wanted to nap. She wanted to eat chocolate. She wanted the knives. It was difficult to remember which of these ideas were acceptable and sane.

She has little memory of the incident itself. There was a sense of freedom, like dashing down a slope, out of control, unable to stop. The bright triangle of the blade. Blood on her shirt. Blood on the countertop. A high-pitched hum. Someone sobbing. A blare of lights and sirens. A cold, sterile room.

°

On their last day in the mountains, Simone puts her foot down.

"It's a perfect morning," she says. "Come with me."

Lila is sprawled in the embrace of an armchair. Even in normal times, she is not outdoorsy. She dislikes the chaos of bushes and brambles. She finds the expanse of open sky alarming—too much air, too much light. She treats the natural world with the same dubious, dutiful attention that she might give an exhibit of unpleasant abstract art at MoMA. But Simone is holding out a second fanny pack, smiling her eager smile. With a sigh, Lila climbs to her feet.

The morning is chilly. The path winds downhill through dappled shade. Simone points out a hawk circling in the distance. She points out deer droppings, neat piles of black pellets. She offers Lila a chivalrous arm to help her over a fallen log. Her face is aglow with hope. This, Lila knows, is what Simone wanted all along. The two of them together. Hale and hearty. Clean air in their lungs. Blue sky overhead.

Lila grits her teeth. She is already dizzy from her medication, and it's a struggle to keep her footing. Simone's words slide past her on the slick breeze.

"I'm going to sit for a minute," she says.

"Oh, come on. We're so close to the lake. You can make it."

"You go. Go without me."

Simone meets her gaze, and they engage in the sort of silent argument that is the special province of long-married couples.

"I'll wait here," Lila says.

"Fine. Holler if you need me."

As Simone crunches off down the trail, Lila sits on a stone. She can smell the lake, murky and deep. She has no desire to approach that gelid body of water. Simone hops over a tree root and disappears down the hill. Lila closes her eyes.

Someday she will have to deal with the devastation the past few weeks have wreaked in her marriage. It was Simone who found her. Prone on the kitchen floor. She had lost too much blood, lost consciousness. Her wrists were canyons of pulp and sinew.

A crimson puddle gleamed on the tile. It had soaked her clothes and matted her hair. Simone was unable to wake her. She called 911 and sobbed all the way to the hospital.

Lila leans back against the rough bark of a tree. The branches sway in the wind, and she can feel the movement deep in the trunk. In recent days, Simone has looked at her without recognition. Lila understands this. To her wife, she has become two people in one body. The victim and the attacker. Simone's dear, familiar partner and a dangerous stranger. Simone is old-fashioned, protective, quixotic. She would defend Lila with her life against any exterior threat. But there is nothing more interior than mental illness—in the bloodstream, in the brain. Simone cannot intervene between Lila and herself. Instead, she has been hovering. Eavesdropping on Lila's phone calls. Keeping track of her pills. Watching her every move.

A crackling in the bushes catches Lila's attention. She wonders if her porcupine has returned one final time. The leaves shimmy and dance, and she waits, holding her breath. But the underbrush is empty. It is the wind, nothing more.

Her fingers drift automatically to her stitches. She taps each one in succession, counting them like the beads in a rosary.

°

That night, on the highway, Simone drums her thumbs on the steering wheel in time with the music on the radio. She always goes into another world when she drives. To Lila, it seems to be a pleasant, hypnotic state, Simone's foot pulsing in rhythm on the pedal, her brain busy with the stream of headlights. Lila herself is a nervous driver, happy to cede the wheel.

The moon rises, a dry curve of bone. Lila fumbles in her purse. Before leaving the cabin, in a fit of mischief, she stole the book about porcupines. Now, penlight in hand, she flips to the right page. As the miles slip past, the engine shuddering, Simone drumming, Lila reads. She learns that porcupines mate back to belly—not face-to-face, as scientists once believed. The old joke is true: *How do porcupines have sex? Very carefully.* The females give birth to small litters, between one and four porcupettes. For obvious reasons, the infants emerge with soft quills, more like modeling clay than fired ceramic. These usually harden by the second day of life.

The quills, as it turns out, are minor marvels. They are unique, in fact, in the animal kingdom. Each porcupine carries thirty thousand spikes on its back. Each spike is coated with an antibiotic substance, as potent as penicillin. When scientists first discovered this, they could not figure it out. Nature is rarely benevolent and never altruistic. It makes no sense to bundle a weapon in the same package as its cure. According to the book, a woman in Tennessee was stabbed in the arm during an encounter with a porcupine. The quill dug itself into her bicep. Two weeks later, it emerged from her palm. By that point, she had almost forgotten about it. The spikes are a strange mixture, at once harmful and harmless. As long as they avoid vital organs, they can pass through living tissue without damage.

Eventually, a biologist solved the riddle. He postulated that porcupines must climb trees. No one had ever witnessed them doing this, but it was the only way the situation made sense. If porcupines climbed trees, they might fall. If they fell, they could end up impaled on their own armament of spikes. Lila catches her breath, imagining it. The slip of a paw. The shock of empty air. The earth lurching upward. The collision. She pictures the animal on the ground, sprawled among the tree roots, bruised and battered and pierced like a pincushion.

In the book, there is a photograph of a porcupine lolling on a leaf-strewn branch, its feet slung casually on either side of the limb, its eyes half shut, dozing in its airy cradle. Against all odds, these creatures are happiest high in the air. They climb trees for food, for shelter, even for fun. Over time, their bodies have adapted for this purpose. Their claws are long and curved, their paws soled with rubbery pads. Their stomachs are capable of digesting bark. And the quills—as the biologist hypothesized—have transformed too.

Lila closes the book and clicks off her penlight. She leans her head against the cool window. The paperback is a comforting presence, clutched in her palm like a talisman. She imagines the injured animal prone at the foot of a tree. She pictures it rolling to its feet. Whimpering, bleeding, limping away. Finding a safe place to curl into a ball. Licking its wounds. Porcupines have evolved to climb trees and to fall. They have evolved to suffer and to heal. The quills will do what they are designed to do: they will travel through the dark pulp of the body, slicing the flesh, rending the muscle, and leaving behind no lesions, no bruises, no pain, no scars.

°

In ten years, Lila will return to the Adirondacks. In Simone's company, she will come back to the mountains.

This will not be a spur-of-the-moment trip. The two of them will prepare months in advance, deciding to visit for just a weekend this time. They will rent a new cabin. A different view. A river instead of a lake. Autumn instead of spring. They will organize their schedule for recreation and beauty. They will travel at the crescendo of the fall foliage, when the trees flicker and glow like lit candles.

On a chilly evening, Lila will leave Simone snoring in an armchair, her reading glasses askew. The trees will surge overhead, messy jumbles of gold. The sky murky. The horizon darkening. Grabbing a flashlight, Lila will escape into the breeze. She will stride down the trail, leaving the cabin in her wake, pushing a sheaf of gray hair from her eyes.

She will be restless, eager to get away from the heat of the house, the fluorescent bulbs, and the garish paintings on the walls. Away from Simone, too, who will watch her with concern throughout the trip, speaking low and touching Lila tentatively, as though she is an unexploded bomb. Simone will even start counting her pills again—two yellow, with breakfast.

Lila will understand this concern while simultaneously resenting it. In her everyday life, she will no longer be a creature locked in darkness. Knitting, gardening, lunch dates with friends—she will have hobbies again, plans for each day. Sometimes the shadows will start to close in around her, but she can recognize them now for what they are. She can call Dr. Conroe, increase her medication, exercise self-care, and wait for the light to return.

But here in the Adirondacks, there will be echoes in the air. For the first time in years, Lila will be aware of her scars—faint tattoos on her wrists. She will not feel quite like herself: unsettled, unmoored. Not depression, but distraction. Not pain, but the memory of pain.

As the sky dims, Lila will click on her flashlight. A cold wind will wash down the slope, and flecks of red and yellow will whirl around her like rain. Somewhere nearby, Lila will hear the rush of the river. She will hear birds calling. She will hear a scuffle overhead—an incongruous sound. Her heart will give a startled jump.

A scratching. A snort. A crunch of twigs. Lila will take a deep breath, grip her flashlight, and point the beam upward.

A shape on a branch. Brown and white. Paws clutching the bark. A thicket of quills. Lila will laugh, a brash shout of joy. High in the tree, thirty feet in the air, will be her old friend, the porcupine. Despite the stiff breeze and the leaves coming loose in torrents, the animal's pose will be casual. The tree will sway, and the porcupine will sway too. When the beam touches it, its pupils will contract. The quills will lift, indicating alarm, arching outward like a dandelion gone to seed.

Lila will step closer, peering through the haze of evening, still grinning. Above her head, the porcupine will shift position. She will watch its claws dig into the wood. Disturbed by the flashlight's beam, the animal will grab hold of the trunk and begin to climb. It will ascend clumsily yet rapidly up a trellis of branches, the quills undulating and clattering. As falling leaves thicken the air, Lila will stand still, caught in a posture of helpless wonder. Before her eyes, the porcupine will scale the trunk, mounting into the upper branches, moving without fear or hesitation toward the stars.

Mother, Sister, Wife, Daughter

Our father gave each of us a different reason for his departure. He told Katherine that he was taking part in a worldwide sailing race. He told Emilia that he was looking for treasure so our family could become even richer. He told Gracie, the oldest, that a dear friend needed his help on the other side of the ocean.

We knew better than to believe anything he said. Our father was a storyteller, a wishful thinker, a chronic promiser who never followed through. He loved nothing more than spinning a tale with himself at the center, believing in the moment that he was what he pretended to be: a treasure hunter, a rescuer, a good man. He pulled each of us aside, all seven of his daughters, and we listened stone-faced and only nodded. No matter how he dressed it up, he was leaving us.

We were stair-step in age: Gracie nine years old, Rosalind only three, with Carla, Dolores, Leah, Katherine, and Emilia in the middle. We lived in a big house—a mansion, really, though Mother said that word was vulgar—on the California coast. A private stretch of beach. Our own pier. Father moored his yacht there during the summers. He used to take us on day trips to the deep water, all seven of us armored in bulky life jackets, screaming and laughing as the prow sliced boldly through the waves, casting up cold shocks of spray. He taught us to fish, even Katherine, who was a vegetarian. He called us his brave girls, his amazons, the apples of his eye. That was something else he loved: giving out lavish compliments, as bright and insubstantial as fool's gold.

We watched him sail away. It was early morning, and a brisk, steady wind blew off the ocean. We stood together on the western terrace, high above the water, huddled close for warmth. Rosalind, the youngest, cried. The sun was rising behind the house, throwing shadows across the beach. Father's yacht cut a sharp wake across the gauzy surface of the sea like a run in one of Mother's silk stockings. We watched him until he melted into the fog along the horizon, swallowed up by gray.

°

People said that there were so many of us daughters because our parents kept trying for a boy. Perhaps this was so. We did not know; we never could get a straight answer from our mother or father about anything. Father would smile and tell us whatever we wanted to hear: that every one of his girls was worth a hundred boys, that you couldn't have too much of a good thing.

Mother was more difficult. She faltered and trailed off. Her mind did not move in straight lines. "Well, you see . . ." she would say, leaning languidly against the arm of the sofa. "There are many things in this world . . . I suppose . . . Let me say that between a husband and his wife, decisions are sometimes difficult . . ." She would go on this way for a quarter of an hour and communicate nothing.

All of us were built on the same template as our mother: strong and sturdy, with heavy black hair and round faces. Our father did not seem to have given us any of himself—not his slight frame, not his darting eyes, not his Cheshire cat grin. He was an impish figure, dwarfed by our tall, voluptuous mother. The only one who resembled him in any way was Emilia, and then only in manner—she was mischievous like him, a prankster. It was just like our father to withhold his genetic makeup. He was always doing that, keeping back what we most wanted.

After his yacht disappeared from sight, the seven of us gathered in our parents' room. Mother had taken to her bed. She was a strange mix of opposites: a diaphanous, dithering personality inside the robust body of a farmhand or milkmaid. Hale and pink-cheeked, she languished beneath the covers with a hankie to her nose. The bed could hold all of us, a king-sized canopied behemoth that Father had ordered specially, each of its four posts carved to resemble a sword. We climbed up on the opulent quilt, surrounding our mother like a litter of kittens seeking warmth. Only Gracie, the oldest, elected to stand.

"When will Father be back?" Leah asked.

"Well, you see . . ." Mother began. "He and I have had many talks . . ."

"Will he come home soon?" Carla asked. "He wouldn't tell us."

"It isn't always possible . . . What I mean is that it may be some time before . . ." Mother trailed off, dabbing her eyes with her handkerchief.

"He's never coming back, is he?" Gracie asked, standing apart.

Rosalind began to cry again. Gracie gathered up her little body and carried her out of the room.

°

Father had promised to write or call when he got where he was going. But Father promised lots of things. He once swore to Gracie she'd get a pony, that it was on its way, being shipped cross-country on a special train, coming soon. He said these things for months until she understood that it was never going to happen. He told Leah that he'd give her the moon, but it remained in the sky night after night, unclaimed. All Father really wanted was the generosity of the offering itself. Follow-through did not interest him. Still, it was hard not to believe him when he ignited the full arsenal of his charm. In spite of ourselves, we each craved the white-hot glow of his attention.

There was no way for us to contact him. He was out on the open ocean now, without an address or a phone number. Shortwave radio might have worked if he were near the shore, but he wasn't; we'd watched him travel beyond such things.

Without Father, the house seemed bigger than ever. Twenty-one bedrooms, fewer than half of them occupied. Two grand, winding staircases at the front entrance and a third in back for the servants. The decor was lovely but lacking in personality. Matching upholstered chairs. Heavy damask curtains. Bland portraits of people we did not know. Ours was new money, and it showed, according to one of Gracie's former friends who'd turned her nose up on her one and only visit to our house.

Now it was just ourselves and our mother rattling around that vast estate like beads in a rainstick. There were, of course, the butler and the gardener and the chauffeur and the maids and the cook too, but they rarely spoke to us or we to them. Dolores always tried to be friendly, asking after their children and remembering their birthdays, but it did no good. We were their bosses, more or less, and there's nothing worse than making small talk with a little girl who could get you fired.

It was summer. Father abandoned us in the middle of June, when Gracie, Dolores, Katherine, and Leah were out of school. Carla, Emilia, and Rosalind were too young to have attended anyway. He abandoned us when we had nothing to do but wander the house and notice all the signs of his absence. No surreptitious wink at the dinner table. No quick step on the stairs. No outrageous stories before bedtime.

Leah believed he would come back soon. She spent hours on the western terrace, staring out at the shifting waves until her eyes ached. Carla brought her snacks and sat with her sometimes, less hopeful but unwilling to give up. Gracie said he was gone for good, and the sooner we accepted it, the better. Emilia refused to commit herself either way. She always kept an open mind about everything. She carried a coin in her pocket and tossed it every time someone brought up our father. Heads, he'd be back tomorrow. Tails, never.

Dolores and Katherine suffered nightmares about sea monsters and whirlpools. They often woke up screaming. Our bedrooms were all in the same section of the house, the eastern wing, overlooking the rose garden. Dolores and Katherine would run down the hallway after each bad dream and clamber into bed with Gracie.

Little Rosalind took it a step further—she flatly refused to sleep alone and began each night curled at the foot of Gracie's bed among the stuffed animals. After a few days, we all followed suit. We dragged our sleeping bags out of a closet and took over Gracie's floor en masse. We slumbered each night in a mesh of limbs and breath, slipping in and out of one another's dreams.

°

Clara had learned a skipping rhyme at school:

Mother, sister, wife, daughter,
Waiting there beside the water.
All the men set sail at dawn.
How many days will they be gone?

Clara, Katherine, and Emilia were skilled at double Dutch, and they would chant the rhyme in unison, then count each slap of the rope on the floor. Sometimes the numbers went into the hundreds before the skipper's foot caught and they began again.

°

A week after Father left, the chauffeur vanished too. Micky was his name, and the summers were always an idle time for him. Mother and Father kept him on year-round, living in the servants' quarters, since he was necessary during the academic year, ferrying us to school and ballet and Mandarin and gymnastics and dressage.

We did not notice his absence. To us, he was as much a part of the vehicle that drove us where we needed to go as the steering wheel or the windshield wipers. Close-cropped hair. A thick neck, ropy with muscle. That was all we ever saw of him.

Then the butler informed Mother that Micky's room was empty. One of Father's best cars, a black Jaguar, had disappeared too.

The police came. Mother rose from her bed, swathed in a satin dressing gown, and received them in the living room—two men in middle age, both potbellied and slow-moving. Mother shooed us away, which was a useless endeavor in a house as big as ours. There was always somewhere else from which to eavesdrop. We tiptoed around through the drawing room and lined the wall in the corridor.

"A betrayal of this caliber . . ." Mother was saying. "And after everything . . . my husband, you know . . . the past few days have been . . ."

The policemen asked for the chauffeur's employee records. Mother had no idea where any paperwork could be; Father always took care of such things. Here the butler intervened, and Mother swept down the hallway to her bedroom again.

It was exciting to watch the policemen pacing up and down in the rose garden and circling the fountain, looking for clues. But Emilia overheard them talking as they got back into their car. She reported to the rest of us that the officers did not expect to find Micky. They'd been alerted too late, they said. He and the stolen vehicle had probably left the state by now.

"There's not much they can do at this point," Emilia told us.

"But he's a thief," Gracie said, outraged. "He *stole* from us."

"If Father were here . . ." Leah began. She trailed off, and in that moment she looked just like Mother, head tilted to the side, mouth open.

°

Summer brought days of unbroken sunshine and powerful wind, billowing off the water in violent, unpredictable gusts. We spent the breeziest hours indoors, playing hide-and-seek or listening to

Gracie read aloud. On calmer mornings, we walked the length of our private beach, gathering driftwood and sea glass for Katherine's art projects. The surf was too wild for swimming, but we had our own Olympic-sized pool on the leeward side of the house, sheltered from the wind. Little Rosalind wore arm floaties. Gracie was sleek and lithe in the water. Clara and Katherine drifted on inflatable rafts, holding hands to stay close like sea otters slumbering among the kelp beds, paws entwined so they would not be separated.

Father had left us in the past—quite often, actually—but always provided a return date. He would roar off in one of his Jags or Lambos and be gone a week or two. He usually said he was traveling for work, but of course he didn't work; he didn't have to.

Even when home, he had been a rare commodity. The estate was large enough that Father could spend days in the office or the blue room or the gazebo without any of us happening upon him. Sometimes he would come charging into the playroom without warning and chase us around, pretending to be a monster as we screamed with glee. Then we wouldn't see him for a while. He would take his meals in the library, and we caught only hints of his presence—a slammed door, a squeak of shoe on marble.

We hadn't missed him during his previous trips or his perpetual distancing and cloistering at home. But we missed him now. He'd never sailed away before. The fact that he'd taken the yacht this time, rather than one of his fancy cars—the finality of his wake slicing across the sea to the horizon—left the seven of us bereft.

Dolores took to shadowing the gardener, asking how to deadhead roses and what sort of fertilizer they required. Hamish had been there for as long as we could remember, and we knew he did not like children, or maybe just girls. He had a way of squinting incredulously at us whenever we spoke to him. Dolores persisted, following him around until Gracie pulled her aside and said, "Hamish isn't Father. You can't just pick some other man to replace Father."

Dolores cried in her room all that afternoon but joined us in the evening on the beach, where we each wrote a letter to Father, the little ones dictating theirs to the older ones. Then we lit a fire on the sand and burned our messages, watching them disintegrate and rise on the smoke in a whirl of ash and embers.

°

Three weeks after Father left, we found Hamish dead. It was actually Rosalind who found him, but she did not know what she was looking at, a boot lying at a strange angle among the rosebushes. She was only three. She continued playing with her dolls until Katherine came to find her for lunch. Then there was screaming and running and calling the police, and Mother appeared in the living room once more, still in her dressing gown.

She dabbed her eyes with her hankie throughout the interview. This time the officers were a man and a woman. We'd never seen a policewoman before and were dazzled by her air of authority and the casual way she tapped her gun holster.

"A loyal gardener . . ." Mother said. "The roses, you understand . . . I don't know what will happen to them now . . ."

The seven of us stood in the corner of the room, all of us touching, Gracie's hand on Katherine's shoulder, Emilia's arms around Rosalind's middle. The officers did not ask us a thing. They explained to Mother that it looked like a heart attack. He was an elderly man, Hamish. We hadn't thought of him that way—all adults looked elderly to us—but now we realized that he'd been gray-haired and wizened as long as we'd known him.

We watched through the drawing room windows as the officers got back in their vehicle. An ambulance had come to take away the body. It purred quietly down the drive, no lights or siren. There was no emergency here.

Dolores was teary and touchy that night. "It wasn't my fault that he died," she shouted over dinner when Gracie reminded her to eat her vegetables.

"Nobody said it was," Gracie said mildly.

"I just wanted to learn about roses. Roses are *interesting*."

"You didn't give him a heart attack by following him everywhere or asking him things," Gracie said. "He was old, so he died."

Father was the one who first explained death to us. He told us that all living things perished and there was no God. He told us that we'd better learn what brought us joy and seek it out, because a human life was a fleeting and precious thing.

And then he left us. The implications about where he found his own joy—or no longer found any joy at all—were clear as day.

°

We were all a little in love with the pool boy who came once a week to skim dead leaves off the surface and change the filter. He had a tattoo of a ship on his forearm. He smelled like chlorine. We would gather at the windows of the morning room whenever he appeared, pressing our noses against the glass and doodling hearts in the condensation left by our breath. He never noticed us, intent on his work, eager to finish up and thunder away on his motorcycle.

With Father gone, the pool boy's appearances took on an extra importance. We all sympathized with Dolores to an extent; we might not have been desperate enough to ask grumpy Hamish about roses, but ours was an overwhelmingly female world now, missing that dash of otherness that Father had always provided.

The pool boy was the second to die. On a cloudy morning in July, Leah rose early with the intention of continuing her vigil on the western terrace. She was still waiting there for Father, though not every day; sometimes she joined us now for games or arguments. The rest of us were slumbering when Leah slithered out of her sleeping bag. She picked her way across our bodies sprawled over the floor.

As she padded along the hall, she glanced down through the broad mullioned windows and saw what appeared to be a shark in the swimming pool below. She drew closer to the glass, reluctant and curious at the same time. Something dark floated in the clean turquoise water—recently cleaned, in fact, skimmed and filtered that very morning by the same figure who somehow, we never found out exactly how, pitched headfirst into the pool once his work was done and drowned.

°

Two officers came, both women this time, resplendent in their uniforms. They wanted to speak to each of us alone, but we flatly refused to be separated, and Mother was in too much of a state to make us.

"I can't cope . . ." she kept saying, leaning back against the plush cushions of the couch. "I really can't . . . I don't understand . . . if only . . ."

In truth, there was nothing we could tell the policewomen,

much as we wanted to. We'd stayed up late the night before, using a Ouija board to see if the spirits had news about Father. Perhaps the ghosts that lived in our house (we'd never encountered one, but we were certain they existed) could see farther than we could, across the ocean. The results from the Ouija board had been equivocal: a series of letters that did not spell a word. Clara said they were clues. Gracie said they were nonsense.

After our midnight séance, we'd slept late, even Rosalind, who was barely out of her toddler years and usually woke before dawn. Only Leah had seen the body. She ran to find the butler, who hurried to remove the offending item from the pool with the help of the maids and the cook. All of us were annoyed with Leah for not coming to us first. By the time we woke up, we'd missed the whole thing.

The officers returned to their vehicle, and once again the ambulance drove off in funereal silence.

°

"We might be cursed," Dolores said that night as we lay sleepless on Gracie's floor, staring up at the glow-in-the-dark star stickers on the ceiling.

No one answered.

°

The police did not catch the chauffeur. Gracie overheard the maids whispering about it, but she could not glean any specifics, just a disapproving tone and a few snickers.

In August, Leah abandoned her post on the western terrace.

She said that she was sick of seeing other people's boats on the water. She always mistook them, at first, for Father's yacht. He'd been gone six weeks now. Every time a trim little sailboat scudded by or a sluggish barge churned toward the horizon, Leah felt a surge of hope, then a reawakening of loss.

The butler was the only man left in the house. He was British, bald, and snooty, and we half suspected that Father had hired him as a sort of sustained practical joke. Mr. Gantry was so out of place in our California mansion that he almost seemed to have come from another reality, an Agatha Christie novel, maybe. He was even more frightening than the gardener had been. Hamish might have squinted at us disapprovingly, but Mr. Gantry treated us with such icy disdain that he cowed even brash Emilia. We tried to avoid sharing a room with him, though he always hovered in the doorway during meals, forcing us to eat faster than we wanted to. Then he removed the plates and silverware as rapidly and completely as though we'd never been there at all.

"I bet he's going to die," Dolores said on a rainy afternoon. We were gathered in the library, a windowless cave of a room ringed by floor-to-ceiling bookshelves.

"Mr. Gantry?" Clara asked. "Why would he die?"

"Because of us," Dolores said. "We're cursed. I'm sure of it now."

"You're so silly," Gracie said, but she didn't sound as confident as usual. "What makes you think that?" she asked, after a moment.

"First Father, then the chauffeur, then Hamish, now poor Frankie," Dolores said. The pool boy's name had been Frank, but we always called him Frankie, as though by nicknaming him we could manufacture some sort of intimacy.

"Coincidence," Gracie said.

"If Mr. Gantry dies, we'll know for sure," Leah offered. "We'll know if we're cursed or not."

"We are," Dolores said.

"Maybe," Gracie conceded. "If Mr. Gantry dies, maybe."

◦

Three days later, the butler quit without warning. He did not steal a car, as the chauffeur had done; he took only what belonged to him. The maids informed Mother that his room had been vacated in the middle of the night.

For once, Mother was galvanized into something like anger. She threw off her dressing gown and changed into the sort of clothes she used to wear, a conservative pearl-gray dress and stockings. She even put on lipstick. We sat with her in the drawing room as she spent the morning on the phone, hiring a female housekeeper to replace Mr. Gantry.

"Men are inconstant," she informed us. "A woman, however . . . I do hope you realize . . . I want you to go out into the world with clear eyes . . ."

Emilia snuck into the servants' wing, where we were never supposed to go. "Everyone needs their privacy," Father always said. She found Mr. Gantry's bedroom beside the cramped little lavatory the maids shared. The butler's bureau stood empty, but his razor and shaving cream remained in a bathroom cabinet, evidently forgotten. Emilia stole them and smuggled them upstairs to Gracie's room, where we all gathered around to stare at these relics of masculinity, foreign and unknowable, the last of their kind.

◦

Before taking to her bed again, Mother hired a new gardener, a wispy blond woman with a faraway stare. Within days, the roses were blossoming again, no longer leggy and untamed. Mother hired a pool girl, too, who showed up in ripped denim overalls, snapping gum as she worked. We were not impressed. We convened at the morning room windows where we'd so often watched Frankie skimming leaves with his long net. The pool girl wore her hair in a doughy bun. When she noticed us pressed against the glass to stare at her, she stuck out her tongue.

At this affront, Gracie stormed away from the window and flopped on the couch.

"This is all Father's fault," she said. "All of it."

"Why?" asked little Rosalind, climbing up on the cushion beside her.

"It's obvious," Gracie said, with a preteen eye roll. "The curse began when Father left."

The seven of us considered this.

"I don't know if you're right," Dolores said at last. We all stared at her open-mouthed. It was heresy to disagree with our eldest sister. Dolores flushed pink but continued, "What if the curse made Father leave in the first place? What if it was already inside us then? The curse might have done this to him."

"No," Gracie said with absolute conviction. "No. It was Father who did this to us."

◦

Chilly fog alternated with golden sunlight. At the two-month anniversary of Father's departure, Leah made us all join her on the western terrace once more, despite the biting wind. We stood there in silence until Rosalind's teeth began chattering and Gracie led us inside.

Then came the crash that woke us before dawn and sent us skittering into the hallway, Katherine dragging her sleeping bag, caught on one foot.

"It's an earthquake!" Leah cried.

This was California, after all. Father always told us to stand in a doorway or climb into the tub.

"I don't think so," Gracie said. "It's coming from downstairs."

And she was right. Nothing was shaking around us, not the portraits on the walls or the light fixtures overhead. Instead, the clamor seemed localized to the front hall—a sound like we'd never heard, glass shattering and stone falling.

We ran down the stairs and found one of the maids already there, her mouth wide open in horror. The front door had been smashed in by the front end of a vehicle. The doorknob glinted on the floor, severed from the rest. Part of the wall was crumbling from the impact. The hat stand lay in pieces. One of the columns outside had been pulverized; we could see what was left of it through the gap in the shattered remnants of the heavy oak door that Father had ordered specially from Sweden.

Leah bounced anxiously on her toes. Rosalind clung to Gracie's hand, and Dolores began to cry. But Emilia kept her wits about her.

"It's the mail truck," she informed us. "Look, you can see the stripes."

She pointed. The headlights were cross-eyed now, gazing at each other across the concave wreckage of the front bumper. The windshield resembled a spiderweb. Yes, we could just pick out the telltale stripes, scraped and dirtied almost beyond recognition.

The maid wrung her hands. "I saw it happen," she wailed. "I

saw him turning in at the gate. Oh my god. Oh my god, he didn't even try to stop. He just kept coming."

°

The eastern terrace overlooked the front door. We could see the wreckage clearly from there. Every morning, the postman had trundled down our sweeping drive and pushed the day's letters through the mail slot. He usually came before we were awake; we'd actually never seen him alive, only now, battered and bloody, a limp figure crushed against the snowy cushion of the airbag.

Apparently he'd driven straight up the marble steps and slammed full throttle into the house. He took out a pillar on his way, along with a portion of the wall to the left of the door. Not a door anymore—kindling, matchsticks. Even a nearby window had cracked, we could see now, presumably from the force of the impact. The stairs were chipped beneath the wheels of the mail truck. Smoke rose from the deconstructed engine.

"Look what happened," Rosalind kept saying. We looked.

The sound of Mother's weeping carried down the hall. She was distraught at this latest calamity, though her grief seemed to be focused on the ruined door. Our father had loved it so. We left her in the care of the competent housekeeper—a brisk, rotund woman with a voice like warm honey—who had replaced the butler.

An emergency team was busy extracting the body from the smashed vehicle. A stroke, they were saying. The postman must have lost consciousness during the final leg of his approach. His muscles tensed up—there might have been a seizure—and the vehicle careened onward. Hopefully he was dead before the impact.

"It's only women," Emilia said suddenly.

"What?" Dolores asked.

Emilia gestured toward the EMTs darting around the vehicle. One tall, one thin, one fair, one dark, all of them female.

°

Mrs. North, the new housekeeper, hired a work crew to come and fix the front door and the column and the demolished brickwork. She offered them an extravagant fee to turn up the very next morning with ten strong men and a new oak door.

But they never came. We waited for them, gazing through the windows at the empty drive. At noon we abandoned our surveillance and went to swim in the pool. Mrs. North shouted into the phone for an hour. Then, with the help of the maids, she affixed a sheet of plastic over the gaping hole, taping the edges to the wall.

She booked a second crew, but they never came either. Days passed, and the plastic remained, flapping when the wind blew like the sail of a ship.

Over lunch, Mrs. North complained to us as she laid out our bowls of soup. We sat in our usual places around the table, four on one side and three on the other. Father's chair stood empty at the head, as did Mother's at the foot. The only sign of life from Mother's room lately was the trays of food that the cook sent up, which vanished and appeared again a while later, emptied of everything but crumbs.

"I don't understand this behavior," Mrs. North said in her sugary voice, which belied her obvious irritation. "I've tried four different companies now. Seven men were supposed to be here an hour ago. We confirmed the date and time. And then radio silence. It's ridiculous! We can't have a house with no door, can we, girls?"

Mrs. North bustled out to fetch us a pitcher of ice water. In her absence, Gracie leaned in, her face lit from beneath by the reflected glow from the linen tablecloth.

"You know what this means," she said.

"It's us," Dolores whispered in awe. "We're doing this. Men can't be here."

"That's right," Gracie said.

"We're keeping them away," Leah said. "The workmen can't come. They want to, and they say they're going to, but they can't."

"We kill men too," Emilia said. "That's right, isn't it? Hamish and Frankie and the postman all died because of us."

"We kill them, or we make them disappear," Clara said. "Poof. Gone."

"We're cursed," said little Rosalind, her voice high and sweet.

"We're cursed," we all echoed reverently.

°

At midnight, we snuck out of the house, even Rosalind, yawning and rubbing her eyes. She was a wishbone child, not yet grown into the solid limbs and apple cheeks that made the rest of us look so similar. Sometimes, in photographs, we appeared to be a single girl moving through different ages in stop-motion.

On our way outside, we paused at our mother's room. Her hoarse breathing perfumed the air. She still kept to her side of the bed, leaving a blank space where Father used to sleep. We stood over her, all seven of her daughters. Then we left and moved silently in single file to the back door.

The moon rose buttery behind the house. Every window was dark. The grown-ups were sleeping—the women, that is. No men here. We had destroyed them and banished them, every one, with the strength of our curse.

Moonlight glazed the beach. The sand was cold beneath our feet, but the air felt surprisingly warm, like bathwater. No wind. There was the pier where our father had moored his yacht. There was the horizon he had crossed without us. Was that the moment the curse took hold? Did it happen when he first decided to leave us, or when he turned his prow away from us, or when he vanished from our sight?

With a grunt, Gracie yanked off her pajama top and threw it onto the sand. She kicked off her shorts and stood in front of us naked, hands on hips.

"What are you doing?" Dolores gasped.

"There are no men," Gracie said. "No men can get near us."

And then we were all naked and dancing. The moonlight rendered our bodies new, milk-pale, shimmering with eerie power. Gracie pirouetted down the sand, her dark hair tangling in her armpits. Katherine went up on pointe, as she had learned in ballet class. Clara and Leah did the twist, laughing as their bare bottoms wiggled against the balmy air. Dolores tangoed with an imaginary partner while Emilia twirled in place, her arms aloft. Little Rosalind was the wildest of all of us, cavorting and kicking through the gleaming tongue of each new wave that slid up the beach.

"We're cursed!" Gracie shouted to the sea.

"We're cursed!" we screamed, our voices reverberating over the water, bouncing and echoing as though there were more than seven of us. Dozens. Hundreds.

°

How should a story like this end? We could never agree. Seven sisters can't agree on much of anything. We all had our own opinions, our own ideas.

Leah maintained that Father would return one day. He would come home chastened and apologetic, and the curse would be broken. We would nobly forgive him. She would, anyway.

Katherine was certain that Father had already taken up residence in some foreign land. She believed that as long as he lived, we would remain cursed, unable to leave the house for fear of killing or exiling any man we encountered. We would grow old together, seven white-haired crones in a dilapidated mansion with a broken door.

Rosalind thought the strength of the curse would fade as we got older. Eventually we would be normal again, no longer tainted by our father's desertion. We could go out into the world and become like other people, whatever that meant.

Dolores felt sure that Father would come sailing back home many years from now, withered with age and racked by guilt. We would not recognize him, he would be so changed. Thinking him a beggar or miscreant, we would send him away. His heart would break, and that, in turn, would break our curse.

Clara believed that Father would die at sea, probably very soon. His ship would founder and sink, and when he breathed his last breath, the curse would lift. We could leave home then, and marry if we chose, but we would only ever have daughters.

And Gracie told us that the curse would intensify as we grew up. Now, in our girlhood, our sphere of influence was limited to our estate. But as we aged, the curse would ripple outward, spreading to the nearby town and maybe even beyond. Who knew how powerful we might become? As we transformed into teenagers, young adults, grown women, the curse would gather strength and speed, a wild wave splashing to the edges of California. It would wash away the male half of the population, taking them at work, at home, everywhere. Gracie could see it all, she told us. One day the force of our magic would devour countries and continents, surging around the wide world until all the men, including Father, were gone.

Lastly there was Emilia, who always kept an open mind. How would our story end? Each time the question arose among us, she took the coin from her pocket and flipped it in the air. She smiled no matter how it landed.

Childish

I have fallen in love with a willow tree. I first saw it a week ago, on a hot, dusty afternoon. You and I were out for our daily constitutional. You move with a walker these days, tennis balls affixed to the bottom. You hunch over the metal frame, a shuffling figure with a cap of white curls.

It was one of the last warm days of autumn. The trees were shedding their leaves in spirals of crimson. I strolled at your side, the two of us moving at a gentle, incremental pace. We were on our way to the hobby shop. Passersby darted around us in a steady stream. My arm rested on your back. Long ago, my skin was darker than yours, clay to marble. But time has weathered us both, like wind on stone, eroding us to the undifferentiated granite of old age.

Inside the hobby shop, you settled into a chair, catching your breath. I walked between the aisles. The air smelled of wood shavings and bleach. The fluorescent lights buzzed dully.

To this day, I am not sure how I stumbled into making stained glass. It is an odd pastime for a man like me, a little namby-pamby. But I like it. I have done it for decades. Tracing the outline on the panel. Applying pressure with the blade. Wrapping each shard tenderly in foil. The soldering iron. The smell of melting copper. It is a meticulous business, with no room for error. Over the years, I have filled our house with splendid lampshades and windowpanes.

I had finished my most recent bit of glasswork and was looking for something new. On that autumn day, I moved along the rows of tools, batteries, rubber bands, and hoops of wire. At the back, the shop owner was crowing about some difficult project. Seated at his desk, he pushed a sheet of paper at me.

A lampshade pattern. A willow tree. It had never been done, he said. It was too complex, too fragile, ever to be assembled. Many had tried and failed. Three thousand pieces, some no larger than a dime. The finished lampshade would comprise the canopy of the tree, falling nearly thirty-six inches from the crown to the tips of its swaying branches. A two-foot circumference. Almost barrel-sized, this creation. The bottom edge was not smooth but intentionally rumpled and curved, mimicking the natural unevenness of plant growth. Staring down at the pattern, I could almost hear the branches creaking. Thresh and ply. Glints of sunny gold.

Ever since, the willow tree lampshade has taken hold of me. The past week has been strange. I have all but lived on the sun porch, my workspace. On warm days, that room, with all its windows, grows as steamy as an oven. No air conditioning, just an ancient, rattling fan. I have bent over the table, cutting the glass, manipulating the foil, sweat beading on my back. I have worked until my hands start to tremble.

The pattern aches to be finished. It has followed me out of the sun porch, into my daily routine. As I refill your pill organizer, as I prepare our meals, as I collect the mail, my brain is aglow. You have laughed at me for being inattentive, arranging the shards in my mind when I should have been listening to you. At night, lying beside your slumbering form, a part of me is still at the worktable, blade in hand.

°

At the age of ninety-one, you have come down with Alzheimer's. The disease is a force of nature. Like a tornado, it has devoured you. It has erased your memory, your history. It has laid waste to the landscape of your mind.

You have forgotten little things, like people's names. You have forgotten big things, like the nature of time—the movement of the clock, the changing of the seasons. You have lost things I did not know could be lost: Your sense of humor. Your understanding of our relationship, the fact I am and always will be your husband. Your ability to recognize yourself in the mirror.

In addition, you have a bad knee, a bad hip. Your knuckles are permanently swollen, changing the shape of your hands. The arthritis makes your movements awkward. Whenever you grab for something, there is a hint of squirrel about you. Wet weather makes you ache. You limp and totter. You are blind in one eye, and the other is no great shakes either. Your skin is fragile. A scrape, a brush, and you begin to bleed. You still have a bruise on your leg from a year ago, an inopportune collision with the table. Maybe it will never completely fade.

But none of this bothers you, because of the Alzheimer's. You are unaware of your litany of incurable maladies. The tornado has gobbled up your cares. You have forgotten your dementia, your osteoarthritis, your congestive heart failure. You are not burdened by the memory of what you have suffered or the anticipation of what you will continue to suffer. No past, no future. You live moment by moment. A moment of pain. A moment of hunger. A moment of laughter. A moment of sunlight. A moment of pain. A moment of pain. A moment of pain.

◦

This morning, I worked on the willow tree for hours. One whole hemisphere of the lampshade has come into being, a network of branches weaving and dancing across a bowl of blue. Glasswork is always magical. I am building something out of nothing, shaping a puzzle out of thin air. Beyond the window, the sidewalks were streaked with cold rain, printed with the shapes of leaves. The sky hung low, an oppressive gray. Autumn has begun to deepen and darken.

When I emerged from the sun porch, I heard you laughing. I rounded the corner to find James in the living room. You sat on the couch, and he stood over you, engaged in some kind of playacting. When he saw me, his demeanor altered. His arms fell to his sides, his face sobering. At the age of sixty, James is a spear of a man—tall, slim, and angry. He wears his gray hair clipped close, his beard nattily trimmed. He still had his work clothes on. His tie was askew, a smear of ink on his cuff.

"I had an idea," he said. "I thought I'd give it a try."

"Oh?" I said.

"Look here."

He pointed. There were squares of color on the wall, the dresser, the hutch. Squinting, I saw that James had gone around my house, putting up Post-it Notes. Each bore a single word: *CLOCK, LAMP, BOOK.*

"It might help," James said.

I nodded. "It might."

You have misplaced your words. You often trail off in the middle of a sentence, unable to come up with a central noun or the correct verb. You will open and close your mouth like a goldfish. Sometimes you give up the struggle, folding up your thought and tossing it away. Other times, you spit out an unexpected, nonsense term: *milk* instead of *keys* or *girl* instead of *bird.*

James circled the room, pointing. *COUCH, WINDOW, LAMPSHADE.* You clapped your hands like an audience member at a show.

"Well," I said. "Thanks, I guess."

He shrugged. "No trouble."

"You got a minute?" I said.

He checked his watch.

"Come see the lampshade I'm working on," I said. "It's going to be a masterpiece."

"No time. I'm running late."

He leaned over you, cupping your chin in his palm.

"Bye, Ma," he said. "I'll see you in a couple days. You hear me, Ma?"

You looked at him blankly.

"I don't have children," you said.

He straightened up and met my eyes. For once, I knew exactly what he was thinking.

°

I prefer to remember James as he once was. Lean and brown. Light-boned. He would fit on my lap, brow against my throat. I remember coming home from work, my back stiff and shoulders bowed, the dust of the commute still in my mouth. You would be in the kitchen. You were always immaculately dressed; I didn't notice it at the time, but I remember it now. You danced between the range and the table, tending the pasta, a wooden spoon in one hand, a romance novel in the other. James would sit by your feet, engaged in one of his interminable wars, every surface littered with army men. God forbid anyone ever disturbed their formations.

I remember him splashing in the wading pool in the backyard. I remember him raking leaves into maroon piles. He crafted mud-and-snow forts each winter. Once, when he was ten years old, he and I spent a whole week assembling a model ship. We hung the network of rigging, pinning it to the mast. I had to use a magnifying glass to manage the tiniest spars. James painted the hull and the deck. As he worked, I watched him grow still, no longer jiggling one leg or picking at his fingernails. In those moments, I could see the resemblance between us. That focus, that capacity for silence, was something we shared.

You have lost all those things, of course. Your memory is a knitted scarf that is perpetually unraveling. You have lost any recollection of your pregnancy. The taut bulb of your stomach. The butterfly brush of the fetus kicking. The nausea that kept you bent over the toilet. You have lost the birth—long, difficult, bloody. (I was not with you, of course. I hovered and paced in the waiting room, unlit cigar in hand. That was what fathers did back then.) You have lost James in diapers. James on the seesaw at the playground. James in the full regalia of his Boy Scout uniform. James in the dozy light of evening, bent over the piano, practicing his scales. You have lost your memories of a boy who was small enough to be held. You have lost your memories of yourself when you were strong and steady enough to hold him.

Sometimes I pity you. Sometimes I envy you.

°

A few nights ago, I awoke to a thump. I reached automatically for you, but your side of the bed was empty. There was a dent in your pillow, the blankets askew. For a moment, still bleary with sleep, I wondered if you had died. Ascended directly to heaven. Vanished from this mortal realm. Popped like a soap bubble.

But no—you had fallen out of bed. You were lying on the floor, staring at the ceiling, hands folded across your belly.

"You all right?" I asked anxiously. "Nothing broken?"

"I don't think so," you said.

I groped for the clock. Four in the morning.

"I'm on the ground," you said.

"I know."

You could not muster the strength to sit up. You struggled like a bug on its back, your limbs waggling. You groaned in frustration. James has been telling me that you must work on your "core." I don't know where he picks up these things. I don't know where your core might be.

I climbed out of bed and stood over you. You gripped my hands, and we engaged in a bizarre little dance, me leaning forward, you arching upward, your body swaying and pivoting at the hips, nothing changing. I was too weak to lift you.

You began to laugh. I sat on the edge of the mattress, and you lay helpless on the rug, and we laughed until the tears ran down our faces.

I did not call James. I did not call an ambulance either, since you weren't hurt, just stuck. At 7:00 a.m.—a more reasonable hour—I scuttled next door and got a neighbor to help me. A kind, portly man. I caught him on his front walk, dressed in his robe and slippers, out to pick up the newspaper. He trundled after me with a bemused expression. He got you on your feet with a minimum of fuss.

When James stopped by, later that afternoon, I told him everything was fine.

"That's right," you echoed. "We're doing quite well."

I was lying, of course. But I don't know whether you were lying or not. Perhaps the panic of that dark hour had already drifted from your mind, caught in the current of your forgetting, wafting on the river, away and away.

°

There are a lot of things I have not told James.

I never told him how I found out about your heart condition. He knows about it now; he knows about the cardiology visits and the pills you take. Congestive heart failure. Chronic, yet manageable. It leaves you weak, slow, and weary. But I never told James how it started. How your heart wasn't up to snuff. How it couldn't pump properly. How the leftover liquid began to settle elsewhere—your lungs, your belly, and finally your legs. Twenty pounds of excess fluid. I woke up to a damp bed. Moisture was soaking the sheets, oozing out of your calves.

I never told James that I have lost my sense of smell. Anosmia, my doctor calls it. A common occurrence in old age. It shouldn't be an issue, my doctor says. Except that I'm responsible for changing your diapers. For knowing when it's time to change your diapers. James is aware that you are incontinent. But sometimes you have to slosh around in a soup of your own fecal matter and urine for far too long.

I never told James that you try to cook, even now. A few weeks ago, I found you wandering around the kitchen, carrying a pot of tepid water, your arms shaking beneath the weight. All the flames on the range were ablaze. Your manner was bewildered, the liquid splashing down your front. You wanted to make pasta, but you did not remember what to do next. I got there just in time to snatch up a dishcloth that was sitting on the stovetop, inches from the fire. It had begun to blacken and smoke. Since then, I have removed the knobs from the range.

°

Yesterday James stopped by again. This time, we got into a quarrel. He came over to fix the gate. He usually turns up with a specific task to perform: restock the fridge, check the plumbing. He decided to stay for lunch. I took him out to the sun porch and showed him, at last, the willow tree lampshade—half-finished, the branches vanishing into empty air. He gave me his sweet, sideways smile.

At lunch, he and you were in a mischievous mood, laughing together over my little peccadillos. Even after all this time, you still find amusement in the way I put ketchup on my scrambled eggs, the way I organize the spare change in my pockets into piles on the countertop. For a while, everything was easy and calm.

Eventually, though, I was due for my scolding. I could just about set my watch to it. James has a few complaints. He doesn't like me leaving you alone during the long afternoons. The doctor said I shouldn't, not even for a brief spell. But if I put you in front of the television, I can grab a free hour here and there. You can't manage the stairs to the front door on your own. (James doesn't like that either—the stairs, though there are only four.) So you putter around the house, watching one of those reality shows where people dance, while I lounge in the backyard, just being. Tasting the frost in the air. Watching the leaves walk on the wind. Being alive.

James doesn't like that we don't have some busybody nurse coming by to check on us. They call themselves "angels," those people, which is too self-congratulatory for my taste. James doesn't like that I'm in charge of your medications. You have seven in all, each administered differently (after waking, at bedtime, with food, without food). He doesn't like that I'm the one who does all the cleaning either. My work doesn't meet his standards. I suppose that with his young eyes, he can see cobwebs in corners I have missed.

In short, James wants you in a nursing home. He wants it now. He wants it yesterday.

"It's time," he said. "You know it is, Dad."

"Over my dead body," I told him, and I meant it.

We were shouting by then, both standing up, him on one side of the table, me on the other. You sat between us, your head bowed, as though praying.

"They'll prepare all your meals," James roared. "The medical services alone—"

"No," I said.

"She needs supervision. You aren't able—"

"No," I said.

"You'd still be with her, for God's sake. You'd have the freedom to do what you want, and she—"

"No."

James made an explosive gesture, his hands rising and falling like a tiny bomb had gone off somewhere inside his person.

"Why not?" he said. "Tell me. Give me one good reason."

I drew in a breath.

"Our house is a place for living," I said. "A nursing home is a place for dying."

I don't know if he understood. He slammed out of the house soon after. I went to the window, watching him stride down the street.

°

In the old days, before Alzheimer's was a disease—before it had its own name—I remember my mother talking on the phone. I was a boy of nine or ten, underneath the table, hidden behind the fall of a tablecloth, reveling in the shadowy coolness. My mother sat at the countertop, the phone crooked between her shoulder and chin, smoking a cigarette and exhaling clouds toward the ceiling. She was in her thirties then, with coal-black hair and fine, burnished skin. I always liked eavesdropping on her conversations. This time she was gossiping about an elderly relative.

"He's in bad shape," she said. "Something will have to be done soon."

There was a pause as she dragged on her cigarette.

"The poor thing," she went on. "He's getting childish."

At the time, I did not understand this phrase. But I do now.

You have been succumbing to Alzheimer's for the past few years. I have watched it all. The process is something between a disease and a time machine, aging you backward. Like a child, you now wear a diaper. Like a child, you eat greedily, with abandon. You wrinkle up your nose at the greens on your plate, but you can devour an entire pizza single-handed. (A trim woman always, you have begun to gain weight. I don't have the heart to stop you. Less fat, less salt, your doctor has instructed me. But you do so enjoy them both.) Like a child, you are entranced by pretty things. Costume jewelry. A jangle of music on the radio. A gleam of sunlight caught in a panel of stained glass.

Recently, over lunch, you kept rediscovering the rich red fabric of your blouse.

"Who gave me this shirt?" you said. "It's lovely."

I reminded you to eat your broccoli. I had sprinkled cheese over it to make it more appetizing. But you just sighed.

"My hands are sore," you said. "Right here, at the joint. It's hard to hold the fork."

I reminded you that you had arthritis. I reminded you that your doctor had prescribed some pills.

"Oh?" you said, not much interested. Fingering the crimson fold of your collar, you exclaimed again, "Who gave me this shirt? It's lovely."

°

James and I drove to visit a nursing home on a wet day in November. Rain pattered the windshield of his car. In the passenger seat, I sat silent. James fiddled with the radio, changing the station every few minutes. He whistled energetically between his teeth.

You were not with us. We had left you at home, not wishing to discombobulate or unsettle you more than necessary. James had brought a friend of his to stay with you, to keep you company in my absence. A lady friend. James never married, but he does not lack for female companionship either. This one was named Madeline. She was blond, with smeary makeup. Her voice was bright and ringing, like a struck gong, and she shouted everything, evidently assuming you were deaf.

"We'll watch a little TV together," she roared, smiling.

You flinched.

"The boys will be back before you know it," Madeline cried.

You turned away.

In the car, I could not get comfortable. Rain streaked the window, obscuring the view. I kept picturing the expression on your face when you realized I was leaving you. Your eyebrows pooling together. Your mouth open.

The drive took over an hour. James kept telling me facts about the facility. He had found it online. He was enchanted with it. He was sure I would like it too. He was glad I was listening to reason at last.

I gritted my teeth. I stayed silent. Eventually, I dozed.

James woke me in the parking lot. I opened my eyes to see a bush that had been sculpted and trimmed into the shape of a heart. There was a placard with the facility's name: Garden Villas. A fountain played somewhere, the sound carried on the breeze. I blinked, gathering my wits. I saw a massive brick building coated in ivy. A woman with white hair was seated on a nearby bench, either reading or dozing. The rain had stopped, but the sky was still clotted with clouds.

For the next hour, James and I toured the grounds, the lobby, and the cafeteria. We met a few members of the staff—secretary, nurse, nutritionist. James showed me the medical wing. He showed me the pool. There was a patio where a man in a wheelchair was feeding the sparrows. He scattered seeds across the paving stones, and the birds filled the air with raucous song.

James held my arm as he steered me down the long, carpeted halls. His face was alight with optimism. There was a bounce in his stride. He had done his research. He explained that people of all ages and abilities were welcome at Garden Villas. Some residents lived fairly independent lives. Some could no longer drive. Some could no longer walk. Some could no longer feed or bathe themselves.

"You'd be happy here," James said. "I really believe you would."

I said nothing. I smiled. I nodded.

After a while, my son found an administrator and disappeared into a side office for a private chat. I let them go with relief. My body ached from the unaccustomed exertion of so much walking. My face hurt from false grins.

Still, I was proud of myself. I was playing the long game.

My plan is simple: I will dupe my son into a false sense of superiority. It takes two flints to make a fire, so I will give James nothing more to spark against. I will be agreeable. I will give my son the hope he so desperately needs. On the drive home, I praised Garden Villas to the skies. I even tucked a brochure for the facility into my pocket. I let James have this battle so that in the end, I could win the war.

°

That night, you were anxious. You did not remember that I'd been gone, but on some level you were still disturbed by it. You clung to me, leaning hard on my shoulder, causing a cascade of aches throughout my skeleton. I did not complain. I patted your back and reassured you, over and over, that all was well.

I had my own reasons for wanting to see Garden Villas. But I know I will never live there. I will keep you in our own familiar place, with our own habits and routines. I will keep you with me—together, independent, alive.

At home, you navigate with ease. We have lived in our house for decades, long enough that you know instinctively how to get to the bathroom, the kitchen, the sun porch. You will pivot without thought and reach into the silverware drawer. You can't come up with the word *spoon*, you can't articulate what the utensil is for, but your fingers know where to find it nonetheless.

Our house remembers things for you. Your mind is chaos, but there is structure around you—physical, tangible, true. You have forgotten much of your identity, but your fashion sense is there in the contents of the closet. Your artistic streak is present in the knickknacks on the mantelpiece. Your love of nature can be found in the numerous seascapes on our walls. Each piece of furniture was carefully chosen by you—the former you. Each is a kind of external memory. You are constantly confronted with some vital aspect of yourself.

I know I am right. James might not agree. The doctors might not agree. But they don't know what I know. They don't know about this kind of love. They don't know what sixty years of marriage has done to me. What it has done to you. These days, you no longer refer to me by name. I doubt you remember what it is. You no longer think of me as your husband either. Classification of relationships is beyond you.

Instead, you use the word *he*—"he makes stained glass," "he can't abide rainy days"—and you reach for me. You reach for me reflexively, automatically, expecting me to be there at the end of your fingertips. Like an extension of yourself. Your shadow. You no longer remember our wedding day. You do not recognize your old friends in photographs. You have forgotten the purpose of your house keys, your credit card, your phone. But you know me. You always know me. I am closer to you than words. I am closer to you than memory.

°

Lately I have awoken to find coils of ice on the windows. While at work on the sun porch, I have watched a fine mesh of snow falling. The branches are bare now, stark against the sky. I have labored day and night at the willow tree. I have stood at the worktable until my shoulders burn and my ankles swell. I have listened to you laughing in the kitchen. The TV flickers on and off. Sometimes I hear James's voice in the house. Sometimes I hear nothing at all. Sometimes I lose track of what I have actually done to the lampshade and what I have merely planned to do. Even in my dreams, the pattern appears, looming up beneath my fingers.

The other day I stopped by the antique store and found the perfect base: wrought iron, sturdy, with the suggestion of a tree trunk in its round, grooved stem. Each morning, I arrange a few more gleaming shards. I wield the soldering iron with a certain amount of urgency. I know my time is limited. Sometimes it seems as though the process of making the willow tree is the process of getting ready to die. I am getting my affairs in order. I am finishing my last gift to you.

I will die first. Caregivers usually do. The stress and strain will have their way with me. It might be a heart attack; it might be a stroke. I am hoping for something sudden and painless. Here one moment, gone the next.

When I am in the ground, James will take charge. You will be bundled into a nursing home. Garden Villas—a nice place. I am glad to have seen it. You will enjoy the craft room. The cafeteria. The patio, ringed by evergreen trees.

When I am gone, you will forget me. That is my hope, anyway. I can picture you, settled in. You will spend your days at the window, watching the clouds billow past, listening to the radio play. A few of our old things will be placed strategically around the room. This will liven up the impersonal space, adding a dash of color and comfort. The rug from our den. Your favorite painting of a seascape. Now and then, your gaze will stray to the willow tree lampshade, set in pride of place.

By this point, the disease will have finished its work. You will be childish. You will have lost the last vestiges of your adult mind. You will think the way children do. A world in which everything is still wondrous, yet to be discovered. A world too new for the possibility of memory. A world too safe for the possibility of loss. Staring at the willow tree, you will say, "Who gave that to me?" And again, softly: "Who gave it to me? It's lovely."

Starlike

Somewhere in the woods, an owl is screaming. The cry recurs at irregular intervals, ragged and breathless. The sky is a chalkboard slate, the moon a pastel smudge directly overhead, offering no directional guidance. I have finally admitted to myself that I am lost in the wilds of Tennessee.

In the distance, a brook babbles unseen. I move with caution, peering through the gloom for fallen logs and mud slicks. I am forty, too old to be trailblazing at midnight. But I needed a break—from my husband's brothers, and from my husband.

There is a pale beech stump, roughly the size of a man, that I have passed at least five times, scaring the life out of me on each reappearance. I have gone beyond concern, beyond panic, into a kind of quiet resignation. My body will be found days from now, tumbled in the ivy, scavenged by black vultures, and pearled with mushrooms.

I am a planetary geologist, which seems like it should be helpful in this situation. I know about the helium rain, laced with neon, that falls on Jupiter. I know that a day on Venus lasts longer than a year. I know about the alluvial plains of Tennessee and the loess-covered river terraces that surround the city of Dyersburg. But I do not know the way back to my brother-in-law's house.

At the crest of a slope, the ground tips beneath me. I skid helplessly downward, grabbing a tree branch to steady myself and wrenching my wrist. It might be sprained. When I get my bearings, the brook has grown louder. There is a flash of silver in the gloom and a damp, earthy musk. I have reached the water's edge.

And there, in the distance, is the house, the porch light glinting between the leaves. I break into an ecstatic jog, stumbling through the underbrush. Deep in the woods, the owl shrieks like a murder victim. Clutching the stitch in my side, almost sobbing with relief, I tug open the front door.

There is a body on the couch, still and silent. Another curled in a basket chair in the corner. They are all here, of course—all four of my husband's brothers, out cold, one in the armchair, another laid out on the floor, filling the air with their snoring and the collective fume of alcohol leaching from their pores.

Baylor and I have been in Dyersburg for fifty-six hours. In that time, we have never been alone. His brothers have occupied every minute, roughhousing, fishing, singing the fight song from high school, playing darts, eating fried things, and swimming in an ocean of liquor.

I creep down the hall to the guest bedroom. Baylor is tumbled in a heap of sheets, his breath a sour vapor. I climb into bed beside him. It seems like years since we left Boston. The journey here might as well have been our final passage to hell: taxi and plane and taxi again, ill-fitting chairs, enclosed spaces, no privacy, canned air, noise and bustle, waiting and waiting to end up somewhere I did not want to be.

°

When I first met Baylor, fifteen years ago, he was not an alcoholic. We were both in grad school then, and he rarely drank at all. Sometimes he smoked marijuana, but who didn't? Occasionally he took pain pills too. It wasn't hard to get his hands on a prescription for codeine or OxyContin; he'd hurt his back playing football in his teens and could always feign a painful flare-up. During the crush of final exams, he would pop a handful each evening, playfully mixing his meds, going a little over the line of an acceptable dosage. Then he would quit, just before I began to worry.

Sometimes it was speed instead. Diet pills, ADD medication, even cocaine. Baylor would binge for week, eschewing sleep, studying with supernatural vibrancy. He would snort a line in the men's bathroom with his fellow MBA students, all of them glimmering like dragonflies. He would keep me up at night talking and talking and talking. My head would spin as I tried to follow his theories on climate change and the South after the Civil War and the male libido—all of which were connected, in that moment, in his mind. Then he would quit, just before I began to worry.

At that time, I did not perceive the pattern. Baylor had a thousand justifications for his actions. The diet pills kept him alert. The painkillers helped him relax after a tough exam. The cocaine intensified our lovemaking. The marijuana helped him cope with the dead air in between semesters. He would be sober for a month, even two or three. He would take up a new substance and put it down again, treating each as an isolated incident.

I believed him every time he quit. I did not know any better.

°

I wake up and have no idea where I am. A blazing window. Cork paneling. A deer head hangs on the wall, glaring at me in an accusatory manner. Beside me, Baylor is flung across the mattress, every limb akimbo. He looks like a man dropped from a great height, falling not to his death but into sleep. I decide not to wake him. I will let the liquor simmer in his blood, boiling away like stock in a stew.

My morning routine has a clockwork consistency. A control freak, Baylor says, but I prefer to think of myself as precise, like a fine Swiss watch. A series of stretches. Twelve-step skin care. A brief meditation, aided by an app on my phone.

Down the hall, a clamor indicates that Baylor's brothers are awake too. I have no desire for conversation. Clutching a blanket around my shoulders, I step onto the side porch. The air is soupy and cold. Moss coats the trees. The sun is not yet visible between the branches, though the eastern sky is soaked with glow.

Baylor grew up in a trailer park on the outskirts of Dyersburg. His brothers all settled within a few miles of the double-wide where his parents still live—except Baylor, the outlier, who moved to the mysterious North with me. The father is a shy mumbler, the mother a wine-addled cipher, but somehow they managed to generate five huge, loud, charismatic sons. Tall and barrel-chested, Baylor and his brothers all have the same raucous, head-thrown-back laugh. The same galloping stride. The same broad, capable hands. All of them, like Baylor, have begun to manifest the telltale gut of an alcoholic in middle age. The differences between them (a beard, a tattoo, a limp left over from a motorcycle accident) are minor compared to their astonishing similarities. The oldest is Emil, then Jimmy Lee, then the "Irish twins," Cade and Hank, and finally Baylor, the baby.

They do not, however, go by their given names. The monikers that fly around when they get together are impossible to track. Baylor is both Lil Boy and Big Daddy. When he has done something annoying, he is Baylor Richard Murphy. When he has done something hilarious, he is Captain Jump Up Sit Down Underdog Willie. And, of course, he is often Bo, for short.

Over the years, I have given up trying to keep the brothers' lives straight. I am aware that one of them recently had a cancer scare that turned out to be nothing. One of them breeds hunting dogs. One of them can't hold down a job. Two of them own an auto repair shop together. None of them have kids, though a few are married and might be on the verge. Baylor tries to keep me updated on their lives, but it's hard to parse the family code. "Hankie thinks that Jujube is doing better," Baylor might tell me, or, "You'll never believe it—E-dog says that Sammy Boy has been hiding money from his wife." By the time I figure out who Hankie, Jujube, E-dog, and Sammy Boy are (Hank, Cade, Emil, and Jimmy Lee, respectively), the point of the story is lost.

Now the door bangs open behind me, and a figure strides onto the porch—Cade, our current host, dressed in boxer shorts and an undershirt, a cup of coffee in hand. He nods to me. I settle on the porch swing, leaving room for him, but he elects to remain standing. On closer inspection, his boxers are covered with cartoon bunnies having sex in a trillion different positions. The odor of cigarettes hangs about his person.

"Good morning," I say.

"Is Bebop still sleeping?"

"What?"

His grin fades. "Baylor. Is Baylor still sleeping?"

Mentally I add Bebop to the list of my husband's nicknames. In the distance, a group of wild turkeys begins to sing, hooting and burbling. The sun is rising behind the trees. Cade lives on forty acres of thick forest that blocks any view of the neighbors. He shifts his weight, the boards creaking. I wish he would put on some pants.

"Are you having a rough time?" he says.

"I beg your pardon?" I say, startled. I was not prepared for emotional honesty. Not now. Not here.

He takes a step toward me. "Is it hard being with us? Being in Tennessee?"

"Yes," I say. "It really is."

"I know you ran away last night. I saw you heading into the woods after Baylor and the others passed out. I wondered if you were planning to hitchhike home to Boston."

I manage a laugh, which comes out shaky.

"Glad you found your way back," he says. "Poor thing! We try our best with you. We do."

For a moment, I see my husband in Cade's eyes. There is Baylor's solidity, a touchstone of frank openness. An instant later, however, the spell is broken.

"Come inside and have a Bloody Mary," Cade says, flashing me a mischievous grin.

"Oh, I don't drink."

"Just this once. Have two. Have ten."

"You know—" I begin, but he interrupts me.

"Pretty please," he says. "E-dog and I made a bet a while back.

I'm still hoping to win. Fifty bucks if either one of us could get you wasted. Man, I'd give a lot more than fifty bucks to see that. Little Miss Priss on a tear!"

He throws back his head and guffaws. It is my husband's laugh, note for note.

°

Even now, I am not sure exactly when Baylor became an alcoholic. It was hard to see the pattern unfolding in real time. At some point, he turned to drink as though he'd been dating around for too long and was ready to settle down. He'd tried those other girls—cocaine, marijuana, pills—but this was love. This was the real thing.

Ten years ago, newly married, we moved to a cozy apartment on the west side of Boston. Baylor found a job at a prestigious marketing firm. I began teaching at Boston University, working my way up the ladder toward tenure. We lazed in bed on Sunday mornings doing crossword puzzles. He made me laugh the way I used to in childhood—a full-bodied, uncontrolled, snorting laugh I thought I had outgrown along with my Hello Kitty wristwatch and training bra. I taught him about the solar system and the existence of quinoa. We made love often, linked by tidal locking like Pluto and Charon, always facing each other, spinning in a private orbit of two.

I did not notice the change as it was happening. It was slow. Gradual. Baylor would stop by sports bars on weekends to catch up on "the game." (I never knew what game it was, or even what sport; I was content for him to share this interest with other people, like-minded people.) He would go out after work with "the boys"—his coworkers, always referred to that way, though many of them were female. He came home wasted and amorous, kissing my neck and expounding on my beauty, never an angry drunk, only affectionate and even more boisterous, the life of the party and a dynamo between the sheets. He took up wine as a hobby, buying excellent vintages to share with me over dinner, then drinking a few more glasses once I went to bed. A beer with lunch. A shot of whiskey to settle his nerves. His career did not suffer; he even got a promotion, due in part to his boozy socializing with the top brass.

There was no benchmark, no line in the sand, no moment when I could have pinpointed his descent in action. Maybe addiction is always like that—only discernible in hindsight, with the clarity offered by distance and retrospection.

°

In the afternoon, we visit the local swimming hole—all five brothers, both parents, and three wives, including me. The day is steamy, hung with shimmering curtains of humidity. I set up a beach chair and apply sunscreen and bug spray. Baylor's parents have aged significantly in the past year, shuffling cautiously across the grass to place their lawn chairs. The mother immediately falls asleep, but the father engages me in small talk, though his voice is so low and his southern drawl so thick that I cannot catch a word. I just smile brightly, nodding along, until he dozes off too.

The brothers take turns hurling themselves off a rope swing into the water. Jimmy Lee belly-flops, earning jeers and hollers. Farther down the beach, Cade crashes through the shallows, attempting to catch a minnow in his hands. They have a thousand inside jokes, almost their own language, like twin-speak expanded to include five. Whenever one of them salutes, the other four strike body builder poses. Jimmy Lee and Emil appear to communicate exclusively in quotes from *Calvin and Hobbes.* Baylor and Hank keep karate-chopping each other. At one point, Jimmy Lee screams, "Fire in the hole!" and at once, in unison, all five of them drop to the ground as though felled by bullets.

In truth, it is difficult for me to keep the brothers straight today, dazed as I am by the sunlight and the heat, overstimulated by voices and movement, hulking bodies, unkempt brown curls, jiggling beer guts, identical booming laughs, now tossing a Frisbee, now leaping off the rope swing again. The other two wives are no help. One of them has been texting since the moment we got here, thumbs flying, long plastic nails clacking against the screen. The other slathered herself with baby oil and stretched out on a towel. I can almost hear the sizzle of her skin broiling.

Baylor keeps shooting glances back at me, shading his eyes with a hand. Tennessee has always been a minefield for us. At home, we do well enough. We move seamlessly around each other. I go to bed at ten on the dot, while he sleeps whenever and wherever the mood strikes him. He works long hours; I set my own schedule. On weekends we hike through the nature preserve, and Baylor sweetly feigns interest as I classify the sedimentary strata of every rock that catches my eye. I return the favor by letting him show me incomprehensible memes on his phone every five minutes. In public, I can be standoffish, while Baylor charms everyone he meets. He has talked his way into free dessert, into a tour of the back rooms of my favorite museum; he "could sell sand to a camel," in his own words. We still have explosive, spontaneous, no-holds-barred sex. We are living proof that opposites attract. We balance each other out.

In Tennessee, however, our system invariably begins to break down. During previous visits, Baylor and I have found ourselves fighting over everything under the sun. My use of five-dollar words. His dirty socks. The way I pick at my food. The way he flirts with waitresses. We have squabbled over our finances. We have quarreled over our decision—made long ago, and only revisited here in Dyersburg—never to have children. We have fought over his drinking. His drinking, his drinking, his drinking. More than once, Tennessee has nearly detonated our relationship.

Now Jimmy Lee hefts a cooler from the back of his pickup. The brothers swarm around it, and the air resounds with the crackle and hiss of beer cans opening. Baylor flops down on the grass beside me, pressing an ice-cold can against his neck.

"Tell me something about Jupiter," he says.

"It's big," I say shortly.

"Oh yeah? How many moons does it have?"

"Seventy-nine."

Baylor runs a hand through his damp curls. "Jupiter is near the asteroid belt, right?"

"Right."

"And how did the asteroid belt form again? I know you've told me, but I forget."

Against my will, I smile a little. This is Baylor's usual peacemaking strategy—drawing me out on my favorite topic. The annoying thing is that it works.

"Gravity makes things circular," I tell him. "Gas and dust swirl around until they settle into a ball. That's how the planets formed. But not the asteroid belt. It's too close to Jupiter, and Jupiter is almost big enough to be a star. Its gravity is so intense that a rocky planet couldn't form near it. So instead, there are millions of asteroids orbiting the sun in a wide cloud."

Baylor stares up at me. The sun has brought out his freckles, a dusting across his nose and forehead. “Millions?” he asks. “Really?”

“Some of them are the size of pebbles. Most are around a kilometer across.”

“What does the word *asteroid* mean?” Baylor asks, his voice soft.

“Starlike. They look like stars to us, especially when they fall out of the belt. When they hit our atmosphere. Shooting stars.”

“Starlike. I never knew that.” Baylor runs a finger down the length of my arm, leaving goosebumps in his wake.

“Bo!” Jimmy Lee yells. “We need you to be tiebreaker over here.”

My husband bounds to his feet and joins his brothers.

°

There was an afternoon in autumn, perhaps ten years ago, when I caught a glint of light where none should be. I was at my desk, working on a lesson plan, when I saw something shining in the soil of my fiddle-leaf fig tree. On closer inspection, the gleam was coming from the tiny gap in between the plastic pot and the pretty basket I’d bought to cover it. I fished out the offending object: a bottle of bourbon.

Baylor had taken to hiding stashes of liquor around our home. I knew he was drinking, and he knew that I knew, but he still hid the evidence from me. Addiction is furtive by nature. In that moment, I felt compelled to discover exactly where each bottle might be.

And so I set aside my papers and scoured the apartment. I

got down on my hands and knees to examine the underside of the couch. I peered into the tank of the toilet, where Baylor had stashed a quart of vodka a few months back. In the kitchen, I disarranged the cans and spice jars. In the mud room, I groped inside each of the boots.

Our apartment was not infinite in scope. In less than an hour, I had located a bottle on top of the refrigerator and another under the bed, swathed in a bin of Baylor's winter sweaters. Two more bottles were hidden in the bathroom, standing incognito among Baylor's toiletries.

I set all five in a row on the mantel—biggest to smallest, like children in a class photo. The bottles gleamed in the light. I weighed my options. I could leave them in pride of place where they were, a silent accusation for Baylor when he came home. I could tuck each one back where I had found it and say nothing. I could pour the bottles down the drain, rinsing each one carefully, patting it dry, and carrying it out to the recycling bin, as I did with my yogurt cups and milk jugs. I could smash the five bottles on the floor, leaving a glorious mess of congealed liquor and glittering shards to greet Baylor on his arrival.

All at once, a great weariness fell across my shoulders. The situation was as well choreographed as the orbit of planets around the sun. I had done all these things before, every single one. I had pitched a fit, screaming and sobbing. I had begged Baylor to think of his health. Once I printed out photographs of diseased livers and taped them up all around the apartment. Once I got hold of a list of surgical patients waiting for liver donations and handwrote my husband's name on top, pinning it to the fridge. (The fight that followed was epic. Baylor accused me of being a drama queen, which may have been accurate.) Once or twice, I drank myself blind along with him, getting sloppy on purpose to make a point. I'd dragged him to AA meetings ("too much God talk"). I'd made appointments for him with a therapist ("too much jawing about feelings"). I'd coddled him, cooking his favorite meals and behaving as though the latest relapse was nothing more serious than a bout of flu.

But nothing I did could shift Baylor from his path. I could see that now. He was caught in the gravity well of alcohol. I pictured the void of space like a blanket, strewn with orbs of different shapes and sizes. As each planet settles into the cloth, nearby objects roll toward the ensuing depression, pulled by gravity. The largest objects—like Jupiter, like the sun—create a hollow as deep and unforgiving as a mineshaft dug straight down through solid rock.

Sometimes the Earth carves a perfect circle through space as it spins around the sun, circumscribing the rim of our star's gravity well. Sometimes Jupiter or Saturn reaches out grasping fingers and warps our orbit slightly, pulling our world a few degrees outward, changing our path from circle to oval. But the modification is minor, and the primacy of the sun's gravity remains, keeping us close.

If I made enough of a fuss, Baylor might pretend to change his ways for a short while. He might promise to cut back or stick to wine, but eventually, inexorably, he would return to the status quo. Every option before me—to pour the liquor out, to drink the stuff myself—was, at its core, a minute variation in the orbital rotation, like a faint tug from distant Jupiter, scarcely strong enough to register. A gravity well is an irresistible thing, bending even the fabric of space-time to its will.

°

My last morning in Tennessee is cool and sweet. The air smells as though it has been scrubbed clean. I reach for Baylor and find his side of the bed empty. Then I remember. The brothers dropped me, their parents, and the other wives off after the swimming hole and went out together to "raise a little hell," in Cade's words. I did not ask what this meant; I did not want to know. I spent the evening reading in silence. Very late, Baylor called to stay that he'd be sleeping over at Jimmy Lee's place. He did not add that he was too drunk to drive back to me; I gathered that much from the slurring of his speech. He told me he loved me. He told me again and again.

Dragging my suitcase onto the bed, I begin folding my clothes. Jeans, headbands, and lacy underwear—soon these things, like me, will be back in Boston where they belong. In ten hours, I will board a plane and leave this place in my dust. Like a loving wife, I pack for Baylor too. In filling his suitcase, I exercise far less care—wrinkling his slacks, incorrectly matching his socks into pairs, and shoving his toothbrush among the T-shirts without sleeving it in a plastic bag. I doubt he will even notice, but these gestures relieve my spirit anyway, petty revenges for my bruised heart.

As the sun climbs the sky, I get out my laptop and work on a lesson plan about asteroids. My conversation with Baylor sparked an idea. Next semester, I will give a lecture on asteroid families. I have done research on the subject: a whirling cluster of rocks that all share common orbits and spectra. Their coloration is identical: black for carbon or red for nickel-iron. Asteroids in the same family were once a single organism, but something broke them apart—an impact with another body in space or the tempestuous gravitational pull of nearby Jupiter, cratering a larger asteroid into many smaller ones. There are more than 120 such families in the belt, and they even have their own surnames: Nysa, Flora, Hungaria. Excellent fodder for a lecture.

I am waiting for my cell phone to chime. Whenever he wakes up, Baylor will text me. I pick up the phone, making sure it isn't silenced. Surely he will reach out soon. It's almost noon, and even the most hungover of the brothers must be awake by now.

Baylor and I always check in regularly. When he's at work, when I'm on campus, scarcely an hour goes by without one of us making contact. He might photograph the pile of paperwork on his desk and send it to me with a sad emoticon. I might send him a passive-aggressive text about the laundry. These moments matter—me sharing a snapshot of my newly pedicured toes, him informing me that he has just discovered his hair is thinning. The sensation of my phone vibrating in my pocket, containing a note from my husband, a note that tells me nothing important, nothing romantic, can be as intimate as a caress.

Today, however, there has been no word. One of us is giving the other the silent treatment, but I am not sure who is the perpetrator and who is the victim.

°

Fourteen months ago, Baylor got sober. He did it himself, without the benefit of AA or rehab. He did it the "dude way"—which, to my untrained eye, looked excruciating.

First he went on a tear, drinking all the liquor in our apartment and vomiting it back up over the course of a gruesome twenty-four hours. Then he sank into a kind of hibernation. He crawled into bed, emerging only to get himself aspirin while glowering at the sunshine. During that phase, he seemed to be not so much recovering as devolving. His beard grew thick and wild.

The smell of him pervaded the apartment. I brought him water and tried to make him eat. I would tap nervously at the mound of quilts he had piled over his huddled frame, and he would gradually emerge, a sweaty, bleary-eyed wreck of a man.

There followed a few difficult months. Baylor was not drinking. When I asked him how he was, he would say, "I'm not drinking." When I asked him what he was thinking about, he would say, "I'm not drinking." Everything in front of him—the TV, his dinner, his wife—was clearly being compared to the attractions of a good bottle of bourbon and found wanting.

I kept track of his sobriety in my calendar. A circle marked each dry day—the image, in my mind, of an empty glass. He passed four months, the longest stretch he'd ever done. Five. Six. Seven. I was not sure what was motivating him. He had been wanting to quit for years—forever, really. Every addict always wants to quit. Maybe something had shifted in him physically, his liver crying foul. Maybe it was simply time, as though he had been saving up his willpower in some internal vault for years, and now, at last, there was enough accumulated to see him through.

He stopped going to bars. He avoided his weekly poker game. He let "the boys" go out after work without him. In the past, he had stayed up late to drink after I went to bed. Now his secret behaviors included watching infomercials, reading spy novels, and eating all the Popsicles in the freezer.

I was different too. In a word, I was happy. After ten months passed—a nice round number—I stopped waiting for the other shoe to drop. I no longer sniffed Baylor's breath every morning as a reflex. I stopped wincing in restaurants when the waiter set down the wine list. I stopped reaching convulsively for my husband's arm as we strolled past a liquor store, a metaphorical leash, keeping him from bolting.

There is nothing worse than hope. It is an illusion, ephemeral, like the light emitted by a faraway star that has since reached the end of its life cycle, exploding or contracting into nothingness, even as it appears to twinkle on in our night sky.

°

Hours later, I wake for a second time, covered in sweat. The quality of light pouring through the window suggests midafternoon. I am prone on the couch, my neck bent at an uncomfortable angle, a sour taste in my mouth. I push myself upright, brushing sweat-dampened hair from my brow. I am not usually a napper, but the Tennessee heat is as powerful a soporific as ether.

There is another person in the room, planted in the armchair, staring at me. I jump halfway out of my skin. Brown curls. A barrel chest. Clasped hands.

"Baylor!" I cry.

The man rises to his feet. "No, sorry. It's Hank," he says.

I blink, clearing my head. "Where's Baylor?"

"You know, that's a funny thing," he says.

"Funny how?"

"Here." Hank smacks his hands on his thighs. "I'm going to get you some water. That's what I'm going to do."

"I don't need . . ." I begin, but he is already on his feet, clattering in the kitchen. As he hands me a glass, I notice that he is avoiding my gaze.

"Okay," I say. "I'm awake now. What time is it? We have to leave for our flight."

Hank sits down in the armchair again. "Well," he says. "The thing is, Baylor had to have his stomach pumped."

"What?"

"I said, he had—"

"*What?*"

"It happened last night. I guess you'd call it alcohol poisoning."

A sound escapes me, somewhere between a gasp and a groan.

"We took him to the ER. All of us went together." Hank raises a hand, tapping thoughtfully at his temple. "You know, maybe they didn't pump his stomach. Maybe they just gave him that stuff that makes you puke. What's that stuff? I've had it. Man, it tastes terrible."

"Is he all right?" I say. Glancing down, I realize that I am still holding the glass of water. With a bang, I set it on the coffee table. "Where is he? I should be . . . Let me get my purse, and I'll be ready to go."

Hank holds up his palms. "Whoa, whoa. Baylor's just fine."

"He had his *stomach* pumped."

"Happens to the best of us."

"Not to Baylor," I fire back. "It's never been that bad. He's never been *hospitalized* before."

Hank nods solemnly, taking this in. "It just got away from him, I think. We hit Joe's Bar. Stayed up late. Headed over to Big E's place. We noticed that Baylor seemed . . . well. He had blacked out. We couldn't wake him."

"Why the hell didn't anyone call me?"

"We didn't want to bug you until we knew how serious it was." He darts his eyes sheepishly to the side. "And then, in the hospital, Baylor told us not to."

All the fight goes out of me, and I sink back against the couch.

"He's doing good," Hank says. "Really."

"Cross your heart?"

"Hope to die. Stick a needle in my eye."

I nod. The full weight of his news is still sinking in. There is a strange sensation in my chest, as though my heart has become dislodged, slipping to the side. A silence descends. Hank has my husband's calm composure, the ability to weather an uncomfortable pause with equanimity.

"We're not leaving today, are we?" I ask. "We were supposed to leave today."

"Well," Hank says. "That's a funny thing too."

"I bet."

"The doctors seemed to think that it might be hard for him to fly the same day he . . . he . . ."

Hank trails off, looking at me as though I might suddenly go for his throat. I hear the wind scraping against the wall outside. I hear the turkeys in the distance, warbling their dissonant song. The peace of the countryside is a myth.

"He's never had to go to the hospital before," I say again. "We've been through a lot, but never that."

Hank blushes. "There's one more thing. Baylor wanted me to tell you—I told him I didn't feel quite right about it, but—"

"Spit it out," I say coldly.

He is crimson now, all the way up to the tips of his ears. "He's going to stay at Emil's place once he's discharged. He doesn't want to see you." Quickly, he corrects himself, "I mean, he doesn't want *you* to see *him*. Not like this."

"Fine by me," I say.

"Right." At once, Hank is on his feet, moving toward the door. "Well, it's been real nice talking with you."

This little pleasantry almost makes me laugh aloud. He offers it automatically, as a penance, perhaps, for having shoved himself so awkwardly into the middle of my marriage. He fumbles for the doorknob and escapes into the sunshine.

°

Three weeks ago, Baylor told me that he wanted to come to Tennessee. Almost before the words were out of his mouth, I heard alarm bells ringing. He had been sober for fourteen months, he said, as though I hadn't been keeping my own count. He told me that he could not bear to go any longer without seeing his brothers. I was on my summer break, and he had vacation days accrued. It was time, he said.

On the morning of our trip, I woke to a sinking feeling—a crumbling, as of hope deflating. We spent the ride to the airport sniping at each other. The highway was a mass of angry red taillights, winking and flashing like morse code. Horns blared. There was a musical precision to it; one would shrill, another would answer, and a conversation would ensue, back and forth, each side trying to get in the last word. Our driver bawled ceaselessly into his radio. Baylor's shoulders hunched together. My knuckles went white. A quarrel about our respective packing styles carried us all the way to the airport, through the security checkpoint, and onto the plane.

But the real war didn't start until we were airborne. It was a gorgeous sunset, all watercolor hues and smoky clouds. In the window seat, I watched the ground fall away. Down below, Boston was in darkness, the roads a network of glittering lines, reminiscent of the lava rivers on Io, one of Jupiter's moons, the most volcanic world in our solar system. When we reached the cloud layer, my view was swallowed up by gray.

I glanced over and saw that Baylor had ordered himself a glass of wine.

Before I could open my mouth, he snapped, "I don't like flying. You know that."

When he ordered his second glass, he said, "I'm going to drink this week. No choice, once my brothers get involved. Might as well start now."

By the third glass, he had his headphones on and was humming along to the music. I would nudge him to be quiet, and he would pause momentarily as I gritted my teeth, counting. Seven, eight, nine, ten—and he would be humming again.

The plane climbed above the clouds. Through the window, a milky landscape emerged, pale peaks and ghostly valleys. Bulbous puffs drifted eerily above the plateau. The upper atmosphere appeared to be a wild place, judging by the shapes carved out of the cloud layer by the wind—whorls and loops, towers and hillsides.

Baylor ordered another glass of wine, and I wiped the tears from my eyes.

°

That night, the silence in Cade's house is oppressive, the guest bed too wide. The television is full of nothing but love stories. I do not want to think about my husband. I do not want to picture him nestled, ashen and shaky, in Emil's blankets. I do not want to wonder whether anyone is taking care of him as I have so often done—bringing him tea, aspirin, a cool cloth for his brow. I do not want to think at all.

My cell phone rings. I fumble for my purse and answer without bothering to check the screen. I know who it is. I'm sure

Baylor has been picking up his phone all day, almost dialing, and putting it away again.

"Hi." He clears his throat and tries again. "Hey, babe."

"You sound terrible."

"Been better."

"This is a new low, huh?" I ask, unable to keep the rancor out of my voice. "I thought you hit bottom last time, but I guess not."

There is a pause, and then, without anger, he says, "There's always somewhere further down."

I get to my feet and walk to the window. The woods are a silvery mesh. A flowering tree releases a cloud of white petals, floating on the air like snow.

"Our flight is at four," Baylor says. "Tomorrow afternoon."

"Fine."

"I'll pick you up. Hank will drive us out."

"Okay."

"You know I love you," he says.

"I know."

He waits for reciprocation. I do not offer it.

"I can't talk much," he says. "They put a tube down my throat. I'm pretty sore. Listen, honey—"

I interrupt him. "I'm not going to take care of you this time."

"I'm quitting," he says pleadingly. "For real. For good. I mean it."

I breathe steadily, my eyes closed.

"I've learned my lesson," he says. "This whole thing has shown me the light. I'm on the wagon now. Forever. I promise."

"If you ever drink again, I'll kill you," I say.

"What?"

"I will kill you."

The words come out in a rush, as though someone else is saying them. Baylor takes in an astonished breath. I hang up and turn off my phone.

°

At midnight, sleepless, anguished, I step outside. The night is full of wind, a chaotic breeze swelling this way and that. I walk into the grass. In the distance, an owl shrieks, shrill and grating.

My own words to Baylor ring through my mind. I hear my voice, hardened by emotion into a rough tenor: *I will kill you.* In this moment, however, the words come back to me differently. I hear myself saying, *I will leave you.*

Because that's what I meant, what I should have told him, what I will tell him once we're back home and somewhat recovered. *If you ever drink again, I will leave you.* That is the truth I have come to understand during my final trip to Tennessee.

Saturn glimmers overhead, the ringed planet, first spotted by Galileo Galilei's telescope. Venus is visible too, a fiery hellscape of ochre-colored sulfuric acid that looks serene from this distance. Light pollution usually obscures the Milky Way in Boston, but here I can see it clearly, a beaded quilt thrown over the treetops.

Before my eyes, a pinpoint of light detaches itself from the sky and falls. I would make a wish, but I know it is not a star. It is starlike, an asteroid wrenched from its family, untethered from Jupiter's thrall, achieving escape velocity, plunging through miles of inky void to enter our atmosphere. Maybe it will burn up in the air, charring and crumbling into harmless ash. But I hope it survives the terrible descent. I hope it beats the ground hollow when it lands on the other side of the world.

Petrichor

The first sign was a sandwich. Tuna fish on rye, homemade. Hannah sealed it in Tupperware, slipped it into her purse, and left for work. The sandwich was unimportant at the time, discernible as the turning point only in retrospect.

At the office, everyone was murmuring about this new virus. It was still in Asia then, an ocean away, but the media could talk of little else. "Much ado about nothing," Hannah said, leaning against the copier as it shuddered and squeaked. "They're just trying to scare us. Anything for a headline. Tomorrow they'll be freaking out about North Korean nukes again." She believed this, believed that the media had become a perpetual motion machine, powered by panic, that created an endless supply of its own fuel.

But still, throughout the morning, she found herself googling viruses. The body count in Asia was rising, she learned. Viruses were not living things at all, she learned. They inhabited a nether realm of existence, inert until they came into contact with life, which activated them, inducing them to replicate. *Zombies*, Hannah thought, and turned off her computer for lunch.

After one bite, she threw her sandwich away in horror. The celery crunched, the mayonnaise oozed, everything looked and felt normal. But the whole thing was wrong in a way she could not initially define, something she had never in her thirty-six years of life encountered. There was a terrible sweetness, a misalignment of sandwich and smell: an aftertaste, or maybe an afterthought, of peaches and cream.

°

Next came the roses with a potent aroma of peanut butter. Hannah leaned in to feel the velvet petals against her face and recoiled in confusion. Her morning coffee tasted like spaghetti. On a fitness walk with her sister, Hannah kept pausing, sniffing the air, wondering aloud if a fire was burning somewhere near. But no—it was pollen on the wind, not smoke, according to both her sister and the internet.

Strange, but not yet frightening. Hannah examined her nose in the mirror, familiar, freckled, and flat. Was the glitch in her nostrils or in her brain? Perimenopause, her sister suggested. Cancer, WebMD offered.

And still, the news could talk of nothing but the virus, which had reached the shores of Europe, battering Italy and Germany. The body count rose by the day, by the hour.

Hannah woke in a panic on Sunday morning. Something was missing—something so primal and essential that she could not immediately identify it. She counted her limbs and digits. She laid a palm on her chest, checking for a heartbeat. She inhaled deeply, trying to calm herself, but the feeling persisted—a raw absence, as if some fundamental aspect of the world, or of Hannah herself, had been erased.

Another inhale. Deeper, choking her lungs with air. She understood now what was lacking. The lemony odor of her apartment, the lingering tang of fabric softener in her sheets, the pleasant stink of her own garish sweat. Gone.

°

"Anosmia," her doctor said, and then chuckled. "It's a funny word, isn't it?"

Hannah did not return his smile. "How do we fix this?"

The doctor gave a longwinded, hand-wavy reply that meant *I don't know.*

"How long will it go on?" Hannah asked, trying to keep the desperation out of her voice. "I can't just stay like this forever."

Her first thought had been to call the police. The loss felt as violent as theft, as intimate as a break-in. Someone had stolen one of her five senses.

"We'll keep an eye on it," the doctor said, nodding sagely and ushering her out of his office.

In another month, everyone would recognize anosmia as one of the first symptoms of the virus. Just then, however, Hannah's private suffering seemed unrelated to the news coverage of the first recorded case found on American soil, a couple hundred miles north near Seattle.

°

She took the rest of the day off work. The internet told her that food would now lose its savor, which was true; everything tasted like cardboard. She spritzed perfume directly into her face and smelled nothing, though her sinuses ached afterward. She took a long walk along the river, pausing to breathe intensely when she spied a dead fish. Everywhere, anywhere, the air was blank and meaningless.

Her friends offered their condolences, but politely, briskly. Even her sister did not seem particularly interested. Jo kept changing the subject to the virus, which was spreading through the Pacific Northwest like a wildfire. It would reach their small Oregon town any minute, if it hadn't already. Jo was considering pulling her children out of school as a precaution, but she and her husband could not agree.

Sleepless, Hannah sat up late. She couldn't bear the thought that she would never again inhale the spice of a freshly peeled orange or the bright, brassy scent of her niece's hair after a long day in the sun. It occurred to her for the first time that vision was the favorite child of the English language. Every color had a synonym. There were a dozen descriptors for the quality of light alone—*glitter*, *gleam*, *shine*, *flash*, *shimmer*—but not a single word for so many of the things she had lost: the mouthwatering, sugary bouquet of a bakery, the sting of fresh nail polish, or the omnipresent fume rising from the ocean. Why were there not more nouns like *petrichor*? Hannah had learned the word in childhood, a musical encapsulation of the smell of rain on dry earth. Her late mother had loved its specificity and rhythm, rolling the *r*'s down her tongue.

Now Hannah whispered it like a mantra, "Petrichor, petrichor," and wept.

°

Without smell, she was reduced to taste, a lesser version of the olfactory rainbow. Smell infused the world with context and significance. Smell offered a thousand shades, while taste provided only five: sweet, sour, bitter, salt, and umami.

On her lunch break, Hannah sat on a bench outside, despite the drizzle. A couple walked past, nestled under a single umbrella, both wearing cloth masks. She watched them, wondering if they were doctors, though they were awfully young, and dressed in jeans, not scrubs. Was the woman wearing perfume? Did the man have stinky feet? Hannah would never know. Without smell, the world stood at a remove. She might have been a filmgoer watching the biopic of her own life; everything was flattened as though on a screen, lacking the verisimilitude of odiferous reality.

Hannah opened her lunch. Since the onset of her anosmia, she had packed meals that encompassed the sad little spectrum that was left to her. Today: sliced apple for sweet, sauerkraut for sour, gouda for umami, sautéed Brussels sprouts for bitter, and dried seaweed for salt. As a kindness to the unimpaired noses of her coworkers, Hannah ate outside now, even in the pervasive Oregon rain.

She had prepared the Brussels sprouts according to her late mother's recipe, sautéed in oil and liberally spiced, though, as she chewed, she realized she might as well have eaten them raw. Plain bitterness, nothing more. Sauerkraut: the bracing tartness of vinegar. Gouda: a round, meaty contentment. The apple gave no lingering aroma of the forest, no multifaceted juices, only bare sweetness, unaccompanied. Smell was a wide-open gift, billowing on the wind, available for the taking. Taste was stingy and small, cloistered in the hollow of the human mouth.

Hannah saved salt, her favorite, for last. Dried seaweed on her tongue. Crunchy, melting into spongy. She waited for the top note of salt. Waited. She probed the seaweed, the feel of it, nap and grain, but no taste—nothing but texture.

Where was salt?

Salt was gone.

°

She lost sweet that same afternoon. Umami and sour had vanished by the next morning. Bitter lingered long enough that Hannah thought, even hoped, that it might stay with her forever; a bitter world was better than an empty one. She sipped coffee all the way to the doctor's office, relishing each charred, earthy mouthful.

Ensconced in the plastic coffin of the MRI machine, Hannah thought of Bergamo, Italy, the latest virus hotspot. A doctor over there had described it as a war zone, bodies filling the morgue, crematoriums at capacity, funerals unattended because the loved ones of the bereaved were sick too. A military caravan had carried the dead through the streets; no other vehicles were large enough. Would that happen here, in the small town where Hannah had lived since childhood? Neither she nor Jo had ever felt the inclination to leave their bucolic home.

Her brain was fine. The doctor showed it to her on a screen. To her the image was a Rorschach; to him, a diagnosis of good health. He pointed: "Here, you see, and here?" No lesions, no tumors, nothing at all to explain her symptoms.

Hannah reached for her thermos of coffee with shaking

hands, took a lukewarm sip, and found that bitter, too, had abandoned her.

°

Schools closed. Businesses went remote. At Hannah's office, a few junior members of staff lost their jobs, no longer needed to restock the copiers or fetch coffee. Hannah's own work was easier at home, streamlined by solitude.

She told no one about the vanishing of her sense of taste. It was too profound, too achingly personal, and at the same time too silly, given the backdrop of a world teetering on the brink. Her sister caught the virus and was in bed for a week, followed by her husband, who was sick for even longer. The kids either didn't catch it or didn't show symptoms. They went feral, from what Hannah could tell over the phone, snarling and gibbering in the background as Jo coughed wetly into a tissue and her husband moaned in the other room.

Virtual meetings were a joke, fifteen faces stacked in boxes like fish in an aquarium, the boss droning on, the chat filled with reports of whose uncle tested positive, whose grandmother was on a ventilator. Hannah wore pajama bottoms off-screen, under her smart blazers. She kept her feet bare. She found herself watching her own face almost exclusively, the turn of her throat in the light, the flutter of her restless fingers as she gestured. She wondered if the others were all doing the same, each narcissus granted a private rectangle in which to gaze.

The normalcy of her own face was both reassuring and haunting. There was her broad nose pointing down like an arrow, her thin lips, her elegant brows; she looked the same as always. No one would know that her tongue was as dumb as her fingertips now, all its specialness gone. No one would know that food had become a chore, the dull answer to a nagging question. Hungry? Food. Without smell, without taste, the stuff on Hannah's plate was not a meal; it was matter, mere solid substance, differentiated only by temperature and texture, hot or cold, dry or damp, crisp or soft. She might as well have snacked on clay and sand.

Her dreams were filled with creamy cakes, steaming plates of nachos, the grease of fresh pizza, and the snap of peanut brittle. Hannah woke with a hunger that could not be satiated. Wasn't there a Greek myth about someone in a similar quandary: starving and parched, surrounded by fresh water and ripe grapes, just out of reach?

The CDC claimed that outdoor activity was fine, probably safe, almost certainly safe, even recommended, so long as one was masked and maintained a six-foot distance from other humans and did not step into the contrails left by fast-moving joggers or cyclists. Hannah took long walks around her neighborhood, despite the persistent rain. She gave other pedestrians a wide berth, crossing the street to avoid them, eschewing even eye contact, as though a momentary gaze could be infectious. In her slicker and rain boots, she moved with urgency. She had the nagging sense that she was looking for something out there.

She lost weight without meaning to, without thinking about it, noticing the change only when she saw herself in her reflecting pool during a Monday meeting. Hollows beneath her cheekbones, the gaunt jut of her chin. She did not hear one word her boss said, fixated instead on her new, narrow face.

As soon as the first tests for the virus became available, Hannah hurried to her doctor's office. She was desperate for anything that might explain her predicament. Loss of smell was a symptom, she now knew, though loss of taste did not seem to be, and she did not have any of the other usual indicators either—sore throat, difficulty breathing, cough, headache, blood clots, pneumonia, fever, or death.

The results were negative. However, the doctor explained that the tests were so new as to be somewhat unreliable. In addition, Hannah had first developed her anosmia long enough ago that even if she had been infected then, the antigens from the virus might not show up in her blood now.

"What does that mean?" Hannah asked. "What's happening to me?"

"We'll keep an eye on it," the doctor said. "It's hard to know what's what. This virus is unlike anything else I've seen. This virus . . ." His gaze lifted to the window, and he never finished the sentence.

°

Then came the day when the volume on Hannah's laptop stopped working—at least, that was what she thought at first. Everyone in the morning meeting seemed to be mumbling, their voices tinny and fractured. "What?" she said, leaning close to the speaker. "Are you on mute? What did you say? Can you repeat that?"

You're yelling, Hannah, someone wrote in the chat.

Their voices drifted further away. Mouths moved. Her boss was gesticulating, one hand rolling in midair, everyone else nodding along. Hannah tilted her head right and left, doglike, watching herself onscreen. No sound came from her laptop.

Something's wrong with my connection, she typed into the chat. *I'm going to sign out and back in again.*

She went to fill the kettle while her computer was buffering. She used to prefer coffee, but tea was a comfort now in a purely tactile way—the heat in her palms, the cloud of steam against her cheeks. Besides, tea had never offered much in the way of smell or taste, whereas every sip of coffee was a brief but devastating loss.

Leaning against the counter, Hannah watched the rain bejewel the windowpane. A gray, dreamy day. She wondered if she ought to call her sister, if she had the bandwidth to take on that litany of understandable but overwhelming complaints. Jo had recovered quickly from the virus, but her husband was still bedridden, and the kids were home all day now. No school, no playdates, no routine, the impossibility of working remotely with children at one's elbow, no privacy, no end in sight.

Hannah reached for her phone and saw steam gushing from the spout of the kettle, a frantic, silent blast.

For a moment she did not understand. Everything was breaking down—first her laptop, then the kettle. And the rain, that was broken too. A downpour splattered the kitchen window, urgent drops that smashed into shards and distorted the world outside, but there was no accompanying rhythm, no patter or splash.

Hannah snapped her fingers. Silence.

She clapped her hands. Silence.

She put her palms over her ears, tried to locate the thump of her own heart.

"Help me," she said, and she felt her larynx tighten, her tongue lift, the mechanism of her voice functioning like always, producing nothing she could hear.

°

During the MRI, tears welled up and poured down in a slow waterfall. Hannah did not wipe them away, even as they dripped into her ears; she was not supposed to move. Last time, there had been electronic creaks and groans as the machine took scans of her brain, but this time she was caged in suffocating stillness.

The journey to the emergency room had been a farce. Hannah intended to drive, but the simple act of picking up her keys left her reeling; the absence of the cheerful jingle of metal on metal, that homey, everyday chime, was more than she could bear. Instead, she booked a rideshare on her phone, but that presented its own problems. Standing on the street corner, Hannah was bewildered by the lack of ambient sound. She stared into the trees, watching birds open and close their beaks like defective automatons in a museum exhibit, their electronic music stilled by age and disuse. Wind gusted; Hannah could feel its breath, but there was no accompanying rustle of leaves. A plastic bag wafted past in eerie silence.

Probably her driver honked. Probably he called to her and waved. Only when the man got out of his car and approached her, red-faced, did Hannah snap to attention. Beady eyes, maybe he smelled like cigarettes or sweat, he seemed to be yelling, flecks of spittle, was it possible he was singing opera? She had so little to go on.

"I can't hear you," she said finally. "I can't hear anything."

It was impossible to tell if she had pitched her voice correctly—too loud, too low? Her voice was theoretical now.

To her surprise, the driver smiled. He began to gesture at her, changing the configuration of his fingers and bumping the heels of his palms together. Sign language, Hannah realized. She had never studied it. Why would she? Was learning ASL part of the man's training to become a rideshare driver? That seemed unlikely.

"I just lost my hearing this morning," she told him. "I don't know what you're saying."

He stared at her in alarm, obviously concerned that she might be insane. She did not blame him; what was happening to her did sound insane.

How long had she been in the MRI machine? She opened her mouth to ask the technician, then remembered that she would not be able to hear the answer. What if they had forgotten about her? What if they had all gone to lunch? What if they had left for the weekend? What if she died in here?

She breathed, waited, breathed and waited.

○

They sent her home without a diagnosis. *We'll let you know*, the technician scrawled on a piece of paper. The lobby was overrun by people who were coughing—or pantomiming the act, anyway, lurching forward in a spasm, hand over the mouth. Hannah could not hear them, left to imagine their hawking and rheumy breath. Flushed faces, fevers. She wrapped her scarf around her face to protect herself from germs and hurried out with her head down.

○

At the window, Hannah sat for hours, watching people go by and imagining the click of heels, the carillon of children's voices. Enough passersby wore masks now that the occasional bare face seemed indecent. It was mostly men who went about this way, mouth and nose exposed and spewing particles. Sometimes a husband and wife would walk past, the woman masked, the man apparently unwilling. Hannah observed it all, cataloguing these little injustices.

Framed in a window across the street, a fat tabby lolled in

the sunlight, sometimes grooming its luxurious mane, sometimes charting the paths of birds, sometimes locking eyes with Hannah with an expression rather like sympathy. Two indoor cats, they kept watch over the street together.

Finally the doctor got back to her with results. The takeaway from all the scans—the MRI, the audiologist's report, the painful probing of nose, mouth, and ear—was that medical science was stumped. According to every metric, Hannah was a healthy woman. The only thing that belied the numbers was her own experience, her own testimony.

Poss. psychosomatic, the doctor wrote at the end of his email. *Referring you to psychologist.*

Hannah resisted the urge to throw her laptop across the room. She vowed to find a female physician who would take her experience as truth, who would not treat her as hysterical. Just as soon as she could make an appointment among the thousands of sick and dying people infected with the virus, desperate for aid.

°

A steady rain settled in for weeks, unrelenting. Hannah no longer took walks around her neighborhood. Though the CDC continued to recommend outdoor exercise, it was too frightening in her current state. Everything startled her. An airplane in the corner of the sky made her flinch. A jogger in her peripheral vision triggered some latent prey response; she would cower like a zebra on the prairie flanked by a lion. There was never any warning now—no distant grumble of airborne engines, no car horn, no footsteps. She kept whirling around to see what was behind her. Anything could be back there, a mugger, a truck bearing down on her, a tornado.

The shock of her loss—her many losses—left her weary and timid. She slept often and suddenly. Fatigue overtook her on the couch, in the bath; she had never been a napper, but she had also never been so tired. There was less of a delineation now between dreaming and waking, between day and night. The sky was always gray, rain fell, her senses were muted and muffled as though in a nightmare, it was hard to keep track of what was real. Her orbit shrank: bed to couch to kitchen stool and back again. She ordered groceries online and sanitized them as the internet had instructed. The news was filled with the virus, so she turned it off; her own suffering was so intense and bizarre that she could not summon empathy for others, even the dead.

She was not sure how the hours passed, but they did.

At the emergency room, she had taken a hearing test, sitting in a fabric box with headphones on, the technician staring at her through a thick pane of glass. Hannah was supposed to raise her hand each time she heard a beep or buzz. She did not raise her hand once. The technician shone lights in her ears and measured the bounce of her eardrum with a sharp-edged machine. Everything about her auditory system appeared normal, the cochlea vibrating, the minuscule bones dancing. But the signal was not being transmitted to her brain.

It was the same for her nose. The air was rife, as rife as it had always been, with the molecules cast off by tuna sandwiches and rose petals and underarm sweat, sucked up by Hannah's nostrils with each breath and scanned by her olfactory nerves—and then a malfunction, a lack of communication, the data sitting in somebody's inbox, never passed up the chain.

Taste too. So many chemicals in every kind of food, in water, in metal, in paper, in human skin, all the things Hannah had licked and nibbled in vain over the past few weeks, searching for stimulation. Her taste buds were doing their job, collating and categorizing the data, but her cerebral cortex never got the memo. Her body was healthy, her brain was healthy, but one could not communicate with the other.

This raised a terrifying question: Was she a body, or was she a brain? She had always thought of herself as the former. She had believed that her mind and flesh were inextricable, smelling and tasting and hearing the whole of the world together simultaneously. But now she was beginning to suspect that the real Hannah consisted of nothing more than the three pounds of gray matter tucked in the cocoon of her skull. Her body was a vessel—not the essence of herself but a mere vehicle. The real Hannah was a tiny pilot locked in a windowless, soundproof room, receiving information from the outside world only through a network of nerves.

She did not see. Light entered through her corneas, blazing on her retinae, transfigured by her photoreceptors into electrical impulses, whizzing up the optic nerve to the cockpit. She did not feel. Touch receptors in every inch of her skin sent signals along the bundled fibers of the spinal column. The tiny pilot got these precious messages and knew, from a distance, what lay beyond that protective sheath of bone. Everything Hannah had ever experienced came to her secondhand, delivered through the tubes and wires of her nervous system. One by one, these links were breaking down, leaving her brain, that tiny pilot, marooned, insensate, inside the useless vehicle of her anatomy. What had she lost? What could she yet lose?

°

Her father had died when she was six. She still missed him, a vague ache, though she remembered only a little about him distinctly anymore: his bristly beard, a sneeze like a cannon blast, and the smell of peppermint soap.

Her mother died when Hannah was in college. After the funeral, empty of tears, she and Jo sat up late, drinking wine and arguing about the soul. Her sister believed in heaven. She believed that their parents still existed in some recognizable form, spirits or ghosts or angels, waiting for their daughters.

Hannah did not. She was the analytical one. Like most siblings, she and her sister had grown up both in sync with and in opposition to each other. Jo was a romantic, a daydreamer, hopeful and well-liked. Hannah lived in her senses, in reality, believing what she could perceive. Her parents were gone, but she would remember them. In this way they would live on—in the minds and memories of their loved ones.

That night, she and Jo stayed awake until dawn. Neither of them wanted to face the possibility of sleep, which would lead inevitably to the terrible awakening on the other side, the funeral over, nothing left to plan and prepare for, only the unending, aching absence of their mother. So they sipped their wine, got another bottle.

At one point, Hannah's phone rang. She checked the screen—another grieving relative—and did not answer. Slumped on the couch, Jo snickered. Then she straightened her spine and, in a dead-on imitation of their mother, chirped, "Ring ring!"

"The Mommings!" Hannah gasped, beginning to laugh. "Oh my god, the Mommings!"

She had almost forgotten. Their mother had been sick for years, long enough that she had lost much of what made her unique, including the little quirks her daughters had loved and mimicked throughout their childhood. Certain everyday events—a particular sound, a smell—would elicit specific reactions from their mother, a combination of words and gestures, offered the exact same way every time they happened.

The phone was one of them. Whenever a telephone sounded in her presence, their mother would lengthen her spine like a ballerina and sing out on a high note, "Ring ring!" She would do it in public, in a work meeting, on the bus, anywhere.

Peanut butter was another one. Their mother preferred the oily, organic kind that required stirring, and whenever she opened a new jar she could be found circling her hips in concert with the knife and chanting in a deep bass, "PB for me!"

When Hannah and Jo were young, they had cataloged all the Mommings and could reliably make each other laugh to the point of wetting their pants by imitating them. Now, pouring more wine, they named and incarnated each one.

"Moment of silence," Hannah said, bowing her head solemnly. Their mother had done this in a restaurant whenever there was a crash of dishes hitting the floor.

"Nothing better," Jo purred in honeyed tones, laying her palm on her belly. The taste of chocolate provoked this response and no other.

"Boom," Hannah said, shimmying her palms like a hummingbird's wings. Their mother's reply to thunder—low voice, jazz hands.

Both sisters were crying now. Hannah could not tell if it was the laughter or the grief or the wine.

"Oh, oh," Jo said, leaning forward, spilling from her glass. "We forgot the best one." She mimed a chef's kiss with her fingers and murmured throatily, "Petrichor!"

It was not raining that night, but for a moment Hannah could have sworn she smelled the pungent musk of parched earth melting beneath a drizzle. And for a moment her mother was there with them, standing at the window, gazing out at the night sky, inhaling the first caress of moisture against the dusty ground—the heady aroma rising, suffusing the air. A little miracle, rain after a dry spell. Certain stimuli were so perfect and holy that they required pause and acknowledgment, both gestural and verbal. That was the glorious truth beneath the silliness of the Mommings. Their mother had loved the world so much that it moved her to celebration.

°

Hannah opened her eyes. She closed her eyes. There was no difference.

Reality had been blown out like a candle. Her bedroom was gone. She was in the void of space, she thought, still half awake, blinking and blinking. Absolute emptiness, lacking even the stars.

Hannah could not breathe, and then she could. There was air here, that was lucky. How long would it last, though? One lungful, two?

Her hands grabbed for purchase. She discovered fabric, bunches of it. Some part of the universe remained, then. She sucked in another breath. Air flowed easily into her lungs; it did not seem to be running out. She registered the weight of her own body. So gravity persisted. Hannah herself persisted. She was not floating in outer space—that was her pillow under her nape, damp with sweat. Her calves slid against the mattress. She could feel (but not hear) the anxious knock of her heart.

It was not gray; it was not whiteout or darkness—it was absence, blindness, a woman lying on her back in bed, missing four of her five senses, clutching at the mattress for dear life, tethered to the world by touch alone.

°

Hannah was lost her in own apartment. Shuffling, arms held out like a sleepwalker, toes gripping the carpet, she could not find the front door. Her shoulder bumped against the lamp in the corner. Her fingers brushed the plane of the window. She turned, trying to locate the wall, and barked her shins on the coffee table. The couch was in the wrong place. Everything was in the wrong place.

Hannah collapsed on the floor, cross-legged like a child, and screamed as loud as she could. She felt her throat scrape, tongue rise, pushing the breath out like a bellows; she was making sound she could not hear. Screamed. Screamed.

A tremor beneath her. The door opening, she hoped, or being broken open. And then hands, other people's hands, pulling her to her feet.

°

Probably a hospital. All Hannah knew for certain was the bed, scratchy sheets, a thin pillow, and a needle taped inside the hollow of her elbow, attached to a plastic tube.

Hands came and went. Doctors and nurses, Hannah assumed. She could not access time; she might have been in that bed for hours or days. Weeks, even. She had never before understood the relief of a clock, the simple but vital ability to quantify the vast, shapeless wash of consciousness. Without time, there was only now, and now was unbearable. Hannah groped for her jugular vein and took her own pulse, just to have something to count. The present moment was torture, but the future was coming, heartbeat by heartbeat.

She tried to picture her surroundings, to give herself the

comfort of a mental image at least. She imagined the reek of bleach, the beep of machinery, the murmur of concerned voices. She blinked often, waiting for her sight to come back on like a light switch being flipped. What was more quintessentially human than sight? People said "I see" when they meant "I understand"; it was that primal.

Gradually she came to know the different hands. They changed every so often, according to some tidal rhythm. There were the cold, quick-moving ones, the fingers hard and inhuman. There were the hammy pincers, crushing Hannah's wrist to find her pulse. There were the slim, kindly ones, which announced their presence in the room each time by squeezing Hannah's toes through the sheets, then tapping her elbow in a friendly way before examining her IV port and taking her vitals. All the hands wore rubber gloves. Every so often they would do something shocking, like injecting Hannah's shoulder with a solution that burned like venom. Once a clever, nimble hand settled in the cup of Hannah's palm and began to change shape, kicking its fingers like a Rockette's legs. Sign language, she guessed. Helen Keller, she remembered. The hand contorted against her skin for a while as Hannah said aloud, over and over, "I don't understand." Eventually the fingers went limp and withdrew.

Sometimes the hands urged her out of bed and pulled her limbs this way and that like a child playing with a doll, stripping off her gown and replacing it with an identical one. They steered her into the bathroom at intervals, controlling her path with a viselike grip on her upper arm. They bathed her with a rough sponge. They gave her trays of food—presumably it was food—which she chewed and swallowed obediently. No smell, no taste, and she could not even see it. She scanned the surface with fluttering fingertips: a carton of milk, a fruit cup, a sandwich. Her tongue, no longer a subtle sensor but a blunt instrument, added few details: some kind of condiment soaking the bread, maybe mayonnaise, maybe mustard, and in the middle a mysterious lukewarm substance that could have been deli meat or fried egg.

And then, without warning, a new hand—gentle, with a dry palm—slipped into hers. A pulse of recognition. Until that moment, Hannah had not believed that she would know her sister's touch. She had never paid attention to the tenor and quality of Jo's hands. Why would she? But she was certain—as certain as though she could see Jo's rosebud mouth, smell her lavender shampoo, hear her husky voice, taste the salt tears that flowed down her own cheeks.

She gripped Jo's palm in both of hers, and her sister responded in kind.

°

Nothing came next. Nothingness, rather. One morning, or afternoon, it was impossible to tell, Hannah lay with two fingers against her throat, counting her pulse. It was daytime, she thought, because of the heat on one side of her face, probably from a window, sunlight through glass, though it could have been an electric light, a trick. Hands came, taking away the lunch tray, adjusting the sheets with a tug and tuck, and patting Hannah's shoulder in a reassuring manner—or maybe not, maybe it was just a tactile good-bye, offering no comfort, only communication.

The nurse's hands left, and then the heat. Had the sun dipped behind a cloud?

And what about the bed, that reliable presence, the last sure thing in the universe, pressing always against her back? Where had it gone?

Her fingers still lay against her jugular, but there was no pulse. She could not feel her throat with her hand; she could not feel her hand with her throat.

She had the sensation of falling, as in a dream, a lurch into empty space.

°

During that time, that timeless time, Hannah was locked inside her own flesh. Her internal sensors still functioned, but her skin, the largest organ in the body, as she had learned in grade school, provided no information. When she patted the bed, her finger bones spread apart, the muscles inside her palm tightened, but there was no answering touch from the mattress. When she sucked in a breath, she felt her lungs open, but when she blew out hard through her nose, there was no corresponding tickle against her lips. She had evidence of her own existence, but nothing beyond her body could be verified. The tiny pilot was marooned in ghastly solitude.

The many hands of the doctors and nurses, even her own sister, had abandoned her. Probably they were still there, unfelt, restraining her as she thrashed, trying to connect with something, to launch herself out of bed and slam into the floor, to find the wall with her fist; she would break bone if it meant contact. Maybe they strapped her down. Certainly they sedated her. She could feel it happen, the syrupy, somnolent warmth spreading through her bloodstream from one shoulder.

Sleep was a balm, the same as ever; her senses bloomed there. She dreamed of sitting in her father's lap as a child, scraping her forehead against his beard. She dreamed of baking with her mother, side by side in the kitchen, licking the cookie dough off the spoon in flagrant disregard of doctors' recommendations. "If this is what kills me," her mother said, "tell them I died doing what I loved." Hannah dreamed of running down a hill with Jo, young and strong, breathless with glee. She dreamed of the icy cocoon of the MRI machine. "Here's the problem," the doctor said, handing her a scan of her brain, a translucent sheet of black that showed the chalky bowl of her skull, which held not lobes and neurons but a doll-sized figure, its bones shining white, its posture contorted, waving in panic, signaling to be rescued.

Waking up was an emergency, every time. Hannah shrieked without sound and flailed without contact. "Let me die," she roared silently. "Kill me!" But they did not, would not. They only sedated her again and again, lulling her back into the warm bath of sleep, where the solace of memory and dream awaited her, overlapping and melting into one—dreams as true as memories, memories as immersive as dreams.

°

On a balmy, sun-swept morning, Jo enters the hospital for the first time in months. Vaccinated and boosted, she is no longer in danger from the virus, so the CDC says. Still, she wears a mask, mostly out of habit. For months, as hundreds of thousands of people died across the country, Jo donned a mask every morning, then slipped masks onto the delicate faces of her children, checked the straps, and pinched the folds of foil tight over their noses, as regular as prayer.

At the welcome desk, a pimply young man takes her temperature by scanning her wrist with a laser.

"I'm going to see my sister," Jo tells him. He nods absently.

For months, the hospital has been besieged, running out of

beds, running out of ventilators. No visitors have been allowed in, not even the partners of women in labor. Jo has called and called, annoying the nurses, who have more important things to do than report the same thing every day: "No change, she's sedated now."

Sometimes Jo wished that she could be sedated too. When she woke in the morning already counting the hours until she could go back to bed, when the death count was always the headline of the day, when her husband was too sick to stand up and her children were too antsy to sit still for remote learning, when Jo was slated to lead virtual meetings while her youngest was running around naked, heedless of the camera on her mother's laptop, when the house descended into such an alarming state of filth that Jo would have called child services had she encountered it at someone else's place, when her boss was on a ventilator, when her father-in-law died of the virus, when the world shrank and darkened to a pinpoint, no light at the end of the tunnel, only more of the same, absent of joy, absent of hope, Jo needed her sister. So much happened while Hannah lay in the hospital, more alone, it seemed, than any human has ever been.

At the door to her sister's room, Jo pauses. Not knowing what else to do, she knocks. She is not sure what she will encounter inside—a wasted shell, riddled with bedsores, prematurely aged, fingernails overlong, hands gnarled? How much of Hannah is left?

There is a nurse in the room, changing the IV bag. Jo was not expecting to see anyone else. She waves, and he waves back, dressed in bright-blue scrubs.

Oh, Hannah. As thin as she was in her childhood, "all bones," their mother used to say. Elbows wider than her upper arms. Her beesting breasts, so like Jo's, have shrunk to mere suggestion, a prepubescent swell. Someone has been washing her hair, which shines and curls around her throat, oddly luxurious. Her expression is peaceful. She is pale, so pale, as ashen and still as a porcelain doll.

"How is she?" Jo asks.

The nurse shrugs. "There might have been some new activity on the last scan. I don't know. She's not usually one of mine. I'll tell Dr. Alves you're here."

He rustles out of the room.

Jo takes a seat by the bed. She entwines her fingers through Hannah's, hoping against hope for an answering squeeze. Last time, Hannah clung to her like a lifeline. This time, however, her sister's hand is limp, and Jo must make do with the reassuring fact of bodily warmth, proof of life.

"It's time to wake up," Jo says. "You have to wake up now."

In truth, the whole world is waking up. Jo's children are back in school—thrilled to be dropped off each morning, waving goodbye like teenagers heading off to a rave. Her husband is back at the office, thank god. Jo loves to miss him, to miss the kids. Absence is necessary to affection, she understands now. Her work has stayed remote, which she does not mind. After school, she takes her children to the park, the zoo, the beach. Outdoors is better, the CDC says. The virus is not gone, the CDC says. Before the pandemic, Jo did not even know what the acronym stood for, but now she quotes the CDC's pronouncements in everyday conversations, as though they are old friends. She cries often these days, sometimes from relief at seeing her children laugh on the playground, shaking off the caution they have absorbed like oxygen during the pandemic, and sometimes due to an emotion Jo cannot quite name—a kind of uncurling, the tears she could not shed when things were at their worst now finally released.

One day Hannah will learn all these things. She will learn what she missed. Her senses will return, Jo is sure. She cannot contemplate the other possibility, the outcome that is not recovery. One day, she and her sister will fall into each other's arms again. They will leave this hospital together, stepping into the world with the raw astonishment of newborns, overwhelmed and delighted by every sensation, the flicker of sunlight through the leaves, the distant smoke of a barbecue, the hiss of bicycle wheels on pavement. Changed by what they have endured, stripped down to their essentials, they will revel in the simple, honest gift of the world the way it has always been.

Jo wipes her eyes, then goes to the window and opens it, letting in a gust of clean air. The sky is papered over with gray, the wind humid and slow. A droplet strikes the glass. It has not rained in weeks, a rare dry spell that appears to be drawing to a close. The clouds darken, coalescing.

There is a sound from the room behind her. Three sharp sniffs. Jo recognizes the noise as one of her sister's unique quirks. Hannah would do that, *sniff sniff sniff*, when the aroma of pancakes wafted up the stairs, when their mother wore too much perfume, when their father brought home flowers as a surprise. Not one, not two, always three inhalations, canine in their quickness.

Jo turns, hardly daring to believe. Hannah's eyes are closed, but one hand—yes, one hand has begun to twitch. The fingers swivel like the fronds of an anemone in a strong current. The elbow bends.

Another droplet smacks against the glass. The smell is overpowering, mud and stone, promise and renewal. As Jo watches, trembling all over, her sister lifts a hand to her mouth. Hannah touches her thumb against her fingertips and unfolds the palm.

Her muscles are atrophied, but the gesture is unmistakable, a perfect imitation of their mother's joyous, reverent chef's kiss.

And then Hannah speaks, her voice weak, just one word. But Jo cannot hear it over the roar of the sky opening, the sudden, wild music of the rain.

The Body Farm

It began with a letter. At least, that's when it began for me. I worked the night shift and came home weary. The house was dark and silent when I pulled up in front. The sun rose bloody that morning, as though it knew what was coming. Heavy clouds soaked up the crimson light like a bandage over an injury.

I entered the house on tiptoe, listening for movement. You weren't awake yet, my beautiful boys, four years old then. The mail lay scattered around my feet, pushed through the slot in the door sometime before dawn. I gathered it all up, noting absently that among the bills and catalogs was an electric-blue envelope of thick card stock, addressed to Beatrice. A yowl signaled the arrival of the cats, the only ones awake, three night-black silhouettes twining around my ankles. I stacked the mail on the kitchen counter with the blue envelope on top. I didn't give it another thought as I went upstairs.

Beatrice was sound asleep in our king-sized bed in her usual pose, flat on her belly with her knees bent and shins lifted in the air. I have never seen anyone else sleep like that. Once I took pictures to show the friends who did not believe me, but Beatrice made me delete them.

I went to check on you. Technically you had separate rooms, but you always slept together. That morning you were tangled in a heap of sand-brown limbs in Theo's bed. I lingered in the doorway, watching you dream, Lucas's feet twitching, Theo snoring delicately. The sky brightened by the second. Soon your eyes would open at precisely the same moment, and at once you would both be talking, updating each other on your dreams, wondering what to have for breakfast, and continuing your ongoing, interminable debate about which one of you the cats loved more. There is no foggy transition between states of mind for children that age: one minute out cold, the next entirely awake.

As I stood in the doorway, the exhaustion of my long night fell over me. I staggered back down the hall and collapsed into bed beside my wife, dozing off as the house woke around me.

°

You did not know much about my work then. This was fine by me. If asked, you would both report that I did "science"—Lucas thickening the *s*'s with his adorable lisp. The specifics of my job were not important to you. You were scarcely out of your toddlerhood, sapling-skinny boys with identical crooked grins. Your existence revolved around the central hub of our house, our yard, your toys, and the cats. You knew that Beatrice (Mommy) stayed home with you, reading books about dinosaurs, making play dough from scratch, and kissing away your "boo-boos," real or imagined. You knew that I (Mama) went to work and then came back again. What I did out there in the world, away from you, was inconsequential and vague. Your biggest concern about my job was that I always smelled like antiseptic when I returned. You both refused to get in my lap until I'd been home for a few hours, enough time to accrue the odor of cats and curry from dinner and a residue of Beatrice's perfume.

At that time, I had worked at the Body Farm for nearly ten years. The official name is the Anthropological Research Center, but nobody ever calls it that. From the outside, the place is intentionally anonymous. A flat concrete building. A bland, unspecific name. There's nothing else nearby—no offices, certainly nothing residential, just a blank strip of highway forty miles north of Lyle, Iowa, our hometown.

Visitors to the Body Farm are limited to the occasional police detective or forensic anthropologist. Sometimes teenagers from Lyle sneak over at night to see if the stories are true, but these would-be oglers inevitably find themselves stymied by the high concrete walls and motion-activated lights. Honestly, the smell alone is usually enough to deter them.

Behind the walls, the Body Farm comprises forty acres. The area was chosen for its variety: a stretch of forest, a stream, a meadow, zones of unbroken sunshine and perpetual shadow, a wetland, and a dry, high slope—as great a range of types of terrain as can conceivably be found in a single biome.

During that fateful winter, this idyllic stretch of midwestern greenery was inhabited by 127 dead people.

The purpose of the Anthropological Research Center is simple. Within its walls, corpses decay in every conceivable way, and my colleagues and I observe and record it all. How will a body deteriorate if we bury it in a shallow grave on a windy hillside? Will the data change if the corpse is nude, half dressed, wrapped in plastic, or slathered in sunscreen? What is the exact, mathematical progression of larval growth? What happens to the internal organs after four days, seven days, two weeks? What happens to the bones?

New corpses are always coming in. Thousands of people have signed up to donate their bodies to the Anthropological Research Center after death. (My own will stipulates the same.) Whenever a new cadaver arrives, the other researchers and I debate where to place it. Our aim is to study decomposition in every possible locale: riverbank, direct sun, partial shade, tall weeds, swamp. Each season of the year brings new information. Corpses are different from day to night, winter to summer—there's always more research to be done. Should the cadaver be stripped naked this time? Should it be injected with heroin or OxyContin? Should it be hanged from a tree? What kind of data will be most beneficial? What gaps currently exist in our research? Once the corpse has been laid to rest—perhaps buried in sand, perhaps floating in the creek—its decay will be charted until nothing remains.

I'm one of eight on the team. Georgina is our botanist. Hyo specializes in fungi and bacteria—"the slime lady," she calls herself. Kenneth trains law enforcement officers in the science of decomposition; they come from all over the world to learn at his feet. Luis focuses on microbes, a new and fascinating field, with groundbreaking applications for antibacterial medicines and anticancer chemotherapeutics. Jackson and Cal, both MDs, share the study of the corpses themselves. They dissect and photograph festering skin, weigh liquefied organs, slice up bones, and keep samples of blood at every stage of putrefaction. Then there's LaTanya, who has the most difficult job of all. She serves as liaison, publicist, spokesperson, and official witness, testifying in court cases on behalf of us all and translating our data into digestible, user-friendly language.

I am the Body Farm's entomologist. I spend my days among beetles and blowflies. I know the life cycles of pyralid moths and cheese skippers. In cold weather, I check for winter gnats and coffin flies. At a glance, I can tell the difference between species of insect eggs. The shelves in my office contain preserved larvae at every stage of maturation, lovingly coated in chemicals that won't dehydrate the samples or change their color. My drawers hold trays of beetles, bright as pennies, and velvety moths arranged by size.

It's disgusting work. But the grotesqueness of the Body Farm stands in direct proportion to its worth. Months, sometimes years after a corpse has been found, my colleagues and I can pinpoint the time of death, cause of death, manner and likely location of death, and more, offering a cornucopia of distasteful but salient facts. Killers have been convicted on the strength of our research.

The dead can't speak for themselves. The story of how someone died—and, even more important, what happened to their body afterward—has fallen to me and the other researchers to uncover. I help put away "bad guys," as you would call them. I name the nameless. Too many children die at the hands of a parent. The number one cause of death for pregnant women is homicide, usually by an intimate partner. How can a person walk around knowing these things and not participate in a solution? I get answers for the bereaved. I reunite the dead with their loved ones, bringing anonymous bodies, badly decomposed, home to the family who declared them missing months earlier. The dead can't speak, but insect activity communicates loud and clear.

Still, I do not talk about my work with most people, and

certainly not with my children. I have never told you anything about the Body Farm, my beloved twins—not until now, writing this letter, my confession.

°

On the day the blue envelope came, I woke with a foul taste in my mouth. Working the night shift always leaves me disoriented and bad-tempered. My colleagues and I take turns handling this unpleasant but vital task.

I climbed out of bed and washed my face in the bathroom sink. There was a bang, and one of you—I could not immediately tell which—dashed through the door and slammed into my legs. I let myself be climbed like a tree, then taken by the hand and led downstairs, where a glorious mess greeted me.

Given the bitter wind howling among the rafters, Beatrice had decided that this was a good day to make bread from scratch. She always spends the winter baking, chasing away the midwestern chill with the warmth of the oven and the comforting aroma of yeast and sugar. Flour coated the kitchen floor and hung in the air in a fine mist. Both of you were covered in it too, your curls powdered like the wigs of British lords. Music jangled from the radio. Scuffling around in the snowfall of flour, you two were playing the mirror game, imitating each other so closely that I could not tell who was leading and who was following.

At the counter, Beatrice kneaded a sticky lump of dough. A smear of flour painted one cheek. I leaned in for a kiss and realized that her eyes were bloodshot and swollen. She had been crying.

°

She and I did not have a chance to talk until your nap time. You were on the verge of giving up this relic from your toddler years. When Beatrice was on her own with you, she often let you skip it rather than risk a dual tantrum. I, however, intended to maintain nap time for as long as possible, until you were in college, hopefully.

I set you both in my lap in the rocking chair in Theo's room and read the dullest, most repetitive nursery rhymes I could find. Against your will, you yawned, your heads drooping and rising again, each blink slower and more prolonged than the last. I nestled your precious bodies, limp in my arms, beneath Theo's blanket. Your faces inches apart. Each of you breathing in the air the other had just exhaled.

Then I went downstairs and found Beatrice at the dining room table, her head in her hands, staring at the electric-blue envelope.

I sat beside her. I rubbed her back. She was crying again, no sobs, just a wellspring of tears that seemed to ooze from somewhere deep down.

"I don't know what to do," she whispered.

I picked up the envelope and pulled out the note inside—the same color and weight, azure card stock. Two words had been scrawled in ballpoint pen:

FOUND YOU

Beatrice wiped the tears away with her palm. "What are we going to do?" she asked, still in that throaty whisper. "What can we possibly do?"

I thought about burning the note or running it through the

shredder in the office. But instead I put it carefully back in the envelope, preserving the evidence.

°

And now I must go further back. At the age of four, you were not particularly interested in how your parents had come to be together. You knew that having two mommies was slightly unusual but not unheard of. Domingo, a boy in your class at the preschool you attended a few mornings a week, had two daddies, and another girl lived with her grandparents, no mom or dad in the picture. Your teacher made sure to read books that highlighted all the different shapes a family can take.

For my part, I'm a gold-star lesbian and proud of it—no boyfriends ever, not even in my childhood, when all it took to become affianced to a classmate was a shove on the playground. I like the term *sexual orientation* (as opposed to *sexual preference*, the problematic phrase used in my youth) because it so closely mirrors my own experience. I was born with a compass in my chest that points truth north. There was never any question about which way the needle would lead me.

Beatrice, however, identifies as bisexual and primarily dated men before we met. That's fine, nothing wrong with men, they just aren't my personal cup of tea. But among her sensitive poets and tattooed drummers, Beatrice happened upon a sociopath. Or maybe that's the wrong diagnosis—I don't know, I'd never met the guy, not then, anyway. A bad egg, a ticking time bomb, pick your metaphor.

They dated in college, long before Beatrice and I found each other. I've seen pictures of Emerson: a corn-fed white boy, strapping and tall, with a receding chin. Beatrice never loved him. She was young, sowing her wild oats and reveling in being out of her parents' house. After one single evening together, this man told her he planned to marry her. He told her he'd been waiting for her all his life.

She has never disclosed very much about that time. Even now, it's hard for her to talk about. Emerson consumed her college years—I do know that. She stayed with him because he made it clear he'd kill himself if she left. No more wild oats. Four years of Emerson walking her to every class and panicking if she didn't answer his calls. He bought her necklaces and bracelets and pouted if she didn't wear them, which made her feel, she told me, like a pet with a collar. He pleaded with her to leave her dorm and move in with him off campus. She was able to hold him off only by blaming her parents, claiming they'd revoke her tuition if she did such a thing, though truthfully they wouldn't have cared either way. In photographs, Emerson is always touching Beatrice, one arm snaked around her waist, sometimes holding her braid in his fist, while she flashes a fixed, panicked smile that does not reach her eyes.

After graduation she found the wherewithal to end it. She took a job in the Colorado mountains, miles from their New England campus. She did not tell Emerson a thing about it until the day of her flight. Then he wept, pleaded, and threatened suicide. He outlined all the plans he'd made for her life—marriage, dogs, babies, nothing she'd ever consented to. When Beatrice held firm, Emerson opened the window of her third-floor dorm room, now bare, all her things packed and shipped already. He flung one leg over the sill, yelling that he'd throw himself out if she left him.

This time, however, she was prepared. She called 911, and Emerson spent the night in a hospital on an involuntary psychiatric hold while Beatrice flew across the country, believing she was finally free.

°

We had a security system installed at the house the next day. You were both ecstatic to have workmen clomping up and down the stairs and looming on ladders outside the windows. Nothing this exciting had happened to you since a fire truck came down the street the previous afternoon. Shrieking and pointing, you shadowed the workmen all morning while Beatrice attempted to nap—it had been a sleepless night for her—and I guarded the bedroom door, keeping you out.

At nap time I tried to sedate you with fairy tales, but my plan backfired. You are growing, always growing up before my eyes. Suddenly you could follow the plot, whereas only a few weeks earlier you would've been interrupting me constantly to ask unrelated questions about the nature of time or farts. Now, however, the story caught your attention, and you sat up straighter in my lap. Your eyes shone. "And then what happened?" you each whispered at intervals. I ended up reading fairy tale after fairy tale right through what should've been your nap time, all damsels in distress and armor-clad knights and a happy ending, maybe with a moral thrown in.

My shift started at three that day. I did not feel right abandoning my family in this moment of crisis, but Beatrice rose from our bed and said she'd be fine, you'd all be fine. The alarm system was armed now, and she had let a few friends know what was going on. They'd be dropping by and checking in throughout the day. She promised to keep you both at home. She promised to text me instantly if anything untoward happened.

In the parking lot behind the Body Farm, I took my vial of peppermint oil from the glove compartment and dabbed a few drops, as always, beneath my nose. Over the course of the workday, I would become inured to the stench of decay, but the first wave was invariably overwhelming.

I passed LaTanya's office on the way to my own. She was on the phone, leaning back in her chair and speaking in her most soothing customer service voice: "I understand, but that's not information we have. I can't help you. I'm happy to share what we do know at this point. However . . ."

She caught my eye, made her fingers into a gun, and shot herself in the head. I laughed and moved on down the hall. I did not envy LaTanya, always on the phone, on the go, consulting with overworked police officers and blustering district attorneys. Every murder case is an emergency, while our work remains gradual and complex and painstaking. Decomposition can't be rushed.

Stepping onto the grounds of the Body Farm was like teleporting to some echelon of the underworld. An elderly woman lay swaddled in a heavy tarp, only one hand visible, curling limply upward, not yet touched by maggots. A teenage boy had been rolled in a pile of leaves, naked from the waist down, his limbs smeared with mud. Corpses in direct sunlight. Corpses on the riverbank. Some were fresh, still recognizably human. Others had decomposed to the point of genetic regression, returning to an amoebic state, pink and gelatinous, perfuming the air.

The afternoon was icy, the sky frosted over with pale clouds. Leafless trees surged in a stiff breeze. I wore my usual uniform—latex gloves, a surgical mask, and cotton clothes that did not retain odors as much as polyester. On the hill lay my first stop of the day: a twenty-two-year-old woman, dressed in jeans and a neon-green T-shirt, half-buried in soil. She had been there for six days, and her organs had melted into soup. Her torso appeared sunken, the ground beneath her stained and damp. Her brain, I knew, was already gone. The bacteria in the mouth worked quickly after death, devouring the palate, then everything else.

I opened my tool kit and took out my forceps. There were several maggot masses. I collected a few samples from each area, then checked the temperature of the flesh; the insects' bustling generated its own heat. I plucked up the wriggling bodies with a practiced motion, dropping each one into a separate jar. As always, I kept half alive and killed half immediately, preserving them for later inspection.

Next I studied the area around the body. Since the corpse lay on a slope, some of its fluids had seeped downhill. Maggots always follow fluids. I dug through the leaf litter with a sterile tool. Insect activity is a fairly reliable measure of time of death, though many things can alter the data: if the body has been moved, kept in extreme cold or heat, or covered with fabric or plastic. Part of my job is to think of every possible factor that could alter the timeline, study each one, and keep records.

Not long ago, I discovered that cocaine in the bloodstream of a corpse will supercharge the maggots, accelerating their growth and maturation, whereas barbiturates have the opposite effect, lulling them into lethargy. A serial killer was convicted on the strength of my data. That's right—a *serial* killer. LaTanya testified on behalf of our team, as she always does, offering glossy photographs and her patented brand of wry humor to put the jury at ease. The result: multiple life sentences without the possibility of parole.

°

Emerson began stalking Beatrice the moment her plane touched down in Colorado. That was not the word she would have used then, however. It was a less enlightened time, lacking the language to describe the many kinds of mental and physical violence people can inflict on one another. If your boyfriend followed you everywhere you went and never let you out of his sight, that was puppy love. If an ex called you long-distance hundreds of times and bombarded you with bizarre gifts and death threats, that was just the natural expression of his heartbreak.

Beatrice stayed in Colorado for two years. She was content there, working at a coffee shop and daydreaming idly about getting an MFA in visual art or theater, something creative. She liked the clear mountain air, the hiking trails, and the breathtaking vista outside her living room window.

Emerson remained in Massachusetts on the campus where they'd been happy together, at least in his mind. Most days he called Beatrice dozens of times, leaving ragged, rambling voicemails. He sent presents at least once a week—a teddy bear with a heart on its chest, a charm bracelet, nothing that suited her taste at all. She figured that eventually he'd wear himself out. Surely he would find a new object for his affections. Every now and then, she decided it was time to reason with him and answered the phone, leading to hour-long arguments that left her raw and shaken.

She has a good heart, your mother. She did not realize that each time she gave in, she was training Emerson to be persistent. Not that I'm blaming the victim, you understand—he should have stopped the first time she said no. Always remember that. And Beatrice meant well; she had compassion for Emerson, no matter how much he hurt her. But if he called fifty times in a row before she answered the phone, he learned that it took fifty-one attempts to force her to submit. If he sent her ten cutesy stuffed animals without reply, then sent another and received a text saying *Please don't give me any more gifts*, he learned that eleven unwanted presents would trigger a response.

Back then, Beatrice still believed she could set boundaries if she just explained herself well enough. Perhaps she hadn't yet been clear, she thought. This is the danger of being a decent person in this complicated world, someone with a functioning conscience. She could not imagine the malevolent mentality of a brute like Emerson. All he wanted was contact, and every time he got it—even if it was "No" or "Stop" or "You're scaring me"—his desire was met and his resolve strengthened.

Beatrice probably would have stayed in Colorado, and she and I might never have met, and you two would never have been born, if Emerson had not turned up on her doorstep one evening, sweaty and disheveled, suitcase in hand.

I wasn't there, of course, but I can picture it clearly. Beatrice has told me the story many times. He tried to push past her into the house. He told her he was sick of "doing long distance" and it was time for them to try living together. Her "little independent phase" was getting him down.

Beatrice was almost too stunned to respond. She managed to bar the door with her foot, keeping him on the porch. He was acting as though they'd never broken up, as though the events of the past two years had slipped his mind. She could not tell if it was a performance or if he really believed they were still together and imagined that she would let him into her home, into her bed.

"Let's order pizza," he said. "The plane food was awful."

"You have to leave," she gasped out. She did not even know how to argue with him—he was so far from reality as she understood it that there was no common ground on which to stand.

There followed an incoherent shouting match, him declaring

that she was acting childish and crazy, her sobbing that he wasn't her boyfriend anymore. Eventually one of her neighbors called the police. Beatrice felt a swoop of hope when she saw the red and blue lights dancing off the buildings. She still imagined then that the law could help in situations like this.

Two officers clomped onto the porch, both men. Emerson spoke first, explaining that he'd flown across the country to see his girlfriend of six years and for some reason she wasn't letting him in. The men looked at Beatrice with their eyebrows raised. This would prove to be a tactic of Emerson's: if he could establish his own version of events with enough confidence right off the bat, anything Beatrice said to contradict him, no matter how true, seemed dubious to their audience. Faltering, she mumbled that she and Emerson broke up years ago. He shouldn't be here, she said.

"I brought you this." He reached into his suitcase and handed her a wrapped package. "Open it."

"I don't want it," she said. "I don't want anything from you. You need to leave."

Emerson threw a glance at the officers, who nodded back sympathetically. He tore open the wrapping himself, revealing a lacquered plaque with HOME SWEET HOME etched into the wood. Beatrice has always hated that kind of schmaltz, of course. Anything in the vicinity of *Live, Laugh, Love* leaves her cold. She believes that people who need placards on the wall to remind themselves about affection or comfort or joy are deeply unhappy. In the past, she had said as much to Emerson. Did he listen to her? Ever?

"You have no idea who I am," she said, with dawning horror.

"I think it's nice," one of the officers said, bristling on Emerson's behalf.

Eventually Beatrice made it clear to everyone that Emerson wasn't going to enter her house that night. The policemen offered to drive him to a hotel a few blocks away. It wasn't technically allowed, but they obviously felt such sympathy for this poor jilted Romeo that they broke procedure to give him a ride.

In the morning, Emerson showed up at the coffee shop where Beatrice worked. He followed her to the grocery store on her lunch break and critiqued her purchases. He introduced himself to her coworkers as her long-distance boyfriend. They were all surprised they'd never heard of him, accosting Beatrice in the break room to ask for details. Hadn't she been dating the clerk from the Taco Bell a few months back? Was she cheating on Emerson? Or did they have an open relationship?

Two weeks later, Beatrice moved to Maine.

°

After Emerson's letter came, things were fraught for all of us. Beatrice flinched every time her phone rang. One of the cats tripped our new alarm system in the middle of the night and Beatrice seemed to forget how to breathe, wheezing and choking beside me as I threw off the blankets and ran to investigate.

The two of you were affected as well. Four-year-olds are as sensitive as tuning forks, picking up and echoing the vibrations of their parents. You each responded differently—Lucas by sobbing at imaginary injuries and ending each day with dozens of colorful Band-Aids on every limb, Theo by charging around the house with a plastic spear and cardboard armor, fighting pillows and shadows and the poor cats, who took to crouching on top of the tallest furniture.

And I was angry. I don't know that I've ever felt such sustained, slow-burning rage. Teeth gnashing. Fists clenched. Even my dreams were fiery and bloodstained.

Our friends rallied around us, offering to babysit or spend the night on the couch. Several of them made noises about involving the police, but Beatrice, with the weary resignation of painful experience, explained that the electric-blue note wasn't signed, and anyway it didn't contain a threat or anything actionable. All her previous restraining orders against Emerson—one in Maine, one in Virginia, and one in Texas—had lapsed.

So there was nothing we could do but wait, all of us, Beatrice terrified, me furious, and both of you keyed up. Tender Lucas. Warlike Theo. We did not know what would come next. It was like waiting for a meteor to fall to earth without having a clue when or where it would land.

In the past, Emerson had sent texts, selfies, handwritten sonnets with improper scansion, and an engagement ring in a velvet box. Whenever Beatrice changed her phone number, he eventually discovered the new one. He lurked outside her previous apartments in his car, smiling up at her window. He sent flowers to each of her workplaces. Once he slashed her tires. He no longer claimed to be suicidal, not since she'd had him involuntarily committed. Sometimes he threatened her, but never in any way she could substantiate to others. He might send an anonymous note saying he'd kill her if she didn't stop sleeping with that trashy line cook from the diner. He might leave a knife on her porch steps. He stayed just on the legal side of things. She couldn't prove he'd been the one to slash her tires. She couldn't explain to the officer behind the desk why it was so alarming that he'd sent her a diamond ring.

Each time she moved to a new town, a new state, there would be a grace period before Emerson caught up. Beatrice could breathe again. She could begin to hope that the last time might have been the last time. Maybe he wouldn't discover her new locale. Maybe she had finally proven to be too much trouble for him to pursue. She would find a job and rent an apartment. She might tumble into a crush, into bed with someone new. She even dated men, which to me seems rather like visiting grizzly territory after having been mauled by a bear. As time passed, she would relax, sleeping through the night again, not looking over her shoulder every time she turned a corner.

And then the call, the knock on the door, the bouquet sent to her desk at work. Can you imagine her fear and dismay? I couldn't, not until it happened under my roof.

°

At the Body Farm, I sat at my desk with the lights off, spinning in circles in my wheelie chair. Would the meteor strike today, while I was out of the house? Armando and Joe—longtime friends of ours, a dear married couple in their sixties—were spending the morning with you and Beatrice, teaching you to grow herbs in pots, which could then be transferred to the garden when spring came. But I wasn't sure this was sufficient protection. Joe was frail, requiring a cane to walk more than a few feet, and I didn't like the bulbous appearance of Armando's nose lately, the distinct thickening and reddening caused by alcohol overuse. Sometimes it's hard for me not to look for a cause of death in the making.

A knock at my office door startled me. Hyo stepped into the room, holding a canister of specimen jars. Her expression was quizzical, her eyes as bright as a bird's.

"Let's go," she said. "It's a perfect morning."

"What?"

She leaned over and flipped on the light. "How long have you been sitting here? Come on, there's work to be done."

"Right."

"You okay?"

"Yes. Fine. It's nothing."

We strolled down the hill, both of us in down coats and latex gloves and surgical masks, muffling our voices as we chatted. We had worked together for years, and our small talk was as comfortable as breathing: slime, larvae, mildew, blowflies. Hyo sported a sunflower-yellow shower cap, incongruous in the wintry air. In theory, this would keep the smell of death out of her dark mane. I wore my own hair pixie-short. Easier to scrub clean at the end of the day.

As we walked, I was surprised by my ability to perform normalcy. My mind was not there, on the grounds; it was back home, hovering around my family like an avenging angel. And yet I made notes on my clipboard and conversed casually with Hyo about the humidity, the cloud cover, and the corpse lying in grass: a man in his thirties, his face melted like candle wax. Despite the cold, phorid flies droned around his torso. Hyo leaned over him and began gathering specimens. I watched her label each jar in her tiny scribble before dropping it into her bag. Beneath her mask, her cheeks were pink from the chill.

"Remember when we first started?" she said. "You always used to put the bodies on their bellies. You didn't like to see their faces."

"That was a long time ago."

She brushed a stray lock of hair off her cheek with her forearm. We were all conditioned never to touch our faces with our gloved hands out in the field.

"I was worse than you," she said. "I couldn't use the word

murder. Remember? I'd say 'dispatched' like we were in a Jane Austen novel."

I put on an upper-crust British accent. "This fellow was dispatched a week ago. The bloat is quite severe. His testicles have swollen to the size of a cricket ball."

Hyo laughed. "God, how things change. I've got no problem with it now. Murder, murder, murder."

She moved up the hill, toward the next corpse on her list. I stood still, the word echoing in my mind.

°

At three in the morning, Beatrice's cell phone rang. I heard her turn over in bed and fumble around on the nightstand, knocking the lampshade against the wall.

"Hello?" she muttered into the pillow.

With a lurch, she bolted upright. I did the same. Even in the dark bedroom I could see that her irises were ringed with white all the way around.

"How did you get this number?" she asked. Then, quickly, she placed the phone on the blanket between us and put it on speaker.

"—always do," a man's voice was saying. A reedy tenor. Clipped consonants. I reached for Beatrice's hand and laced her fingers through mine.

"Did you get my letter?" Emerson asked.

"I did. How long have you been in the area?" She gripped my hand so tightly that I felt my bones scrape together.

"Just got here," he said lazily. "You know, I've come to really enjoy this game we play. The thrill of the chase never gets old."

"It's not a game," Beatrice said. "I thought this time—"

"You thought I wouldn't find you? I'll always find you, honey."

She shuddered convulsively at the endearment. I moved closer, laying my cheek against her shoulder.

"You got *married*," he said. "You changed your *name*. I liked your old name better."

There was an unsettling singsong quality to his speech. I wondered if his voice was always pitched so high or if emotion had altered it.

"I'm going to hang up now," he said. "I'd rather talk to you when you're alone."

"Are you saying—" she began, but he was gone. She checked that the call had ended, then turned her phone off. She tucked it under a pillow, shook her head as though disagreeing with herself, got to her feet, and paced. Finally she carried her phone into the bathroom, holding it between two fingers like a grimy scrap of garbage, and shoved it into a cabinet among the hand towels. Only then, it seemed, could she be sure that no part of Emerson was present.

"Is he watching us somehow?" she murmured to me, climbing back into bed, her eyes darting everywhere. "Is that what he meant? 'When you're alone,' he said. How did he know?"

I stroked her hair out of her face. "He made an educated guess. He assumed I'd be in bed with you. Where else would I be? He's just trying to scare you."

Privately, however, I vowed to check and recheck all our new security cameras. Maybe I'd get one of those bug sweepers I'd seen on spy shows. Who knew what this madman was capable of? The rage burned in my chest like a coal.

"It's never going to stop." Beatrice buried her face in my throat, wetting my skin with her tears.

°

Ours was a whirlwind courtship. Fleeing Texas, Beatrice moved to Iowa. We met at a summer barbecue hosted by one of her new coworkers. Within the week we were engaged. My queer friends teased me for hitching the U-Haul to the Subaru with such stereotypical swiftness, but nothing about this love felt ordinary to me.

I'd always maintained a distance in relationships before. My work made romance tricky. I would wait a reasonable period of time before telling each new girlfriend about my job, hoping first to enchant them with my wiles and sexual prowess. Usually they broke it off as soon as they learned the truth. Other times they stuck around for a short while but urged me constantly to get into another field, something normal, not quite so horrifying.

It has always been difficult for me to explain why I enjoy this work. Initially I took the job because full-time gigs for entomologists are few and far between, and I have no taste for academia. I figured I would see what the Body Farm was all about, help close a few cold cases, and leave for greener pastures as soon as I got an opportunity for fieldwork, ideally in a rainforest where I could make my name discovering a new species of beetle. There are always more beetles to be found.

Most researchers stay at the Body Farm for either a couple of hours or their entire lives. There was, of course, an adjustment period for me. In my introductory meeting, LaTanya informed me casually that if I needed to throw up or faint, that was fine, as long as I didn't do it on the corpses themselves. And yes, I vomited once or twice at the start, I admit. But soon it turned out that I had the right mindset. I could focus on the trees instead of the forest. I learned to turn my attention to the details (the timeline of pupation, the movement of larvae through rotting tissue, or the metallic sheen of healthy adult blowflies) while ignoring the bigger picture entirely (existential dread, gut-wrenching repulsion, and my own fear of inescapable death).

I didn't stay just for the bugs, however. My work matters. I sleep well at night knowing that I'm helping balance the scales of justice. Even as a child I was a righteous soul, beating up other people's bullies on the playground and shattering a neighbor boy's magnifying glass when he used it to fry ants. Now I take on the work that few others are capable of. I look death in the face every day and analyze how it moves, what it wants. I do it for the good of us all.

"I think your work is amazing," Beatrice told me the night I proposed. No one had ever said anything like this to me before. She even enjoyed my interesting insect facts—or pretended to, anyway, well enough that I never knew the difference.

God, I was smitten—I still am, honestly, all these years later. Your mother is a rare creature. The way she listens with her whole body. The way she radiates calm in a palpable forcefield, softening the mood of an entire room. The way she reacts viscerally and audibly to whatever she's reading—laughing and nodding and saying "Oh!" alone on the porch swing, as though the author could hear. Her hopefulness is like a kite rising on the wind, carried irresistibly upward. As a grouchy pessimist, I stand in awe of her innate buoyancy. Nothing else could have seen her through Emerson's madness. Each time she escaped him, she was able to hope, sincerely and completely, that it would finally end.

We married. She took my name. By that point Emerson had been silent for over a year, the longest stretch since college.

He did not make contact when we traveled to Paris for our honeymoon. He did not make contact when we bought our house. He did not make contact when you were born, first Theo, then

Lucas, a vaginal delivery, brave Beatrice laboring for thirty-seven hours. You looked like her even then, my angels, with your identical tufts of black fuzz and crumpled faces. Her nose went to Lucas. Her chin went to Theo. Both of you got her perfect tawny skin.

Seven years of peace punctured by a bright blue envelope. I thought Emerson was gone, I really did. To be honest, I figured he was dead.

°

A second electric-blue envelope showed up a few days after Emerson's late-night phone call. You two found it, rushing to the door at the sound of letters sliding through the mail slot. I'm sorry that I shouted at you. The world dissolved into a crimson haze the moment I glimpsed my babies holding something that monster had touched. I yelled, and then the envelope was in my hands and you both were staring wide-eyed at me from the safety of Beatrice's embrace on the other side of the room.

"Don't take it out on them," she said.

"I'm sorry," I said. I went to you, kneeling down to your eye level. "Mama's so sorry. Mama was being a jerk."

"Mama was being a jerk!" you chorused.

"A-plus parenting, babe," Beatrice said, plucking the blue envelope from my grasp. She gave me a nudge to take the sting out of her words, then slipped from the room.

He had written her a poem, that son of a bitch. I won't repeat his maudlin little stanzas here. Suffice it to say that after reading it, Beatrice went to bed and cried for the rest of the day.

°

I know a lot about murder. I've spent years considering motive, means, and opportunity. There are five classifications of death: homicide, suicide, accidental, natural, and unknown. Though the cadavers we study at the Body Farm usually fall into the "natural" column, our research applies to all the other kinds too. Part of our job is to beat killers at their own game, to think like they do, to think better than they do. The police are fond of saying there's no such thing as a perfect murder, but I don't agree. There are flaws in any system. I helped design this particular system, so I'm aware of its flaws.

Toxicology reports, for instance, are far from comprehensive. During an autopsy, the medical examiner studies the victim's blood. She looks for illegal substances (like heroin and cocaine) and prescription medications (like opiates and amphetamines). But it simply isn't possible to screen for everything. Nobody checks for jellyfish venom or deadly nightshade, for example—not unless there's a specific reason to do so. Other poisons melt away upon ingestion, leaving no trace in the body. Cyanide does not linger in the blood; the only indication is a faint smell of almonds, and even that varies. Ricin, too, kills within days and leaves no sign of its presence.

Then there are the everyday poisons, so ordinary that they fly beneath the radar in a different way. Large amounts of potassium can be lethal, but it also occurs naturally in the body and is always found in the blood. Why would anyone bother to test for a substance that's definitely going to be there? Toxicology reports focus on a couple hundred possible poisons, but there are thousands more in the world. In truth, almost anything can be fatal in sufficient quantities. Too much nutmeg. Too much salt. Too much water.

Even air can be a problem. Once a cadaver came to the Body

Farm, a woman who'd died of cardiac arrest. But given her comparative youth, Jackson and Cal, our MDs, were not satisfied with this verdict. Cardiac arrest means only that the heart has stopped beating. It is a symptom of death, rather than the cause.

So Jackson did a thorough autopsy. He scanned for surface and subcutaneous trauma. He examined the seven locations in which a needle can be inserted without being noticed by most medical examiners. At last, he found an incision beneath the woman's tongue. Someone had injected her with a syringe full of empty air, which formed an embolism and stopped her heart.

And, of course, there are accidents—or deaths that appear to be accidental. The world is a dangerous place. People fall down the stairs and slip in the shower. They get drunk and crash their cars. They leave cigarettes lit and burn their houses down. With a little help, life can be fatal. A loose wire. A stove left on. A push at the wrong moment. An unseen, guiding hand. Even if the police suspect foul play, they can't act without corroboration. Innocent until proven guilty, after all.

Corpses are like postcards, written unknowingly by the killer, full of unintended clues. Fingerprints. Hair. Droplets of saliva or tears. Without meaning to, the murderer might record whether they were right- or left-handed. They might hint at whether they had done this before. (An inexperienced, nervous attacker leaves different marks from one who is confident and assured.) They might indicate their height and weight. (A blow struck by a short skinny woman is quite unlike a punch from a six-foot-tall 350-pound man.) At the Body Farm, my colleagues and I can read these things printed on the flesh in the killer's unique script.

To get away with murder, it's best to dispose of the corpse altogether. A wood chipper and an eight-foot grave. A deep lake, a length of chain, and a cinder block. A concoction of lye and bleach, melting the flesh like warm ice. No evidence at all. No trail for the police to follow. No message for the medical examiner to decode. No body, no crime.

°

What was the tipping point for me? Not Emerson's first letter, or the late-night phone call, or the pathetic poem. Not the nights I lay awake in bed, tossing and turning, finally getting up to verify for the tenth time that every door and window was locked and that you were safe and dreaming in your shared bed. Not the second call, which came one morning while you ate breakfast and Beatrice sat beside you at the table, smiling cheerfully with the phone to her ear so you wouldn't be alarmed. Only heavy breathing, she said later, but that was bad enough. Not even Emerson's third letter, in which he described me as an "androgynous nothing person."

He had always treated Beatrice's lovers that way, as though they couldn't possibly live up to his example or offer any real threat. He would graciously forgive her each time, too, clucking his tongue and reveling in his own magnanimity.

His assault on our family went on for weeks. Another letter on blue card stock, which the two of you avoided like it was radioactive. You collected the rest of the mail and left that envelope in the front hall for me to find on my way to work. More heavy breathing down the phone. A single rose tucked beneath the windshield wiper of Beatrice's car. How did he know which one was hers? I went to the police then, but the officer said exactly what Beatrice told me he'd say. Emerson hadn't done anything illegal. Was I even sure it was him? The car was parked on the street; anyone could have put the flower there. If the guy became violent or trespassed on our property, I should file a police report for sure. Then it would be too late, I said, and the officer raised his hands, palms up, in a gesture of helplessness or supplication.

I fervently hope that you don't remember that brief, terrible phase of your young lives. Beatrice's nerves tautened like a guitar string pulled too far, ready to snap. I subsisted on coffee and energy pills. A bracelet in a velvet box left on the porch. Another electric-blue letter covered in drawings of hearts. A dead bird in the grass of our backyard—had it fallen from a nest in the pine tree, or had a Machiavellian maniac tossed it over the fence as a warning? A midnight call, consisting only of kissy noises and sexual groans.

But the tipping point came when I saw Emerson with my own eyes.

I'm still not sure what woke me. I'd been sleeping lightly for weeks, startling at every sound, but there was no creak of floorboards or tap of branches on the window that night. I slipped out of bed, listening to the ringing silence, the carpet cold beneath my bare feet. Beatrice lay on her belly with her feet in the air. My ridiculous, wonderful wife.

I padded down the hall to check on you both. You were in Lucas's bed this time, sleeping head to foot. I wondered if you'd started out the night that way or if you began with both heads on one pillow and one of you migrated. You were wild sleepers at that age, kicking and rolling in frantic motions that never woke either of you.

I went to the window to make sure it was locked. And there he was, standing on the sidewalk, staring up at the house. At your room.

My heart jolted violently enough to knock the wind out of me. I don't know if Emerson saw me through the curtains. He did not react to my appearance, at any rate. The streetlamp turned him into a copper statue, dressed in a puffy coat, hands folded behind his back, blond hair glittering. He was taller than I'd expected. His stance suggested he'd been out there a long while, despite the cold. An unnerving stillness. Endless patience. As my eyes adjusted to the watery glow, I saw the expression on his face: chin lifted, a small smile.

I read once that geckos can hold a pose for hours, exerting no energy while remaining perfectly alert, ready to launch their tongues at the first appearance of prey with the speed and lethality of a bullet. They are harmless to humans but vicious predators of insects. There was something of the lizard about Emerson as he lurked there on our street, motionless, vigilant, waiting.

I watched him watching us. I stayed where I was for god knows how long. The two of you mumbled in your sleep, smacking your lips and rustling amid the blankets. My leg began to cramp and I needed to pee, but I didn't move from my post at the window until Emerson pivoted on his heel and strode away. I kept my gaze on him until he turned the corner and disappeared into the darkness.

°

Once I make up my mind about something, I act quickly and decisively. I have always been like that. I wanted to buy our house the moment we stepped inside, and we made an offer that same day. Beatrice longed for babies before I did, but the instant I knew I was ready too, we went hand in hand to the sperm bank.

I decided to murder Emerson the night I saw him.

The idea had been bubbling away at the back of my mind for

some time, but I had not taken it seriously. We all think crazy things in the privacy of our weird little brains. To blow off steam, I'd considered means and opportunity. Motive I already had in plentiful supply. It had become a game to play during sleepless nights or quiet moments at the Body Farm. A reverse whodunit, figuring out how, in theory, I might get away with it.

Female killers are not caught as often as male. It skews the statistics. In fact, no one really knows how many women have committed murder. The records track only those homicides that result in arrest and conviction. It's impossible to count the successful killers—the ones who are never found out, never suspected at all.

The evidence of women's prowess in this area is anecdotal but compelling. Cal, one of the MDs at the Body Farm, worked at a hospice facility for years before coming to Lyle. He was shocked, he said, by the number of sweet old ladies who confessed on their deathbeds that they'd poisoned or suffocated somebody decades ago. None of their relatives or friends ever dreamed of such a thing, Cal said. These women made it to old age, to the point of their own demise, with their crimes undiscovered.

In the break room, my colleagues and I debated the gender disparity of murder. Everyone had a different theory to explain it. Luis believed that social conditioning was the root cause. At a young age, boys were encouraged to lash out, to dominate, whereas girls were taught to contain and control their anger. As grown women, this ability allowed them to act with premeditation and cool heads, which accounted for their success and secrecy.

Hyo thought it was a matter of cleanup. Men couldn't properly scrub a toilet or discern when the carpet needed vacuuming. How could they ever hope to leave behind a sterile crime scene? In addition, most women had decades of experience scrubbing bloodstains out of their underwear. Men wouldn't know to soak the fabric first and wash in cold water, since hot would induce the stains to set.

Kenneth, who had more experience with the law enforcement side of things, believed it had to do with ego. Men overestimated their own intelligence and made mistakes as a result, while women often underestimated themselves, leading them to plan more thoroughly and take greater precautions.

Georgina felt it all came down to motive. Women held grudges, she said. They could wait years before taking action, long after any apparent motive had faded from everyone else's minds. Men didn't tend to let things fester that way. They either acted at once or moved on.

And LaTanya said that women were simply the smarter sex, more capable of doing everything under the sun, including homicide.

Now that I have become a murderer myself, I believe all of them were right, more or less.

°

Do you remember the fairy tale that obsessed you during that time? I hope so, since I read it aloud to you daily for weeks on end. You'd found it on one of your shelves, a hand-me-down picture book with no cover, the pages soft from use. I still don't know the title. The spine, like the cover, had been torn away by some other child's hands.

The heroine was a "golden-hearted woman." No other personality traits were mentioned, but perhaps they weren't needed. She caught the eye of an evil wizard, who cursed her, transforming her into a bee. That was the part I liked. Any story with an insect in it gets my vote. She flew unhappily from flower to flower, growing weary, so lonely, until a kind farmer held out his hand and gave her a place to rest. His touch transformed her back into her human shape. They married and lived happily ever after. Heteronormative but sweet.

"What happened to the evil wizard?" you asked every single time I closed the book.

"It doesn't say," I told you.

"Did he die? Did he go to jail?"

"I don't know."

You were never satisfied with this answer. Eventually you would climb off my lap to finish the story on your own, drawing crayon illustrations of the wizard boiling to death in a pot or falling off a cliff. You killed him a hundred bloodthirsty ways and cheered his demise, then asked me to read the book aloud again.

I've heard people say that children can't fully understand death. That's why they crave such cutthroat stories and playact such barbaric things. (Once the evil wizard had his arms and legs ripped off by elephants; another time he got kicked into a volcano.) But I think children are perfectly capable of understanding what death is. They're not naive and guileless; they're clear-eyed about the limits of justice. They know that the world of fairy tales is better than ours.

Real life isn't fair. In my work, I've seen the full measure of what human beings can do to one another, and I've seen the limits of our justice system too. But in a fairy tale, there's no need for cops or courts, since the story itself brings balance. Murderers have their eyes plucked out by doves or drown in the sea, while good people are guaranteed to live happily ever after. The Body

Farm wouldn't exist in a fairy tale. Why would anyone study death and decay in a world where magical retribution is a fundamental law of nature?

That's the reality I want.

The book with no title became your obsession because it broke the most essential rule of fairy tales: it wasn't fair. You wanted to hear the story over and over because it bothered you, not because you liked it. Yes, the golden-hearted woman and the kind farmer were rewarded by fate, as they should have been, but what about the evil wizard? You kept hoping that he might finally be punished this time. And then, when the ending let you down again, you wrote a better one yourselves.

°

My plan was simple. The best plans always are. I bought a burner phone on my way to work, taking a leaf out of Emerson's playbook. He used disposable cell phones so that he could harass Beatrice and threaten her without leaving a paper trail. She would go to the police and show them a string of terrifying text messages, and they'd tell her there was no way to be sure of the source.

One night, as Beatrice slept, I scrolled through her phone. (To be clear, I usually respected her privacy. This was a one-time breach of my moral code, done only in exigent and extreme circumstances.) As I suspected, Emerson had been bombarding her with texts for weeks, from a slew of different numbers—messages she hadn't told me about, not wanting to worry me. Beatrice never replied, but that didn't stop him.

Using my new flip phone, I texted his most recent number, posing as Beatrice. Emerson believed she would do that—contact him of her own volition, after all this time. Can you imagine? I asked to meet him in an isolated spot, late at night. He agreed. We worked out the details of our rendezvous, him and me.

Now I wonder: Was he really so arrogant, or was he delusional? Did he actually believe that one day it would be him and Beatrice, a perfect match, destined for each other? Did he buy the story he kept selling? Or did he see the situation clearly—predator and prey, psychopath and victim—and the poems and diamond rings were simply weapons in his vast arsenal? How much was gaslighting with the intent of causing harm, and how much did he regard as true?

I guess it doesn't matter. Actions are important, not motives. That's what LaTanya always tries to explain on the stand. The jury wants to know *why* the victim was killed, *why* the murderer did it, but the only thing science can reveal, at the end of the day, is *how*.

I met Emerson at midnight, in a place of my own choosing. I wore a hat and scarf and he didn't know it was me until it was too late. I won't go into the details. That is not my purpose, and I don't want you to be burdened with those images.

When he was dead, I wrapped his corpse in a tarp, wrestled it into my trunk, and drove to the Body Farm. It was my turn to take the graveyard shift. We all hate doing it, so we follow a rotating schedule. Temperature, insect activity, fungal growth, humidity—these things don't stay constant after nightfall, and it is essential that we observe our subjects around the clock. But the Body Farm is creepy after dark, even for us. The trees rustle menacingly. Darkness erases the visual markers of death—liquefied eyeballs, putrefied flesh—that we normally count on to remind ourselves that these are corpses, not people. At night, the Body Farm seems to be inhabited by a watchful, unmoving crowd.

In addition, the dead are not always silent. Fresh cadavers

sometimes sigh or groan. I've heard them pass gas. I've seen them twitch their fingers or blink. As they move further through the process of decay, the sounds don't stop; they merely change. Sometimes month-old corpses bubble or belch. In rare cases, they explode, their torsos ripped apart from within by a profusion of volcanic gases.

That night, I parked by the back door, where there are no security cameras. Why would there be? We only ever use that entrance to receive the dead or throw away hazardous waste. To get that close to the building, we have to pass through two locked gates with keypads. The cameras face outward along the walls, keeping teens and miscreants away, rather than monitoring the researchers inside.

I fetched a gurney and wheeled Emerson's corpse through the halls. I did think briefly about keeping him there, on the grounds. I could mock up the paperwork of a new admission. I could smash his face and snip off his fingertips, rendering him unidentifiable. I could find an appropriate resting place for him and watch him molder away until there was nothing left but bones.

There was an odd symmetry to the idea. I imagined counting the maggots that devoured him and measuring the life cycle of the coffin flies that made their homes in his flesh. In life he had been a pernicious soul, causing only harm, but in death he could be useful. His body would provide data and aid the noble cause of science, and I would be able to savor my revenge.

I blame the graveyard shift for that particular line of thought. I am not normally such a ghoul, but the Body Farm is eerie in the wee small hours.

I cremated him. We have our own incinerator, for obvious reasons. I needed to use it that night anyway, since we'd amassed more skeletons than we could utilize, picked absolutely clean by insects and bacteria, nothing left to learn. I burned four skeletons and Emerson, then went out onto the grounds to do my work.

°

I wish I could tell you that it upset me to take his life. That's what I'm supposed to say, isn't it? That it left me nauseated and shaken. That I could scarcely look at myself in the mirror afterward. That it haunts me to this day.

But the truth is quite different. Years at the Body Farm have reshaped my reaction to death. Emerson was a problem for me to solve. At work, I solve objectively disturbing and disgusting problems all the time. What's the most efficient method of removing blowfly eggs from the mouth of a corpse? Use a child's paintbrush. What's the ideal preservative for beetle larvae? Alcohol or naphtha. What's the best way to change Emerson's body from alive to dead? That was the problem before me: a man who ought to be a corpse. I found an ideal solution. Doing so was no more repugnant or upsetting than any old shift at the Anthropological Research Center.

The next few months were difficult. I knew Emerson was gone, but I could not tell Beatrice, who continued to wake up screaming from nightmares and startle every time her phone rang. With the two of you, at least, I could be myself again. Fun Mama. Science-y Mama. When the weather warmed, I took you to the zoo. I hung a tire swing from our oak tree. We worked in the backyard, transferring the herbs Armando and Joe had helped you grow in indoor pots to a vegetable garden by the fence.

"It's been a while since I've heard from you-know-who," Beatrice said on a rainy day in spring. "I'm getting antsy waiting for the other shoe to drop."

"Maybe it won't," I said. "Maybe he's finally moved on."

She smiled at me. Her hopefulness is amazing. I will never stop admiring it.

Flowers bloomed. You splashed in puddles. One morning you found caterpillars, seven of them, crawling around on the parsley we'd planted in the garden. They were black swallowtails—I could tell from the coloration and their choice of host plant. We carried them inside, safe from predators, and raised them by hand. I have never seen such smiles. You named them, loved them. When they melted and solidified into chrysalises, you mourned. When they hatched into miraculous, dewy creatures with midnight-black wings, you laughed. When we released them into our garden, you danced, watching them flit and circle and finally rise, vanishing into the blue.

On the one hand, homicide is objectively wrong. On the other hand, is it? I don't think I'm deranged. I hope you don't think so either, my darlings. I believe you see me as I truly am: a doting mother, a loving wife, and an affectionate friend to my friends. A good provider. A well-balanced person. A conscientious member of society.

The Emersons of this world are a dying breed. That's my hope, anyway. I want it to stop with your generation. It comes down to you, my beautiful boys. You are growing up every moment, and one day, all too soon, you will no longer be interested in fairy tales. You will shed the wild sweetness of these early years. It's hard to imagine you as preteens, high schoolers, adults, but I know it's coming.

You will be good men. That isn't hopefulness on my part—it's decision, intention. Despite our years together, none of Beatrice's optimism has rubbed off on me. I know you'll be good men because I will see to it. Lucas, with your tender heart, so like your mother's. Theo, with your righteous spirit, so much like mine.

"Can Emerson be gone?" Beatrice asked when summer came. "He isn't gone, is he? I'm afraid to let my guard down."

"I think he gave up," I said, pouring her a glass of wine. "Maybe he finally saw how happy you are. How happy we are."

She laughed the way she used to, a cascading waterfall. I hadn't heard that unfettered laugh since the first blue envelope arrived.

°

When I began writing this letter to you, I thought I understood my purpose. I believed I was setting down my confession in case the truth ever came to light. I wanted you to know why I did what I did. At the Body Farm, we only care about *how*, but you, my children, would want to know *why*. And so I have tried to explain. I intended to hide the letter somewhere secret, to be opened in the event of my conviction. Not arrest, you understand—*conviction*. That was my plan at the start, anyway.

But now that I have written it all down, I can see that I will never be caught. It was indeed a perfect murder. I even incinerated Emerson's burner phone, and mine, along with his body—the only extant things in the universe that could possibly connect him to me.

It has been a year since I killed him. Winter has settled in once more, and Beatrice seems at ease in her own skin again. I've seen her shoveling snow without glancing up every time someone walks by. She forgets to turn on the security alarm some nights. The doorbell rang the other day and she ran, excited for the package she'd ordered, throwing open the door without looking through the peephole first. I took her out for a night on the town and she did herself up, highlighter on her cheeks, a slinky red dress I'd never seen before. She wouldn't have been so bold and colorful if Emerson was on her mind. Our lovemaking—well, I'm sure you don't want to hear about it, so I will only say that Emerson had a stifling influence on both of us that has since vanished entirely.

Even now, the police don't realize he's missing. They probably never will. Beatrice mentioned once that Emerson didn't have any family. I'm sure there are no friends to report his loss either. A loner. An oddball. The only person who will notice his absence is Beatrice, and for her it has been a balm, a delicious silence, the cessation of persistent pain.

What, then, have I written here? Not a confession—there would be no point. I will take the truth to my grave. I will let time prove to Beatrice that Emerson is gone, and I will say nothing, not to her, not to you, not to anyone.

And yet, even if no one will ever read this letter, it may still serve a purpose. It could be a blueprint of sorts—a battle plan. Not that I anticipate ever needing to take such drastic action again, you understand. I killed Emerson because I had to. There was no other solution to the particular problem of his aliveness.

But if I were to take the lessons I learned from his death and turn my attention to someone else, another "bad guy," a stranger to me . . . I will admit that during one of my recent graveyard shifts, in the ghoulish lull of the witching hour, the thought did cross my mind. The only tricky part of Emerson's murder was the connection between us, however tangential. There was the slimmest chance that a search of motives could lead back to me.

A stranger, however—someone with no link to me at all—well, what could be easier? Yes, the thought has crossed my mind. There's that neighbor who screams such vile things at his wife after a few drinks. There's the principal of the local elementary school, who has kept his job for a decade despite persistent rumors that he sexually harasses his teachers. There's the woman Hyo told me about, a dear friend of hers from college, trapped in an abusive relationship, too afraid to leave him even after he beat her badly enough to put her in the hospital. Hyo mentioned the man's name to me as she wiped away her tears. I did just happen to jot it down.

And a couple of weeks ago, there was a news story about a serial rapist right here in Lyle, convicted of assaulting eight different women and sentenced to a paltry two years in prison. I did just happen to make a note of his release date as well. God, it would be so easy. No affiliation between any of these men and me. No apparent motive. My rotation on the night watch comes back around like clockwork, and the skeletons are always piling up again, ready to be incinerated.

So maybe what I have written here is a cautionary tale. Maybe it was never intended for you or me. Maybe, all along, I meant it for men like that rapist or the principal or the neighbor—men like Emerson. The fact that none of those despicable souls will read it is irrelevant. A story like mine has power in the mere fact of its existence. A warning. A tremor in the fabric. A new kind of ending.

I don't have to decide yet what I will do. I have all the time in the world to see what kind of person I am becoming. We are all in a process of constant evolution, larvae metamorphosing into blowflies. That's what I love most about insects: their capacity for transformation. A tiny translucent egg sac becomes a half-blind, slow-moving grub, which mutates into a cocoon filled with mush that lies motionless in the soil for days as though dead, then erupts into its final form, a fierce winged creature with a panoramic field of vision and an accelerated perception of time, with feet that can taste the ground. It's the closest thing to magic to be found in this life.

And insects transfigure more than themselves. Without bees, there would be no flowers or fruits. Without bone beetles and coffin flies, the dead would not decay, and the cycle of life would be broken. The work of insects, like mine, is both grotesque and vital. They transmute flesh and bone into mulch and nutrients. They change the dead into the raw materials for new life. There are no plants as green as the ones on the Body Farm, feeding from the richest, most blood-soaked soil on earth.

What happened to Emerson was not legal, but it was right. It was fairy-tale justice. And I suppose, in the end, that's what this story is: a fairy tale. Once upon a time, there was a golden-hearted woman, pursued over hill and dale by an evil ogre. She met a gallant knight—me, of course—and bore two fine sons. They lived peacefully for a time, hoping the ogre was gone, but he came back, as wicked things so often do. Bravely, cleverly, the knight slew the ogre and burned him up. The golden-hearted woman rejoiced. Together they raised their sons to be better men than the men who came before them. And they all lived happily ever after.

Acknowledgments

This book would never have come into being without the support of so many people. Thanks to my family, writer friends, mom friends, readers, students, colleagues, and in particular:

- Scott—unique, brilliant, charming, hilarious, RRM's, Bean senses, playground, Hercules, razor perceptions, to be, handsomeness, best friend. I can't do justice on the page to the marvel that you are and the gift you have been in my life. *Love* isn't a big enough word.
- Milo—the most interesting person I've ever known, a shining light, the only one who's ever made me do a spit take with laughter, my favorite human. I am grateful every day to be your mother. Every day with you is a new adventure.
- Laura Langlie—beloved agent, champion, friend. None of this would be possible without you.
- Dan Smetanka—the most insightful and generous editor I could ever have hoped for. You ask for magic, and because of you, I am able to find it.
- Sarah Bendix—my always friend, my heart, purveyor of

excellent memes, lifeline via text. You taught me what friendship is, how to do it, and why it's worth it.

- Dad—painter, teacher, meditator, sci-fi writer, world traveler, woodworker, gardener, musician, the ultimate renaissance man. You showed me how to notice the beauty of the clouds, how to identify songbirds and fix a faucet, how to love the world, how to never stop learning.
- Joe—no one else could possibly understand all the times that *Bloom County* and *Calvin and Hobbes* quotes are needed. Thank god you are always there if I come across an important fact about dinosaurs. Any day that goes by without a text from you is a lesser day.
- Patsy—legally my aunt, but factually my fairy godmother. You change my life for the better with a wave of your magic wand.
- Lan Samantha Chang—mentor, genius, and all-around stellar human. Thank you for bringing me back to the Iowa Writers' Workshop. Thank you for bringing me home.
- StoryStudio Chicago—a nonpareil sanctuary for writers. I am ferociously proud of my remarkable students. I am forever grateful to be a part of this wonderful community.
- Counterpoint Press—everyone on the team is amazing, but I must especially thank Megan Fishmann, Barrett Briske, Laura Berry, tracy danes, Rachel Fershleiser, and Kira Weiner.
- Laurie—you saved my life, and you continue to save my life.
- My dogs—you can't read, but you are essential to my writing nonetheless.

These acknowledgments would not be complete without mentioning my mother. She died in 2022, and she will never see this book come into being, though I'm glad she had the chance to read a few of the stories before she got sick. I am a writer because of her. I am who I am because of her. She edited everything I ever wrote. She loved me fiercely and unconditionally. She never believed in an afterlife, but I'm going to say it anyway: Thank you, Mom.

The author gratefully acknowledges the following publications, in which some of the stories in this collection previously appeared:

"The Rapture of the Deep" in *Missouri Review*
"The First Rule of Natalie" (as "Selkie") in *Joyland*
"Porcupines in Trees" in *Ninth Letter*
"Childish" in *Triquarterly*
"Starlike" (as "Star-like") in *Arkansas Review*
"The Body Farm" in *Epoch*

© Maia Rosenfeld

ABBY GENI is the author of *The Lightkeepers*, winner of the Barnes & Noble Discover Great New Writers Award for Fiction and the inaugural Chicago Review of Books Award for Best Fiction; *The Wildlands*, a finalist for the Los Angeles Times Book Prize; and *The Last Animal*, an Indies Introduce Debut Authors selection and a finalist for the Orion Book Award. Geni is a graduate of the Iowa Writers' Workshop and a recipient of the Iowa Fellowship. Find out more at www.abbygeni.com.